# THE PENGUIN CLASSICS

FOUNDER EDITOR (1944–64): E. V. RIEU

JOHANN WOLFGANG GOETHE was born in Frankfort-on-Main in 1749. He studied at Leipzig, where he showed interest in the occult, and at Strassburg, where Herder introduced him to Shakespeare's works and to folk poetry. He produced some essays and lyrical verse, and at twenty-four wrote *Goetz von Berlichingen*, a play which brought him national fame and established him in the current *Sturm und Drang* movement. *Werther*, a tragic romance, was an even greater success.

Goethe began work on *Faust*, and *Egmont*, another tragedy, before being invited to join the government of Weimar. His interest in the classical world led him to leave suddenly for Italy in 1768, and the *Italian Journey* recounts his travels there. *Iphigenie auf Tauris* and *Torquato Tasso*, classical dramas, were begun at this time.

Returning to Weimar, Goethe started the second part of *Faust*, encouraged by Schiller. During this late period he finished his series of *Wilhelm Meister* books and wrote many other works, including *The Oriental Divan*. He also directed the State Theatre and worked on scientific theories in evolutionary botany, anatomy, and colour.

Goethe was married in 1806. He finished *Faust* before he died in 1832.

PHILIP WAYNE was, until his retirement in 1954, Headmaster of St Marylebone Grammar School. He translated the complete *Faust* in two volumes, for the Penguin Classics, and prepared a three-volume edition of the works of Wordsworth.

Philip Wayne died in 1965.

# GOETHE

---

# FAUST

## PART TWO

---

TRANSLATED WITH AN
INTRODUCTION BY
PHILIP WAYNE

PENGUIN BOOKS

Penguin Books Ltd, Harmondsworth, Middlesex, England
Penguin Books, 625 Madison Avenue, New York, New York 10022, U.S.A.
Penguin Books Australia Ltd, Ringwood, Victoria, Australia
Penguin Books Canada Ltd, 2801 John Street, Markham, Ontario, Canada L3R 1B4
Penguin Books (N.Z.) Ltd, 182–190 Wairau Road, Auckland 10, New Zealand

—

This translation first published 1959
Reprinted 1962, 1965, 1967, 1969, 1971, 1973, 1975,
1976, 1977, 1979, 1981, 1982

—

Copyright © the Estate of Philip Wayne, 1959
All rights reserved

—

Made and printed in Great Britain
by Richard Clay (The Chaucer Press) Ltd,
Bungay, Suffolk
Set in Monotype Bembo

*Terms for performance or adaptation of 'Faust' in this new translation
may be obtained from Penguin Books Ltd, Harmondsworth, Middlesex,
to whom all applications for permission should be made*

Except in the United States of America,
this book is sold subject to the condition
that it shall not, by way of trade or otherwise,
be lent, re-sold, hired out, or otherwise circulated
without the publisher's prior consent in any form of
binding or cover other than that in which it is
published and without a similar condition
including this condition being imposed
on the subsequent purchaser

# CONTENTS

# INTRODUCTION

## I

THE growth of the Faust-theme in Goethe's mind is described in outline in my Introduction to *Part One*. There I cited the opinion of G. H. Lewes, that the story of Gretchen provided a passionate human drama for every reader, whereas in *Part Two* we should find a philosophic activity and discursiveness apt to interrupt the main epic concerning the soul of Faust. I have found no reason to recant from that view; but I confess humbly that years of close work upon the text have brought me to a better understanding not only of Goethe's wish that the two Parts should be read as one, but of the majestic and sometimes wilful energy with which he engaged upon divagations that now afford a mine of thought for the contemplative reader. Though in *Part Two* we do indeed pass from the passion of lovers to the search after wisdom, it can still be said that Goethe's pursuit of wisdom, even when accompanied by the sometimes rough humour of his irony, is always passionate.

So rich is this *Second Part* in allusions and allegories that whole libraries of commentary have been written about them by German professors, rightly proud of their European giant, and in any case never so happy as when expounding the scriptures. The aim of a short Introduction must be to offer undismayed some sort of perspective for the general reader. To this end it may be best to consider the great and complex work in separate aspects.

## II

AS to the growth of *Part Two* it should be remembered that the whole plan of Faust was fairly complete in Goethe's conception long before the publication of *Part One*. In June 1797 – as with so many things in Goethe's crowded life, we know the very day – he braced himself to overcome the doubts that had beset him during twenty years of interruption in his devotion to what was neverthe-

less the undying main theme of his creative life; indeed, at this
juncture, he had the methodical energy to set out his plan in
numbered sections, of which Nos. 20 to 30 define *Part Two*. In this
the scenes at the Emperor's Court and particularly the encounter of
Faust with Helen had been in his mind from the first, for they
draw on the original legend (see Introduction to *Part One*); and, in
proof of the confident coherence of his vast scheme at this date, we
find him clearly decided as to the death of Faust and the succeeding
fight for his soul; and the scheme concluded with passages relating
to the 'Dedication' and to the two 'Prologues' of *Part One*, all
conceived – and in the case of the profound 'Dedication' written –
at this same time of powerful contemplation.

Eleven years later, in 1808, *Part One* was published. Another
twenty-three years were to pass before Goethe finished *Part Two*,
but he had said as early as 1806: 'The whole is forthcoming, not
yet all written, but composed.' And he told Eckermann in 1831
that the actuating thoughts opening his last Act were over thirty
years old. A little study of this long growth of the complete Faust
can bring us to a sense of wonder at the will-power so touchingly
applied by a great author to his duty. That this enormously busy
man – theatre-director, scientist, cabinet-minister – was by nature
dilatory, makes his persistence the more heroic. Schiller had
spurred him on like a noble friend. The faith of the methodical
Eckermann was a much later encouragement to him. Eckermann
came on the scene in 1823; and Goethe now worked hard at *Part
Two*, from the age of seventy-five to his eighty-second birthday. In
November 1830, he was ill and sleepless and had a severe haemorr-
hage: four days after that he was at work on Act IV. In the New
Year he shut himself away in his 'Garden House' to finish, facing
the always irksome toil of revision, to ensure harmony between
the later and the earlier work. Gravely, humbly, and, even in his
old age, passionately, he felt he must give to his fellow-men the
complete Faust, as the best that was in him. By late summer his
'chief task' was done: and he said that he regarded the rest of his
life 'purely as a present'. It was a present of seven months. Even

so, his genius was still at work, for in the early days of 1832 he took out his manuscript again for critical reading; and on 17 March he wrote to his friend Humboldt, reflecting upon the welding of the earlier and the later work in his *Faust*, and reconciling in an artistic conception the conscious with the unconscious, the inborn with the acquired. When he wrote that penetrative letter he had only five days to live. Then the papers of *Part Two* were taken from a sealed packet, and the complete work published after his death, as he had desired.

### III

A word as to the coherence of the whole scheme may be acceptable to readers already conversant with *Part One*. Gretchen is gone. She only appears at the end in spirit – but this indeed is her essence, in the vast reality of eternity. The intervening marriage of Faust and Helen is no human love-affair but an allegory, which we shall presently examine. What gives coherence to the whole drama is the fate of Faust's immortal soul. Even the Helen episode, which grew to a whole Act (the third, published separately, in 1827), is no detached usurper: not only was it inwrought in Goethe's mind from the old legend, but he certainly conceived the vision and the aspiration of Faust as a link between the two Parts:

> *That comely form enchanting once my mind,*
> *That mirrored magic joy of womankind,*
> *Was but a pale foam-phantom of such beauty.**

And this change must be seen as Faust's spiritual growth, rising from voluptuous delight to the realization of sublime beauty. Similarly with Faust in his bitter desperation; the curse with which he rejects 'a sweet remembered echo' (I, pp. 83-4) is linked in his soul's story till just before the end:

> *Such was I once, before dark ways I sought*
> *And with fell words a curse on living wrought.* (II, p. 264)

* Cf. Pt I, pp. 114, 120, and Pt II, p. 87.

Deep in Faust's nature, as in Goethe's, was a belief in the re-
deeming sanity of action; thus in *Part One* (p. 71):

> *The spirit comes to guide me in my need,*
> *I write 'In the beginning was the Deed'*

and this has its echoes towards the end of *Part Two*:

> *The glory's nought, the deed is all.*   (p. 220)

> *Only the master's word gives action weight,*
> *And what I framed in thought I will fulfil.*   (p. 267)

It is in *Part Two* that we must seek 'Creation's prospect ...
From Heaven through the world and down to hell', intended
from the start (I, p. 37); and again, near the end, Faust, rejoicing in
action, *almost* pronounces (II, p. 270*) the words that in his com-
pact with the Devil were to be his doom:

> *If to the fleeting hour I say*
> *'Remain, so fair thou art, remain!'*
> *Then bind me with your fatal chain,*
> *For I will perish in that day.*
> *'Tis I for whom the bell shall toll,*
> *Then you are free, your service done.*
> *For me the clock shall fail, to ruin run,*
> *And timeless night descend upon my soul.*   (I, p. 87)

Those words draw from Mephistopheles the grave, uncynical
answer, 'This shall be held in memory, beware!'; and the passage
is given full citation here to show how closely Goethe has knit
those crucial moments, for the careful reader will find again (II,
pp. 270–1) the bond, the very clock-finger and the stillness.

The main coherence is seen in the fact that the much erring
Faust is saved.

---

* A fine point of grammar is involved, but a very important one: in
'Then to the moment could I say', Goethe first wrote 'can', and then cor-
rected it to the subjunctive (*dürft' ich*) which bears the sense, 'could I find it
in my heart (to say)', a great difference.

> *For man must strive, and striving he must err.*  (I, p. 41)

To the end Faust errs; for though he could blame the clumsiness of Mephistopheles for the deaths of Philemon and Baucis, it was his own ambition that trusted the issue to such an agent. Nevertheless

> *A good man in his dark, bewildered course*
> *Will not forget the way of righteousness.*  (I, pp. 41–2)

and the sense of this passage is linked with merciful pronouncement at the end:

> '*For he whose strivings never cease*
> *Is ours for his redeeming.*'  (II, p. 282)

Goethe himself set these lines in inverted commas to emphasize them as a fundamental pronouncement; and he spoke, in his eighty-second year, vital words to Eckermann about this passage. 'In these lines the key to Faust's salvation is contained: in Faust himself there is an activity mounting ever higher and purer to the end, and from above eternal love which helps him in his need. All this is completely in harmony with our religious conceptions, according to which we enter into bliss not by our own strength alone, but by the divine grace vouchsafed to us.'

In the closing cadences of *Part Two* come the hymns of medieval Latin character (II, pp. 279, 283) echoing in style those of the earlier Easter Morn (I, pp. 55–7), while the verses of Pater Profundus (II, p. 280) have close relation with those of Gabriel and Michael (I, p. 39). Even more manifest and deliberate is the spiritual echo of Gretchen's prayer:

> *Ah, look down,*
> *Thou rich in sorrow's crown.*  (I, p. 158)

and

> *Ah, look down,*
> *Thou rich in heaven's renown.*  (II, p. 287)

The harmony is complete.

## IV

SYMBOLIZATION and mythological references certainly have
such ample proportions in the *Second Part* of Faust that we must
often allow them to bear us away from the story. Goethe com-
passed no central philosophical doctrine, such as Schiller wished
from him, but he takes leave freely to hang superb speculative
fancies upon his drama, and some of these assert poetically a sub-
stantial significance of their own. Says Goethe himself (to Ecker-
mann, 13. ii. 1831), 'In such compositions what really matters is
that the single masses should be clear and significant, while the
whole remains incommensurable; and by that very reason, like an
unsolved problem, constantly draws mankind to study it again and
again.' The symbolization most ambitious and extensive in this
*Part Two* is that by which Goethe expresses, through the union of
Faust and Helen, his imaginative longing to join poetically the
Romantic Medievalism of the Germanic West to the classical
genius of the Greeks. The loving reverence that Goethe felt for the
Hellenic spirit – and he had already written his noble *Iphigenia* – led
him to adopt here the lofty Euripidean trimeter, with such earnest
that we can well understand his being drawn to make a separate
drama of the Helen motive; and though he remained faithful to his
Faust scheme, it is significant that he abandoned his first notion of
having Helen reborn in Rhineland, doubtless because he could not
subject her to the genial doggerel (*Knüttelvers*, see Pt I, p. 21)
natural to the wit of the German Mephistopheles. It seems indeed
that the spell of Helen inspires even Mephi-Phorkyas to a nobler
style (e.g. pp. 166, 172, 201). Faust teaches Helen Romance, at any
rate in discovering rhyme (p. 190), a lesson derived from a Persian
legend; and the 'sea-girt land' is re-dedicated to Helen (p. 194)
with Goethe's own classical devotion. Helen and Faust have a son,
whose name is taken from an early legend about Helen and
Achilles; but Goethe's Euphorion, hopeful spirit of poetic re-
naissance, is drawn in the likeness of the fiery Byron, always a
greater portent on the Continent than here. 'Byron', said Goethe

(Eckermann, 5. vii. 1827), 'is not antique and is not romantic, but he is the present day itself. Such a one I had to have. Moreover, he was just my man on account of his unsatisfied nature and of his warlike bent, which led him to his doom at Missolonghi.' Though Goethe here desired a general typification, not to be identified too closely with the English poet, he does turn at one place (p. 209) to individual elegy.

The Classical Walpurgis Night, a fantastic approach to the 'Helena' Third Act, is a counterpart to the ghost-ridden medievalism of the Brocken Walpurgis (Pt I, p. 167), but now disclosing to Faust august figures of the early world, as he seeks his way to supreme beauty. Meanwhile Goethe allows himself special humour in the reactions of Mephistopheles to this second Walpurgis; indeed it seems to me a symptom of the devil's declining stature that he who, like Time, 'takes survey of all the world' should now appear ill at ease and not very knowledgeable about the Classics.

> *Though Northern witches I command with ease,*
> *I'm not so sure of foreign sprites like these.* (p. 128)

And though he has quick relish for the sensual Lamiae (p. 129) the Greek's lack of shame about the nude puts him off:

> *We, lewd at heart, can relish the salacious,*
> *But this antique's too lifelike and vivacious.* (p. 109)

> *The sins they lure men to, have light and spark,*
> *While ours are sombre, always in the dark.* (p. 105)

In this same Classical Walpurgis combatants in shadowy strifes of forgotten ages are made to bear Goethe's deep interest in evolution and in geological controversy. The 'Plutonists' or 'Vulcanists' (as, e.g., in Hutton's *Theory of the Earth*, 1785) held that change came chiefly from upheavals due to subterranean heat; whereas the 'Neptunists', such as the contemporary Werner, taught that rocks were precipitates of primeval ocean, and that slow development wrought by water was nature's rule, volcanic

upheaval being only a violent accident. Goethe's Pigmies and
Cranes are to be understood in this sense, as well as the more
specific encounter of the later Anaxagoras and Thales. It is not
pressing the point too far to remark that Goethe, with powerful
foresight in modern scientific theory, was deeply convinced of the
gradualness of evolution: he returns to the subject when, at the
beginning of Act IV, Faust modifies Mephistopheles' plutonic
view of Nature.

> *There verdure teems, a growth that for its gladness*
> *Needs nothing from your tale of seething madness.*  (p. 217)

The belief in a gradual fulfilment of life is dominant in the very
opening of Faust, where the German differentiation of 'being' and
'becoming', hard to set in another language, is implicit in the last
words of the Lord God:

> *Eternal Growth, fulfilment, vital, sure,*
> *Enwrap your minds …*  (Pt I, p. 42)

It lay deep in Goethe's nature to suspect violence as something
accidental and unwise.

The lesser symbols and recondite allusions in *Part Two* en-
courage annotations beyond the scope of this volume, but a few
explanations may be helpful. The Cabiri (pp. 145–7) were early
deities, possibly of Phoenician origin, who were later invoked
against shipwreck. Goethe gives here practically all that is known
of them, even to the worship of their images in pot-bellied jars;
and in this trait, together with the sharp close by Thales and Pro-
teus (p. 147), he seems to be satirizing a cult. But some editors have
seen in this passage Goethe's enumeration of the world's religious
faiths, with a crowning eighth to come. In the next scene (p. 149)
the Telchines present a noble religious peace, symbolizing perhaps
a union of religion and art.

Galatea, with the doves and style of Venus (pp. 153–5 and 151–2),
enters much as in Rafael's fresco – this Goethe possessed in repro-
duction – and she seems to be the harbinger of an exalted aesthetic.

Goethe himself translated the description of her from Philostratus. In the next Act, at p. 176, the reference to the 'hardy race' prepares us to accept the new Faust as one of the Frankish Knights settling in Greece at the beginning of the thirteenth century. The narrative stanzas of Lynceus (pp. 187–8) refer to much earlier movements of warlike races. The hurly-burly strange carnival (from p. 38) achieved by Mephisto's arts, must be taken as satirical symbolization of the story of human society, moving from Arcadian simplicity to aspects of toil and to sophisticated civilization, including poetry, patronage, and the greed that ends the fiery pageant.

Most mysterious of all is the strange quest for 'the Mothers' (pp. 76–9). Even to the faithful Eckermann, seeking explanation here, Goethe 'veiled himself in mystery'. Faust has to seek power to bring back to life the superb beauty of Paris and Helen. That creative power can only be found in the primal intellectual forces that give birth to ideas, and have in keeping forms past, present, and future. Rare genius may wield the key to this region of truth, appallingly lonely in infinity, and come to 'the Mothers', whose tripod may lend a creative spell. Goethe said he had knowledge of these prehistoric deities from Plutarch; this would be from *Marcellus* XX, but another passage seems to have charged his imagination, for there (*de Defectione*, xxii) Plutarch dwells on the thought of a triangle of 180 worlds, with a further one in each corner, surrounded by eternity and compassing a field of Truth; 'wherein lie motionless the causes, forms, and original images of all things, which have been and which shall be'. Time, that touches these spinning worlds, is a mere effluence of eternity. Goethe's free and expansive treatment of this source of forms has doubtless Platonic and Neo-Platonic inspiration. Mephistopheles the materialist here has knowledge but no belief and no power, and so Faust, an idealist striving for fulfilment, says,

> *Well, let us on! We'll plumb your deepest ground,*
> *For in your Nothing may the All be found.* (p. 78)

## V

TOUCHING on just a few of the sometimes difficult but always evocative allusions, the foregoing section may afford some notion of the wealth of imaginative speculation that awaits a reader inquiring and patient enough to read the *Faust* and return to it. Here is a work that occupied for sixty years one of the strongest, most lively and explorative minds the world has known. We may expect lines with strong diagnostic bearing on our modern times, and we shall not be disappointed. Inflation, through the introduction of paper money, is foreshadowed by Goethe at the idle court (pp. 70–5). The theme of the creation of life by scientific synthesis is seen in the birth of Homunculus (p. 101), a brain-spun creature longing for organic life and higher development: the glass bearing his aspiration, its light and its music, is at last shattered at the throne of love, and in his plaintive and fantastic career his being is spread upon Galatea's waves, a passage (pp. 155–6) harmonizing with the Neptunist idea of growth, here re-echoed by Thales and the Sirens. Indeed to ponder with imaginative insight upon the mystery of evolution was natural to Goethe's power and habit of mind. As a scientific worker he designed a theoretical plant, prototype of all botanic growth; and in vestigial anatomy he perceived an intermaxillary bone previously overlooked in relating the human skull to that of the animals. In *Faust Part Two* he is, as a poet, suggestively eloquent regarding the development of earth, of man, and of man's imaginative aspirations; and, years before Darwin, he showed clearly a similar scientific outlook:

> *Then, following eternal norms,*
> *You move through multitudinous forms*
> *To reach at last the state of man.*   (p. 150)

The sudden exaltation of Youth in our day was partly anticipated in the ideas of Fichte, who is satirically represented in the unbounded confidence of the young Baccalaureus:

> *This is the noblest call for youthful soul!*
> *This world was not, until I made it whole.*   (p. 98)

And says Mephistopheles, a little before,

> *If to the young the simple truth we speak,*
> *That food offends the fledgeling's yellow beak;* (see p. 96)

The mischievous reference by Mephistopheles to the 'Absolute' (p. 96) points to the current philosophy of Hegel and Schelling, with its tenet of the 'unconditioned'.

Prolific as is the wealth of evocative ideas in this *Part Two*, we have yet a greater gain; for what matters most is our conviction by sheer poetry, and here, according to Goethe's own precept, the heart must speak.

> *Only from a heart o'erflowing*
> *Comes the power upon the heart.* (p. 201; cf. p. 190 and Pt I, p. 49)

'Some minds', says Lewes, 'will be delighted with the allegorical Helen ... and in their delight ... will write chapters of commentary. But the kiss of Gretchen is worth a thousand allegories.' That backward look sees much truth, but not the whole truth. Gone is the girl from her little garden and her tidy room; but she is of that universe of spirit and thought that her Faust strives restlessly to comprehend. The discovery of wonder goes on. In the shifting world of the Second Faust fresh streams of poetry are forthcoming, most of all, it must be said, where Goethe deals with mountain, woods, and waters, so intimately known in the course of his own life.

The nineteenth century acclaimed this poet as a most edifying moral physician. In the words of Matthew Arnold,

> *He took the suffering human race,*
> *He read each wound, each weakness clear;*
> *And struck his finger on the place,*
> *And said: Thou ailest here, and here!*

But surely Faust, the embodiment of Goethe's life, is engaged in raising passionate question rather than in laying down moral precept; for in Faust question comes from the heart, as well as from the satirical wit, concerning the hidden things of life through which this soul must pass on his way to redemption.

Goethe thought much and reverently of sexual love, but his mind is set, especially in Faust, on universal things. The great psychologist Jung made timely protest against current theory such as would force one to suppose 'that every relationship to the world was in essence a sexual relationship'; and those inclined to undervalue any alternative to Gretchen's love may admit the warning that comes from an author who so constantly acknowledges the inspiration of Faust. Lewes no doubt felt, about allegory, that there was little of poetic sublimity in the cleverness required to recognize pieces in a puzzle. But Goethe was striving with greater things than puzzles, inasmuch as his whole life and thought, with its indefatigable questionings, is cast in the daring images of this his main work. Very acceptable here is the clarity that Dorothy Sayers gives to the point, in her Introduction to the *Divine Comedy*: 'Allegory is the interpretation of experience by means of images,' and again, 'A great poetical image is much more than the sum of its interpretations.' It was in this sense that Jacob Burckhardt wrote to one of his pupils: 'What you are destined to discover in *Faust*, you will have to discover intuitively. *Faust* is a genuine myth, i.e., a great primordial image, in which every man has to discover his own being and destiny in his own way.'* Commentators who can preserve that sense, in a catholicity of interest, can help us much; and it is thanks to an expert like Georg Witkowski that I, for one, understand better the profoundly sincere and modest words with which Goethe, in his eightieth year, looked back at what he had achieved: 'The commendation which the work has received, far and near, may perhaps be owing to this quality – that it permanently preserves the period of development of a human soul, which is tormented by all that afflicts mankind, shaken also by all that disturbs it, repelled by all that it finds repellent, and made happy by all that it desires. The author is at present far removed

* Transl. Alexander Dru.

from such conditions: the world, likewise, has to some extent other struggles to undergo; nevertheless the state of men, in joy and sorrow, remains very much the same; and the latest-born will still find cause to acquaint himself with what has been enjoyed and suffered before him, in order to adapt himself to that which awaits him.'

That which awaits man in the spiritual sense lies at a threshold to which only the imagination of the greatest poets may dare to approach. Among those Dante, Milton, and Goethe had the kind of mind best disposed to such contemplation; but the older poets, it must be remembered, had not to work in a time when the sense of cosmos was shaken by encyclopedic scepticism. That Goethe was through life so fearlessly and ironically critical makes the religious ecstasy of his last scenes the more moving and impressive to us.

There Goethe's meaning must be weighed in every word. For instance, not to dwell long with detail, it is unsafe for an editor to remark that Goethe wrote 'Dr' Marianus, thus differentiating him from the Fathers, apparently for no reason. Goethe was taking devout care; and this deliberate change of title indicates his thought of a historically later worship, in which spiritual studies could lead to true ecstasy. Certainly he who, more than any other poet, had castigated pedantry here means something farthest removed from it.

So is presented the grace of the Mater Gloriosa. The final exaltation of the spirit of Eternal Womanhood, a mystery that Goethe all his days had loved with deepest reverence, brings a conclusion famous in literature. To such a peace was Dante led, and Orestes, at last delivered from the Furies. Here is poetic truth far more sublime than any positivist notion of Faust saved by public works – which scraping of shovels was in any case invalidated by the yet blind ambition of Faust's courageous nature. And so the vast story closes with the divine mercy, which after all is the only happy ending.

\*

I acknowledge here very gratefully critical help that I have enjoyed. In *Part One* I worked alone, but my version of the more recondite *Part Two* has been read first by H. F. Hose and W. D. Evans, and then to their kind care was added, very generously, that of Professor Roy Pascal. My friends have, of course, no responsibility for my shortcomings, which certainly would have been more numerous but for their scholarly insight.

P. W.

London, 1959

# FAUST

—

## PART TWO

# ACT ONE

—

## PLEASING LANDSCAPE

*Faust is stretched on a flowery mead, weary and restless
and longing for sleep.
It is twilight.
The Ring of Spirits, in swaying movement, with little
graceful forms.*

ARIEL (*singing, to the accompaniment of Aeolian harps*).
When the petals, like sweet rain,
 Deck the earth with fluttering spring,
When the fields are green again,
And to men their blessing bring,
Then the little elves, great-souled,
Haste to help, if help they can,
Saint or sinner, for they hold
Heart's compassion for each luckless man.
Ye who surround this head in airy wheeling,
Show now the noble elfin power of healing,
Soothe now the tumult of this mortal heart,
And wash away the stain of horrors past;
Of self-reproach, remove the bitter dart,
And, in the night's four vigils, give at last
This soul the comfort pity can impart.
Pillow his head upon the sweet, cool lawn,
Then bathe his limbs with dew from Lethe's lea,
Soon the cramp-stricken frame will lissom be,
With strength renewed, through sleep, to meet the dawn.
Fulfil, O elves, your lovely task aright,
And lead him back restored to heavenly light.

CHOIR (*with solo, or by twos, or in voices joined, antiphonally and in full chorus*).

When cool airs above the meadow
Load the green-embosomed sward,
Then with haze and fragrant shadow
Falls the dusk, in sweet accord.
Peace, in twilight's whispering sighs,
Cradles human cares away,
And upon these weary eyes
Closes soft the gates of day.

   Deep the falling of the night,
Star holds sacred rank with star,
Lordly beams and twinklings bright
Glitter near and shine afar,
Glitter mirrored in the lake,
Gleam in cloudless night on high.
Bringing stillness in her wake,
Moon in splendour rules the sky.

   Now the heavy hours have vanished,
Joys and pains are passed away.
Breathe new faith, your ills are banished;
Trust the new-born break of day.
Green the vales and hills, displaying
Wealth of shade in peaceful morn,
Seed now seen in silvery swaying
Gives the promise of the corn.

   Rise to wish and will unclouded,
Look on beams beyond the dusk!
Lightly, softly you are shrouded,
Break from sleep as from a husk!
Resolute, now claim your hour,
Though the throng may quail and drift;
For the noble soul has power

To compass all, if wise and swift.

(*A great tumult heralds the approach of the sun.*)

ARIEL.

Hark! the Hours, with furious winging,
Bear to spirit-ears the ringing
Rumour of the new day-springing.
Gates of rock grind back asunder,
Phoebus comes with wheels of thunder:
Light spreads tumult through the air.
Loud are trump and timbrel sounded,
Eyes are dazed and ears astounded,
Sounds unheard of none may bear.
Glide away to petalled bell,
Deep in quietness to dwell.
Deep in foliage, 'neath the rock,
Lest deafness comes from that dread shock.

FAUST.

The throb of life returns, with pulses beating
Soft to ethereal dawn. O steadfast earth,
True through the night, you waited for my greeting,
Breathing beneath my feet in glad new birth,
And, clothing me afresh in joy of living,
In high resolve that banishes misgiving,
You stir my soul to prove life's utmost worth. –
In gold of dawn the quickened world lies gleaming,
The forest is alive with myriad voices,
Through dell and vale the misty shapes are teeming,
But nature's deepest heart in light rejoices;
Now burgeon, freshly quivering, frond and bough,
Sprung from the fragrant depth where they lay dreaming;
On flower and blade hang trembling pearls, and now
Each colour stands out clear, in glad device,
And all the region is my Paradise.

Look up on high! – The giant peaks that stand
In joy of light above the mountain-brow,
Are heralds of the solemn hour at hand,
That brings the blessing down upon our land.
Already, down the soft eternal stair,
The shine has reached the lower Alpine sward,
Where clarity and brilliance are restored,
As downward, step by step, the light is poured –
The dazzling sun strides forth, and fills the air.
I turn, from greater power than eyes can bear.

And thus it is, when hope with earnest striving
Has toiled in aims as high as man may dare,
Fulfilment's open gates give promise fair,
But from those everlasting depths comes driving,
A fiery blast that takes us unaware:
We thought to light life's torch, but now, depriving
Our highest hope, a sea of fire surrounds us.
Such fire! Of love? Or the fierce glow of hate?
The blend of joy and sorrow that confounds us
Sends us to earth: to veil our troubled state,
For benefice of Spring we supplicate.

And so I turn, the sun upon my shoulders,
To watch the water-fall, with heart elate,
The cataract pouring, crashing from the boulders,
Split and rejoined a thousand times in spate;
The thundrous water seethes in fleecy spume,
Lifted on high in many a flying plume,
Above the spray-drenched air. And then how splendid
To see the rainbow rising from this rage,
Now clear, now dimmed, in cool sweet vapour blended.
So strive the figures on our mortal stage.
This ponder well, the mystery closer seeing;
In mirrored hues we have our life and being.

# IMPERIAL PALACE

*The Throne-Room. Council of State,*
*awaiting the Emperor.*
*Enter Court retinue, of all kinds, in splendid costumes.*
*The Emperor assumes his throne; on his right*
*is the Astrologer.*

EMPEROR. Greetings, my friends, and royal good cheer
    To thanes come in from far and wide.
    My Sage I see now at my side,
    But why is not my Jester here?
SQUIRE. Your mantle's train, upon the stair,
    He followed, but fell headlong there.
    They bore this load of flesh away,
    Dead or besotted, none can say.
SECOND SQUIRE. At once, in wondrous little space,
    Another comes, to take his place,
    One richly clad and debonair,
    But so bizarre that people stare;
    The guards now check advance so cool
    With halberds crossed before his face –
    And yet he's here, the daring Fool.
MEPHISTOPHELES (*kneeling before the throne*).
    What thing's accursed yet welcome ever?
    What longed for and yet chased away?
    What lacks our safe protection never?
    What chidden from the light of day?
    Whom may you never bid draw near you?
    Whose is the most beloved name?
    Who comes before your throne to cheer you?
    Who himself outlaw will proclaim?
EMPEROR. Pray save the wit you come purveying.

This is no time for puzzle-playing,
That's something that concerns these lords –
Riddle me that! I'd prize your words.
My Fool, I fear, has travelled far away;
His place is yours, here at my side to stay.
>    (*Mephistopheles goes up and takes his place on the
>                       left hand of the Emperor.*)

MURMURS OF THE THRONG.
Another Fool – New toils begin –
Whence came he? – How's the man got in? –
The old one fell – No fall was graver –
A barrel he – And this a shaver.

EMPEROR. And so, fair greeting to my vassals dear,
From all the realm now come to council here.
You meet when starry influence is high,
And golden is the promise of the sky.
Yet tell me why, in days so smiling,
When all our thought is reconciling
Our cares with arts and masques, beguiling
The time with mummery and joy,
Why we should seek out torment and employ
Our minds with problems? Yet, if thus your will,
So be it: and we turn to duty still.

LORD CHANCELLOR.
An emperor's brow must bear the sacred zone
Whose name is Justice: and to him alone
Belongs it this high virtue to invoke.
What all desire, demand, count as their need,
It is for his royal competence to heed,
And, in his wisdom, grant it to his folk.
But how, alas, can reason serve the mind,
Or grace the heart, or helpfulness the hand,
When fever rampant through the state we find

And evil breeding evil in the land?
Who views our kingdom from this point supreme
May well suppose he sees an ugly dream,
Where law is warped to serve a lawless terror,
And misbegotten shapes increase and teem,
Disclosing to the eyes a world of Error.
One steals a herd, a wench another,
And, from the altar, cross and chalice,
And then, without a qualm to smother,
He lives unhurt to vaunt his malice.
The courts are packed with plaintiffs suing,
The judge sits high, upholstered well,
Meanwhile, with hateful hullaballooing,
Rough riot's frenzies rage and swell.
For him the law is lightly broken
Who has accomplices agreed;
And *Guilty* is a word unspoken,
Except where Innocence has dared to plead.
So is the world disintegrated,
And what is seemly turned to dust;
To stagnant doom that sense is fated
By which alone we reach the Just.
Then men of upright mind, in time,
To bribes and toadies will resort;
The judge who cannot punish crime
Joins with the culprit in his court.
My picture's black, yet darker still
I'd limn it if I had my will. (*A pause.*)
    Reforms must come without delay;
Where all commit and suffer ill,
Falls even Majesty a prey.
COMMANDER OF THE FORCES.
How wild these days of hurly-burly,

Men strike, are stricken, late and early,
Too deaf an order to obey.
The knight has crag-built keep's protection,
The burgher's walls are his redoubt,
And both maintain armed insurrection
And swear that they will last us out.
Our mercenaries, sulky growing,
Loudly demand their hireling pay,
And, but that they have monies owing,
These troops would simply melt away.
Let one resist the common trend,
He finds he stirs a hornet's nest;
The realm they promised to defend
Lies ravaged, stricken, and oppressed.
And thus unchecked is rank disorder,
And half the world is ruined, lost;
Monarchs there are, beyond our border,
But none will think this happens at his cost.

LORD TREASURER. Let talk of allies not delay us,
When subsidies they pledged to pay us,
Like doubtful water-pipes, have failed.
And, Sire, through all your royal lands
Who holds possession in his hands?
For far and wide new owners have prevailed,
With independence flouting royal sway
To please themselves, while all of us look on,
For we, alas, have given rights away
Until our right to anything is gone.
In Parties, this or that their name,
All confidence today is lacking;
Indifferent is their praise or blame,
Their love or hate have equal worth;
For who will give his neighbour backing

When foxy powers have gone to earth,
A pause for Ghibelline and Guelf,
And each will only help himself?
The gold is gone, its portal barred.
Each grabs and scrapes and tries to guard
His hoard. The treasury is void.

LORD SENESCHAL. How wretchedly am I employed!
We daily try to save and store,
When every day our needs are more,
No day without new task for me.
The cooks are well maintained at present
With deer and wild-boar, hare and pheasant:
Supply of victuals shows no slacking
If paid in kind; but wine is lacking.
Time was, our cellars had their wealths
Of cask on cask in vintages most rare;
But noble lords for ever drinking healths
Have drunk them dry and left the cellars bare.
The City Council, too, must have its share:
In lifting tankards shows itself most able,
And ends its banquets underneath the table.
I pay the piper, and these call the dances;
No pity has the Jew for my mischances:
I write him bills for his advances.
They slaughter swine unfattened and unfed,
They even pawn the pillows from the bed,
Our bread is eaten ere it serves our board.

EMPEROR. Wilt tell us, Fool, some misery unsaid?

MEPHISTOPHELES.

By no means, my resplendent royal lord:
One glance upon your train, and faith's restored.
What room for fears, where Majesty holds sway,
And ready power keeps hostile threats at bay;

Where thrives good-will, with strength of wisdom
    crowned,
And manifold activities abound?
Here evil things are powerless to combine,
And gloom is banned where stars in galaxy shine.

MURMURS OF THE THRONG.

Ay, that's a rogue – He knows his way about –
Climbs in on lies – If only not found out –
It's clear to me – Things are not what they seem –
And what comes next? – He'll have some crafty scheme.

MEPHISTOPHELES.

Are there not always wants, the wide world o'er?
Now this, now that, but money in our case;
Which, truly, can't be picked up off the floor,
Yet wisdom delves in treasure's deepest place.
In mountain-veins, old walls, or underground,
Is gold, uncoined or minted, to be found.
And should you ask who'll bring that store to light:
'Tis he endowed with Mind and Nature's might.

LORD CHANCELLOR.

Nature and Mind! – Terms Christian ears resist!
For talk like this we burn the atheist.
Such words are full of danger and despite:
Nature means Sin, and Mind the Devil!
The two breed Doubt, misshapen evil,
Their ill-begot hermaphrodite.
Not so with us! – The royal domains
Of old engender two great strains,
Enthroning their imperial lord:
The Men of God and Knights are they
Who hold all threatened storms away,
With Church and State as their reward.
Thus rabble leaders and their tricks

Receive a check to keep them down:
They're sorcerers and heretics
Who wreck the country and the town:
And these will you, with wanton jesting,
Now smuggle in, our noble court infesting,
You cling to such corrupted hearts,
For you and they are counterparts.

MEPHISTOPHELES.
A speech that shows the learned lord you are!
What you don't touch, is leagues afar;
What you can't grasp, is total loss for you:
What you can't reckon, seems to you untrue.
What you can't weigh, possesses then no weight,
What you can't coin, must be invalidate.

EMPEROR. All this serves little to relieve our need,
To what does all your lenten sermon lead?
I'm tired of everlasting If and How;
Our need is gold; then get it, here and now.

MEPHISTOPHELES.
Your want I'll solve, and make still greater levy,
Thus making light of what in fact is heavy.
The stuff lies there: the problem is to win it;
That calls for art, and who can now begin it?
Yet ponder this: in times of panic flight,
Of land and folk submerged in hostile might,
This man or that, by urgent terror ridden,
His dearest treasure here or there has hidden.
'Twas thus in mighty times of Roman fame,
And evermore, to present day, the same.
There, quiet beneath the ground, lies wealth untold:
The ground's the Emperor's, and his the gold.

LORD TREASURER.
This speech now, for a Fool, is fairly bright,

For there we have the Crown's established right.

LORD CHANCELLOR.

These are the snares that Satan lays, to try us:
With lure of gold, but nothing right or pious.

LORD SENESCHAL.

If only he can bring to court the needful,
A pinch of wrong won't find me very heedful.

COMMANDER OF THE FORCES.

The Fool has wit: wide bounty is his aim,
A soldier will not ask from where it came.

MEPHISTOPHELES.

And should you think yourselves by me deceived,
Here's one, the Astrologer, may be believed.
He knows each orbit, house, and influence well:
Now say, what truths the starry heavens tell.

MURMURS OF THE THRONG.

Two rascals – In collusion, these –
Dreamer and Fool – And, if you please,
So near the Throne – Stale songs and speeches –
The Fool will prompt – And Grey-beard preaches.

ASTROLOGER (*speaks, while Mephistopheles prompts*).

The Sun himself is gold in pure array,
While herald Mercury has gold for pay.
The Lady Venus has bewitched you all,
Her winning glances constantly enthral.
Chaste Madam Moon has whims that never cease,
And Mars, not striking, yet endangers peace.
Still Jupiter remains the finest star,
Saturn, though great, seems small because so far.
Metallic is he, but not prized as such:
His worth is little, though his weight is much.
Ah, when the Sun is married to the Moon,
Silver with gold, the world is merry soon;

The rest will follow: palace, garden-close,
And pretty breasts, and cheeks like summer's rose.
And all these he commands, the man of learning,
Who wields a power that passes our discerning.

EMPEROR. With all his words I task my hearing sore,
But seem no wiser than I was before.

MURMURS OF THE THRONG.
What's this avail? – A played-out tale –
Calendar-quack – And alchemist pack –
I've heard enough – Misleading stuff –
He comes with talk – And is a gawk –

MEPHISTOPHELES.
They stand around and gape and grumble,
Mistrusting treasure-trove and spell;
Of mandrake-roots the one will mumble,
The other of the Hound of Hell.
And how shall one cry out on witches,
Another air his wit in pride,
When soon his sole shall walk on itches,
When soon shall fail his lusty stride?
Within you stir the secret strains
Of Nature's ferment never-ending,
And, from the hidden deeps ascending,
It worms its trail along your veins.
When limbs start twitching, ague-inclined,
When eerie grows the field and floor,
Straight dig and delve, and there you'll find
The fiddler and the golden store.*

MURMURS OF THE THRONG.
Odds life, my feet have turned to lead –
Perhaps the gout – My arm's gone dead –

* A touch of superstitious folk-lore: where someone stumbled a fiddler
was buried, or perhaps treasure.

A devilish twitching in my toe –
Pains in the back, and vertigo –
Here will be found, to judge by signs,
A treasure rich as Solomon's mines.

EMPEROR. Make haste! Not this time sneak away.
Come, test your frothy fabrications,
And show these noble habitations.
If there is truth in what you say,
I'll lay down Sword and Mace as well,
And toil with hands the working-day
To end the task. If lies you tell,
I'll send you packing, down to Hell.

MEPHISTOPHELES.
That path, indeed, I could pursue unaided –
Yet nobody can be enough persuaded
What wealth unclaimed lies hid in many a burrow.
The humble ploughman, following his furrow,
Will turn a precious goblet with the mould;
Or if he chips saltpetre from the wall,
He finds perhaps a wallet lined with gold,
With joyful fright, poor man, at such a haul.
What vaults the treasure-seeker has to blast!
Into what rifts he goes, what chasms vast,
Bold neighbour to the Underworld at last!
In spacious vaults, with must of ages sealed,
Are goblets, beakers, salvers to behold,
Their wealth and splendour to his eyes revealed,
With chalices of rubies and of gold.
And if he stays, in relish of the yield,
He'll find at hand rare vintage, stilled of old.
Yet – if the erudite may have our trust –
The staves have long since crumbled into dust,
Leaving the wine contained in its own crust.

In vivid essence noble wines, as well
As jewels and gold, will come with night to dwell,
And shroud their being in the fearful gloam.
Here wise explorers suffer no rebuff:
What daylight shows is often paltry stuff,
Deep mysteries take darkness for their home.

EMPEROR.

Those you can have. From gloam there's nought to glean.
If things have worth, then let that worth be seen.
Which man's the rogue? In pitch-dark, who can say?
Where every cow is black, all cats are grey.
Those crocks of massy gold, in deep earth's night –
Go, drive your plough, unearth them to the light.

MEPHISTOPHELES.

Take spade and mattock, dig, and not by halves,
Ply your own hands, the toil will make you great,
And raise yourself a herd of golden calves
That spring from earth, enriching your estate.
There, with no check or drag on your delight,
Your love and self you'll deck with jewels bright;
For Majesty and Beauty on their thrones
Are fairer still by light of precious stones.

EMPEROR. Then come, at once! What need to linger?

ASTROLOGER (*prompted, as before*).                    Sire,
I beg you moderate this hot desire.
First end the carnival, the motley game,
For minds distraught will hardly serve our aim.
Let self-command, atonement be our school:
They serve the higher things, who lower rule.
If Good you seek, then first be free from blame,
If Joy, compose the blood, that it be cool.
If wine you ask, send lovely grapes to press,
If miracles, a stronger faith possess.

EMPEROR. Then let these days be given to merriment,
　And thus Ash-Wednesday brings a wished-for Lent.
　Let mirth prevail, and mummery withal,
　More mad than ever, in our Carnival.

MEPHISTOPHELES.
　How Merit comes to be with Fortune twined.
　Is to these fools undreamt-of and unknown:
　Give them the Stone of Wisdom, and you'd find
　Philosophy gone – and what was left, the stone.


## SPACIOUS HALL

*With Apartments leading off. There is decoration and
festal finish, as for the Masquerade.*

HERALD. Look not, as in German revels,
　For dance of Death's-Heads, Fools, or Devils:
　Gay gladness lights your holiday.
　Our Sovereign's quest, in royal excursion,
　For his good gain and your diversion,
　Has crossed the airy Alpine way,
　And won a Kingdom fair and gay.
　Thus, at the holy footstool kneeling,
　At first he begged his power from Rome,
　And gained a crown by this appealing,
　And brought for us a Fool's Cap home.
　We are all born again, translated,
　For every well-instructed man
　Makes snug his head and ears, fool self-created,
　Proclaims aloft his madness, folly-pated,
　And hides, below, such wisdom as he can.
　More crowded grows their thronging and jocunder,
　In love they pair, or sway their ranks asunder.

Musicians, singers, set the precincts humming,
Come freely on! And stand not on your coming,
The monarch, now as ever, is Misrule:
With endless tricks of mockery and mumming,
The world wears motley as the one great Fool.

FLOWER-GIRLS (*song to the sound of mandolins*).
Florentines are we by nation,
Thus arranged in festal sort,
Hoping for the commendation
Of the brilliant German court.

So, our chestnut hair entwining,
With the lure of many a flower,
Wear we silken flosses shining
With the threads of beauty's power.

Services we think to render,
Such as comfort and endear,
For, by art, in fadeless splendour
Bloom our flowers all the year.

Coloured lappets, snipped caprices,
Form a concord by our skill.
If you mock it, judged in pieces,
Yet the whole delights you still.

Fair are we to the beholder,
Flower-girls speaking to the heart,
For the fates of woman mould her
With a nature kin to art.

HERALD. Come, the wealth of baskets showing,
From the lovely heads that bear them:
Flowers on arms and shoulders glowing,
Each may choose, with joy, to wear them.
Swiftly, with your floral wreathing,
Clothe the alley, twine the bower,
Make a garden round us breathing,

Sweet the pedlar as the flower.

FLOWER-GIRLS. Then come buy, with joyous token,
Barter-tricks let none assume:
Gallants with few words, fair-spoken,
Find the meaning of the bloom.

OLIVE BRANCH (*fruit-laden*).
To floral fame I've no pretension,
Envy I shun, and all dissension,
Things against my natural vein.
Yet I am the pith of nations,
Pledging with my rich oblations
Peace to every flowery plain.
May this day's most happy fate
Bring me a noble brow to decorate.

WREATH OF GOLDEN EARS OF CORN.
Ceres' gifts for your attiring
In their loveliness excel:
May the gain of your desiring
Give you beauty's grace as well.

WREATH OF FANCY. Coloured blossoms like the mallow,
Sprung from moss, a miracle:
Fashion can beget and hallow
Even what's unnatural.

NOSEGAY OF FANCY. Now to name my sprays so rare
Theophrastus would not dare.
Charms I bring, in hope to cheer
If not all, yet many here.
She shall gather my caresses,
Who will braid me in her tresses;
Still more joy may she impart
If she sets me near the heart.

CHALLENGE. Let bright fancies, beyond reason,
Grace the fashion of the season,

Strange, fantastic, many-splendoured,
Such as Nature ne'er engendered;
Cups of gold and stems of green
Through the tresses' wealth are seen –
We, the while,

ROSEBUDS.         will hide from sight;
He who finds us wins delight.
When the summer days return
And the buds of roses burn,
Who can turn such bliss away?
All the promise, all the yielding,
Holds, with powers of Flora's wielding,
Eyes and sense and soul in sway.

(*In green bowers and avenues the Flower-Girls arrange
a pretty display of their wares.*)

GARDENERS (*song accompanied by lutes*).
Flowers your foreheads to embellish
Bloom in stillness here to greet you;
Fruits give promise not to cheat you,
Taste, and you shall truly relish.

    Swarthy girls, aglow, cheeks burning,
Tempt with cherries, plums, and peaches;
Buy, for eyes have less discerning
Than the tongue; the palate teaches.

    Ripe the fruit, come look upon it,
Feast of joy for your delight.
Roses are for song and sonnet,
But the apple waits your bite.

    Grant us then that we be mated
To your flowers of youth so fair,
And we offer consecrated
Mellow fullness of our ware.

    Then in arbours wreathed and winding,

Twined with many a tender shoot,
Waits fulfilment for the finding,
Bud and blossom, leaf and fruit.

(*With antiphonal singing, accompanied on guitars and lutes, both Choruses proceed to display their wares, piling them step-wise and inviting custom.*)

### Mother and Daughter

MOTHER. Dearest girl, when first you came
Pretty hoods I made you,
Fair of face and sweet of frame
Softly I arrayed you,
Saw you in my hopes a bride,
Rich in wedded rank and pride;
So my thoughts portrayed you.

Years, alas, have fled away,
Bringing no such blessing,
Fled the troop of suitors gay,
Idle their professing;
Though a dancer felt your charm,
Yet another, arm to arm,
Knew a deft caressing.

Parties, cunning though their aim,
Brought a conquest never,
Forfeits, or the Odd Man game,
Proved a vain endeavour.
Fools today come on apace;
Dearest, give your fond embrace,
Make one yours for ever.

(*Other girls, playful companions of youth and beauty, join the throng, and gay chatter grows louder. Fishers and Fowlers, with nets, rods, limed twigs, and other gear, enter and mingle with the pretty girls. Various attempts in wooing and pursuing, in catching and escaping, give rise to delightful dialogues.*)

WOODCUTTERS (*boisterous and uncouth in their entrance*).
   Make way, give ground!
   Room for the wood-men,
   Brawny lads, good men,
   Who send the trees falling,
   Crashing and sprawling,
   And in our hauling
   Hard knocks abound.
   Give credit ungrudging,
   Look clearly and straight:
   The rough folk go drudging
   For fine folk and great;
   How, workers misjudging,
   Would these keep their state,
   With all their brain-fretting?
   Learn this, you the chosen,
   You all would be frozen
   Except for our sweating.
PULCINELLI (*clumsy, almost half-wits*).
   You are bent double,
   Fools, born for trouble.
   We folk are clever,
   Load-bearing never,
   Wearing our trappings,
   Cocks-combs, and wrappings,
   Light as you please.
   And so, with ease,
   Comfort and pleasure,
   Slippered, at leisure,
   Through stalls we wander,
   With time to squander,
   Staring and stopping,
   Crowing and hopping;

With cries resounding,
Through the press bounding,
Slip we like eels,
And kick up our heels.
Riot repays us:
Whether you praise us,
Whether you blame,
To us is the same.

PARASITES (*fawning and lascivious*).
You sturdy hauliers,
With kinsmen colliers,
Toiling so hard,
Have our regard.
Of bowing and scraping,
Nodding and apeing,
The tortuous phrase,
False yeas and nays,
Hot and cold blowing,
With the mode going,
What is the use?
Whirlwinds of fire,
Monstrous and dire,
Heavens could produce,
No good bestowing,
Had we not heavers,
Coal and log-cleavers
To keep the hearth glowing.
There's frizzling, boiling,
Sizzling, broiling!
The glutton, joint-picker,
Lip-smacker, plate-licker,
Sniffs then at roasts
Or fish fit for fables,

And girds him for toasts
At noblemen's tables.

DRUNKARD (*maudlin*). Today, I reckon, life has merits:
I love it all, no matter what.
Health and song and best of spirits –
Here you are – I've brought the lot.
And so I keep on drinking, drinking.
Here's to you, sirs, glasses clinking!
You at the back, sir, pray come on,
Clink my glass and call it done.

My loving spouse, with indignation,
Sneered at this my motley coat
And, for all my protestation,
Called me masquerading goat.
But I keep on drinking, drinking,
Bumping glasses, ringing, clinking,
Masqueraders, drink! All's one.
On the clink we'll call it done.

Me adrift? – No need to dread it,
Sweet and snug my lot is laid.
If the host won't give you credit,
Ask the hostess or the maid.
So I drink, and keep on drinking,
Come, you others, with your clinking;
Drinks all round for everyone! –
Seems to me, the thing is done.

How and where I'm satisfying
Pleasure, let it be complete.
Let me lie where I am lying,
For I cannot trust my feet.

CHORUS. Brothers all, keep up the drinking,
Give a toast to set 'em clinking,
Stick at board, enjoy the fun,

With him beneath the table, done.

(*The Herald announces various poets: Nature poets,
Singers of Court and of Chivalry, Sentimentalists, and
Rhapsodists. In the crowd of rivals of all sorts, no one allows
anyone else to hold forth. One of them slinks past, muttering.*)

SATIRICAL POET. Now, in my poetic writing,

Guess what I would hold most dear:

To go singing and reciting

Things that none would want to hear.

(*The Poets of Night and Charnel-house beg to be excused
because they have just struck up an interesting conversation
with a newly arisen Vampire, and this might lead to the de-
velopment of a new genre of poetry. The Herald has to accept
the excuse, and he calls on Greek Mythology to fill the gap,
which it does, retaining still both character and charm even in
the mask of modern times.*)

### The Graces

AGLAIA. Grace we bring as flower of living;

Let fair grace be in your giving.

HEGEMONE. Grace be in your glad receiving,

Heart's desire is sweet achieving.

EUPHROSYNE. Closed in tranquil time and place,

Thankfulness has special grace.

### The Parcae

ATROPOS. I, the oldest, here am bidden,

With my wheel, to celebrate.

Deep the dreams and thoughts lie hidden

In life's fragile thread and fate.

That your thread be fine and flowing,

Sweetest flax is purified;

Softness, smoothness, grace, the knowing

Fingers, doubt not, will provide.

Should you plunge in dance and pleasure,

Proud, for exultation's sake,
Think, this thread has proper measure;
Have a care, for it could break.

CLOTHO. Lo, of late, you see me wearing
Shears I am empowered to ply,
For our Eldest's deeds and bearing
Failed, alas, to edify.

Useless yarn, in endless spinning,
Sought the sunlight from her loom;
Glorious aims and hopes of winning
Dragged she broken to the tomb.

Yet I, too, in youth's rash ruling,
Wrought in error far and wide;
But today, all impulse schooling,
Shears I sheathe, here at my side.

Thus I take my curbing gladly,
Smiling on this place today;
In your freedom, blithely, madly
Let your revel have its way.

LACHESIS. I, with light that will not dwindle,
Still control the living thread;
And my constant, flying spindle
Never yet has oversped.

Threads come forth, my spool receives them,
Each I guide upon its way;
Governed by the hand that weaves them
All will circle and obey.

Should I once forget or slumber,
Hope for all the world were vain;
Hours they count and years they number,
And the Weaver takes the skein.

HERALD. Though deeply learned, with antiquarian zest,
You will not know the persons now approaching;

And seeing them, so apt in evil-broaching,
You would proclaim each one a welcome guest.
    These are the Furies, though you doubt the avower,
Fair, sweet of form, of smiling youth and kind:
Consort awhile with them, and you will find
Such venomed doves can wound, with serpent-power.
    Though treachery is theirs, the season urges
That each should wear his folly with elation;
These therefore claim no angels' reputation,
But own themselves as town and country scourges.

*The Furies*

ALECTO. What's that to you? You'll trust us all the same,
Us pretty, each so young, a coaxing kitten,
And whoso has a lass with whom he's smitten,
We'll stroke his ears and teach the sugared game,
    Until we tell him, with no doubtful voice,
She plays with others, goes from flame to flame,
Is thick of wit and crooked-backed and lame
And good for nothing as a bridal choice.
    And then his love, with flutter we molest her:
Her darling – thus the fears of love we handle –
Has told of her, to such a one, a scandal.
They make it up? – But still some thoughts will fester.

MEGAERA. A trifle that! Observe the married creature:
There I begin; and can in every case
The purest bliss by idle whims deface,
So varies mood and hour and human nature.
    And holding in his arms what most should charm him,
Each fool will set his dreams on some new yearning;
From highest joy, now grown familiar, turning,
He shuns the sun, and takes the frost to warm him.
    With practised hand I rule in these affairs,
And bring in Asmodeus, trusty devil,

To sow, when time is ripe, conjugal evil,
And thus I wreck the human-race in pairs.

TISIPHONE.

Sharper than barbed words, I send you
Steel and poison for the traitor.
False your love: then sooner, later,
Havoc comes to pierce and rend you.
　　Then on sweetness falls the sentence,
Love is turned to froth and gall.
Here's no bartering market-hall:
Penance follows on repentance.
　　Warble not the word 'forgive'!
Plead to Echo's rocks and stones,
'Vengeance' is the word she moans:
He that's fickle shall not live.

HERALD. And now be good enough to stand aside:
You'll find what comes so strange and unallied.
A mountain moves relentless through the throng:
His flanks in housings rich, he sways along.
Lithe like a snake his trunk, his tusks immense,
A sight mysterious, but I show the sense.
Upon his neck a dainty woman rides,
And with her wand controls his solemn strides.
Another, throned on high in queenly guise,
Is clothed in sheen too dazzling for my eyes.
Two women, noble but in chains, walk near,
One blithe of mien, the other full of fear;
One freedom lacks, the other's free in feeling.
Let each now speak, her character revealing.

FEAR. Lamps and torches, murky graces,
Light the riotous festal room;
In a whirl of cheating faces
Chained am I, in captive doom.

Hence, you throng of fleering, flocking,
Grinned at grinners, full of spite.
All my foes, with threats and mocking,
Crowd upon me in the night.
　　Here's a friend turned foe: his masking
I detect, his mummer's play;
Made my murder all his tasking,
Now, unmasked, he slinks away.
　　All my thoughts dwell on escaping
To the wide world's utmost bound;
But, from far, my ruin shaping,
Haze and horror hedge me round.

HOPE. Sisters all, I give you greeting.
You have made a merry meeting,
Mummers pleased with passing days,
Yet I know full well your ways:
On the morrow comes unmasking.
And if torch-light fails of pleasure,
Such as brings a special thrill,
Yet in days of lively leisure
Joys await us for our asking:
Lonely or in throngs, at will,
Through green pastures we may wander
Free to rest or work or ponder,
Living free of care or grieving,
Naught forgoing, all achieving;
Everywhere the folk befriend us,
Welcome guests with sanguine powers,
Somewhere fortune must attend us,
All that's best must needs be ours.

PRUDENCE. Fear and Hope, behold them chained,
They who keep mankind enslaved,
Now from common harm restrained;

Clear the way, for you are saved.
   Lo, I lead this living giant,
A colossus, tower-bearing,
Pacing, steady and compliant,
Step by step, his rugged faring.
   In that lofty turret swaying,
Lo, the goddess, with swift pinions
Spread for conquest, now surveying,
As she turns, her new dominions.
   Clothed in splendour, radiant, glorious,
Far and near her beacon rises;
Victory her name, victorious
Goddess of man's enterprises.

ZOÏLO-THERSITES. Hu, hu! I come upon the spot,
To damn you as an evil lot.
And Dame Victoria up there
Shall come in for a special share.
With spreading pinions, snowy, regal,
She thinks herself no doubt an eagle.
Convinced, wherever she may stir,
That land and folk belong to her.
But when some lofty thing is done
I gird at once my harness on.
Up with what's low, what's high eschew,
Call crooked straight, and straight askew.
What need I more, for health and worth:
I'd have it so throughout the earth.

HERALD. Then show, you cur of mongrel birth,
Now smitten by the master-mace,
The instant writhing of your race.
Lo, how this double-dwarf, this ape,
Curls in a ball, a loathsome shape!
The shape turns egg-like! Wondrous view!

Puffs itself out, and breaks in two!
And strange twin-progeny appear;
A bat, an adder have we here:
The one in dust-tracks slides and curls,
The dark thing round the ceiling whirls,
Now out to join her mate she's whirred,
I would not care to make a third.

MURMURING VOICES. Yonder, quick, the dance is on –
My desire is to be gone –
How the horrid spectral race
Flits around us in this place!
Something brushed against my hair –
Caught my tread all unaware –
None has wound or hurt to show –
Yet the terror starts to grow –
Gaiety is crushed and ended –
As the vermin-pair intended.

HERALD. Herald's duties on me laid,
Here, and in all masquerade,
Bid me watch all doors, to guard you,
Lest perdition slink toward you
In this chosen place of bliss:
I'll not budge or shrink in this.
Yet, I fear, through window spaces
Spirits glide and spectral faces,
And from ghosts and sorcery
I can hardly set you free.
First the dwarf had power to shake us,
Floods of force now overtake us.
Meaning, in the shapes that rose,
Could I formally disclose;
But what eludes my keen observing
Must elude my explanation:

Help me to interpretation!
What proud chariot now goes swerving,
Four-in-hand throughout the throng?
Splendidly it swings along,
Touching none; no crowds divide,
None is hurt or thrust aside.
Distant dazzling hues are burning,
As in magic lantern turning,
Errant stars for our discerning;
Hurtling comes the fierce assault.
Back, make way! I shudder!

BOY CHARIOTEER.                    Halt!
Steeds, your wingèd course restrain,
Own your lord's time-honoured rein,
Find self-mastery and your master,
Then, inspired by me, speed faster –
Honour here this noble hall.
See the growing congress, all
Us admiring, crowding round.
Herald up, your fanfare sound,
Ere we go from you afar,
To the throng depict and show us,
Allegories that we are –
And as such you ought to know us.

HERALD. I am at a loss to name you.
Though to picture you I dare.

BOY CHARIOTEER. So begin.

HERALD.                    Then I proclaim you
First a creature young and fair,
Half boy, half man: the ladies own
They'd rather see you fully grown.
You seem a promising pursuer,
Seductive, bred and born a wooer.

BOY CHARIOTEER.

  That strikes a note! Go on, in fancy free,
  Until you find the pretty riddle's key.

HERALD.

  Deep lightning in dark eyes, black midnight curls,
  All heightened by a jewelled circlet's beam!
  From shoulder falls the splendid toga's stream
  To touch the buskin with its flowing furls
  And thread of gold and royal purple gleam.
  A girlish charm you have that calls for banter,
  And yet, for weal or woe, love's devotee,
  Among the girls you'd make a powerful canter,
  And they would teach you soon the A.B.C.

BOY CHARIOTEER. And what of him who sits on high,
  The noble figure on the chariot's throne?

HERALD. His looks a monarch's bounty signify:
  Who earns his favour makes his luck his own,
  And needs no more to struggle for his rights.
  That glance can check the grudging freak of fate,
  And in bestowal of his pure delights
  Is more than ample luck or rich estate.

BOY CHARIOTEER.

  So far, so good; but there you may not rest:
  Complete your picture and fulfil your quest.

HERALD. High dignity is past description's power.
  A visage bright as moon, I see, the flower
  Of health, the mouth superb, the cheeks a-bloom,
  Shining beneath the turban, beauty's plume.
  The flowing robe he wears with royal air;
  To picture such a presence I despair.
  As ruling lord I seem to know his fame.

BOY CHARIOTEER.

  Plutus, whom men the god of riches name,

Now come to us in all his pomp and pride,
The mighty Emperor needs him at his side.

HERALD.

And you, what rank, what nature may yours be?

BOY CHARIOTEER. Profusion I, the soul of Poesy;
The poet I, fulfilled and one content
When, prodigal, his special wealth is spent.
I, too, am lord of opulence untold,
A match for Plutus I, for all his gold.
His festal court I grace with life and pride,
And what he lacks, that can my art provide.

HERALD. A charm you show, in vaunting such a prize,
But show your arts, with proof before our eyes.

BOY CHARIOTEER.

I've but to snap my fingers and, behold,
The chariot is touched with glint of fire.
Thence comes this string of pearls that you admire,
And, for the neck and ears, rich gauds of gold.

*(Snapping still with his fingers.)*

Here's comb and crown, a flawless diadem,
And rings that shine with many a priceless gem;
And spurts of flame I scatter, with intent
To see what kindling answers the event.

HERALD. Now see the charming mob all grabbing rush,
They almost maul the donor in the crush.
The gems he flicks around as in a dream,
And snatchers fill the hall in greedy stream.
But lo, a trick quite new to me:
The thing each seizes eagerly
Rewards him with a scurvy pay,
The gift dissolves and floats away.
The pearls are loosened from their band,
And beetles scurry round his hand.

In haste he flings them off, poor lout,
And round his head they buzz about.
With solid goods before their eyes,
Some grab, and catch frail butterflies.
The rascal offers wealth untold,
But gives the glitter, not the gold.

BOY CHARIOTEER.
Masks you discern, and introduce them well,
But piercing to the truth beneath the shell,
That is beyond a herald's courtly task –
A deeper insight for that quest we ask.
Yet will I keep from any feud or rift:
My questioning voice to you, my lord, I lift.

(*Turning to Plutus.*)

Did you not to me confide
The tempest of this four-in-hand?
You choose, and I the whirlwind ride,
Am I not there, where you command?
Who served with fearless wings your throne,
To bear the palm for you alone?
When troubles called the sabre from the sheath,
How often has the victory been mine?
When laurels graced that lofty brow of thine,
Whose hand but mine, whose art has wrought the
        wreath?

PLUTUS. Is witness needed, gladly will I bear it,
And name you very spirit of my spirit.
Your actions meet my wishes and outfly,
And richer are you, in the end, than I.
I treasure, to your praise and your renown,
The bough of green beyond all other crown.
I speak this word of truth to everyone:
In you I have my joy, beloved son.

BOY CHARIOTEER (*to the crowd*).

　The greatest gifts my hand has to bestow
　Are scattered left and right in lavish share.
　Behold, on many a head the tiny glow,
　The spurt of flame that I have kindled there.
　From brow to brow the lambent flashing springs,
　Eluding most, though here and there it clings;
　But rarely does the tongue of flame leap higher,
　To bear a token like a flower of fire.
　With many, ere they recognize the spark,
　It burns away, and all is sad and dark.

CHATTER OF WOMEN.

　He on the coach, perched up on high,
　That one's a mountebank, say I.
　And, crouched behind, a clown so thin
　You'd think him nought but bones and skin,
　A starveling this, and down at heel,
　Pinch him, and nothing would he feel.

THE STARVELING. Disgusting women-folk, stand back!

　Ill-will from you I never lack.
　When hearth and home were women's zone,
　As Avaritia I was known.
　Then throve the home, with care devout,
　Much coming in while nought went out.
　The coffers were my constant care.
　And who will zeal a vice declare!
　But, following the modern drift,
　A wife has no more use for thrift,
　So she, like all defaulting ninnies,
　Has more desires than she has guineas.
　The husband meanwhile fumes and frets;
　Whichever way he looks are debts.
　The wife, what funds she can recover,

Spends on her back and on her lover.
And, with the evil crowd that woo,
She daintier dines, and drinks more, too.
The charm of gold I then acclaim,
And Greed, male gender, is my name.

LEADER OF THE WOMEN.

Let dragons vie in dragons' greed,
But in the end it's cheating stuff.
He comes to give the men a lead,
When, lord, they're troublesome enough.

WOMEN IN A CROWD.

The scare-crow, clout him off his waggon!
What care we for his gibbet-face?
And shall we flinch at his grimace,
Or fear a lath-and-plaster dragon?
Come on, and teach the clown his place!

HERALD. Obey my wand, keep order there!
And yet no help they need from me.
Lo, of his quick-won ground aware,
Each grisly monster spreads his pair
Of double wings, most grim to see.
The dragons gnash and writhe in ire,
Their scaly gorges spewing fire;
The place is void, the people flee.

(*Plutus comes down from the chariot.*)

Lo, he descends with kingly mien,
And dragons, at his sign serene,
Have gone to bring the coffer down,
Gold-filled, and bearing Greed, the clown.
With wondrous power their load they bring,
And set the chest before the king.

PLUTUS (*to the Charioteer*).

Now is your all too heavy duty done

And freedom for your proper sphere is won.
Not here your place, in wild and tangled maze
Of things distorted: fly these chequered ways,
To where you look clear-eyed on beauty's face,
And claim your soul, can to yourself be true,
Where joy is all in goodness and in grace,
To solitude! – There build your world anew.

BOY CHARIOTEER.

As I, my kinsman near and dear, do love you,
So may I be an envoy worthy of you.
Rich plenty reigns with you; and where I dwell
Each feels he has a glorious gain to tell;
And, wavering, he serves now you, now me,
Inconstant life so shakes his fealty.
Your subjects, frankly, rest in soothing peace:
Who follows me, his strivings never cease.
My action is not secret or concealed:
If I so much as breathe, I stand revealed.
And so farewell: you grace my fortune's tide,
But softly call, and I am at your side.

(*He goes even as he came.*)

PLUTUS. The time is come to set the treasure free.
To smite the locks I take the Herald's rod.
They spring apart! From brazen cauldrons, see
The flow comes welling up like golden blood.
The wealth of crowns and rings and chains comes pouring
In molten blaze that threatens their devouring.

VOICES OF THE CROWD IN ALTERNATING CLAMOUR.

Ay, look! For there the treasures flow,
The coffer brims with gold aglow –
See, vessels melting, and of gold,
And minted money wildly rolled –
The ducats skip as though new-struck,

My heart beats high with so much luck –
There's all I crave for here, and more,
They roll pell-mell about the floor –
Come on, there's fortunes here to make,
Stoop down, and wealth is yours to take –
The rest of us, in action swift,
Will seize the coffer as a gift.

HERALD. What think you, fools? What think you, pray?
There's nothing here but mummers' play.
This night your lust must have an end:
Think you we give real gold to spend?
Your just deservings in this farce
Are less than token-coins of brass.
You dolts, you're ready to receive
As solid truth a makebelieve.
What's truth to you? – A musty dream
You clutch at, with devout esteem.
You, Plutus, lord of mumming mien,
Drive me this rabble from the scene.

PLUTUS. Your wand commands the proper power;
Pray lend it me, a little hour.
I dip it in the molten glow:
Look to your safety, mummers! Lo
It flashes, crackles, sparks in showers,
A glowing wand of fiery powers.
Whoever ventures to press near
Will feel a ruthless singeing sear. –
Now go I forth upon my round.

VOICES FROM THE CRUSH AND THE TUMULT.
We're done for! Mercy me! Give ground! –
Let any flee who can! Alack!
Give ground, you people at the back!
Scorching my face come spurts of flame. –

The fiery wand has made me lame –
We're doomed and done for, one and all. –
Back, back, you raging carnival!
Back, back, mad mob, lost to all sense –
Had I but wings to lift me hence! –

PLUTUS. The threatened rush of folk is turned,
And none of them, I think, is burned.
The flinching crowd
Is frightened, cowed. –
But still, to stablish rule and law
My ring invisible I draw.

HERALD. That is a splendid work you've done.
My thanks for wisdom you have shown.

PLUTUS. Yet patience, noble friend, is needed;
Still threats of riot must be heeded.

GREED. Then we are able, if you please,
To view this circle at our ease;
For women-folk will always take the lead
In gaping or in nibbling, such their greed.
With senses free of rust I stroll at large,
And find a handsome woman handsome still;
And, as today the goods are free of charge,
I vote we go a-wooing with a will.
Yet, since in places over-full of crowd
Not every ear will grasp what's said aloud,
I'll tax my wit, and look for some successes,
In seeing what plain pantomime expresses.
In this, hand, foot, and gesture won't suffice:
I must contrive some fanciful device.
I'll work the gold in shapes, like moistened clay;
This metal's transformations who can say?

HERALD. This fool, what means he, starveling crone?
Does humour dwell in skin and bone?

He kneads, like dough, the mass of gold,
Which, in his hands, is soft to mould.
Howe'er he plies that touch of his,
He only makes deformities.
The women thus he will waylay,
They scream, and all would break away,
With fierce repugnance in their bearing:
The rascal shows his evil daring.
I fear his pleasure proves to be
The overthrow of decency.
My silence here were duty lacking,
Give me my rod, to send him packing.

PLUTUS. He little knows what outer threats portend;
Leave him his silly pranks a little longer.
His lease of comedy is near the end:
Strong is the law, necessity still stronger.

TUMULT AND SINGING.
The savage host takes up the tale,
From mountain-top and wooded vale,
They rise, indomitable clan,
To celebrate their mighty Pan.
With knowledge such as no man knows,
They crowd the now deserted close.

HERALD. Your mighty Pan I know; with that wild god
Full many a daring circuit you have trod.
I know the hidden knowledge that you bring,
And open, as your due, the narrow ring.
And now may best of luck attend them!
A wondrous course their fates could run;
They little know the way I send them,
They march, but foresight had they none.

WILD VOICES. You dressed-up folk, you tinsel-brood!
They come on rough, they come on rude,

With flying leap and rushing rout,
They come, a sturdy crew and stout.

FAUNS. With frolic air
Fauns dance around,
Crisp, curly hair
With oak-leaves crowned.
The parted curls show, peeping clear,
The fine up-pointing tapered ear;
Pretty snub-nose and visage broad
Are not by fairest eyes ignored,
And should a faun his paw advance
Beauty will scarce decline the dance.

SATYR. The satyr follows, jumping in;
A goat-foot he, with scraggy shin.
He favours sinewy legs and thin
To serve his joy: he'll perch and gaze,
Like chamois, from high mountain-ways,
Then, breathing freedom, braced and wild,
He jeers at man and wife and child,
Who think themselves alive as well,
Snug in their deep and reeky dell;
While lofty worlds, serene and pure,
Are his alone to hold secure.

GNOMES. Comes tripping in the little troop,
Not apt to pair, but in a group,
In mossy coats, with glimmer lit
Of tiny lamps, they merge and flit
In separate tasks that they perform
Like glow-worms in a shimmering swarm;
Careering featly to and fro,
With busy zeal they come and go.
    To the Little People we are kin,
Rock-surgeons, skilled in medicine.

Where lofty mountains loom and tower
Rich veins we cup, and store the power.
We heap the metal from the truck,
With cheerful hail: Good luck! Good luck!
We've good at heart, and so intend:
A good man truly we befriend.
But funds of gold do we reveal
For folk who choose to pimp and steal;
And iron we grant the mighty man
With wholesale murder as his plan.
The three commandments being broken,
Men scorn the others by that token.
In all these things the blame's not ours;
So use, like us, your patient powers.

GIANTS. The wild men come, and such their name,
 Hartz Mountain Heights know well their fame.
As stark as Nature, naked, strong,
And each a giant in that throng,
With pine-tree bole in huge right hand,
And round the waist a studded band,
With apron rough, twigs, leaves entwined,
Such body-guard no pope could find.

CHORUS OF NYMPHS (*surrounding the great Pan*).
Lo, he is come,
Of earth the sum,
Essential man,
The mighty Pan.
You joyous ones, your ranks advancing,
Greet him with whirl of lissom dancing.
Since, with a nature grave and kind,
He wills us joys to fill the mind.
Beneath the blue vault of the skies,
Most vigilant are his steady eyes.

Yet breezes cradle him in peace,
With brooks that murmur without cease.
Let noon-day bring him sleep, and now
No leaf will stir upon the bough;
But herbs that breathe refreshing balm
Will load the air with scented calm;
Then dares the nymph no more of glee,
But, standing, slumbers peacefully.
Comes startling then the fearful sound
Of the great voice that echoes round,
Like shattering thunder, raging sea,
When none knows whither he may flee;
And hosts at war dread fears assail,
And in the tumult heroes quail.
Honour to whom our praise belongs,
The god who here has led our throngs.

DEPUTATION OF GNOMES (*to the great god Pan*).

When the precious ore is shining
Threadlike through the veins of stone
And alone our rod's divining
Labyrinthine vaults has shown,
   Troglodytes, we vault our dwelling
Deep within the dark abyss,
You, in sunlight, gloom dispelling,
Grant your gracious benefice.
   Find we now the secret hiding
Of a wondrous spring, near-by,
Rich in promise, source providing
Things the mind can scarce descry.
   All this lies in your fulfilling,
Take it, Sire, in your good care:
Every treasure, at your willing,
Yields the whole wide world a share.

PLUTUS (*to the Herald*).

   Strength must we summon up, and high assurance,
   And what's to come, let come, with firm endurance.
   Indeed your courage ever has been high.
   Most frightful fate approaches, to afflict us;
   Men, and posterity, will contradict us:
   Write down true record that shall testify.

HERALD (*laying his hand on the staff which Plutus still holds*).

   The dwarfs lead Pan, that mighty sire,
   All softly to the well of fire.
   Up from the crater's depth it seethes,
   And, when it sinks and flaming wreathes,
   The gaping gloom new menace breathes.
   Fresh spouts the molten fiery vent,
   And mighty Pan stands well content,
   To watch the prodigy with pride,
   While pearls foam up on every side.
   But is there trust in sights like this?
   He bends, to peer in the abyss. –
   Alas, his beard is swept within! –
   Who may this be, so smooth of chin?
   His hand conceals it from our gaze. –
   And now fate follows ugly ways:
   Restored, the beard is all ablaze,
   It kindles head and laurel leaf,
   Joy of the throng is turned to grief.
   To quell the fire is all their aim,
   But none escapes a share of flame.
   And where the crackling sparks have darted
   Fresh tongues of fire are quickly started.
   Enveloping them thus, the fire
   Can burn a masking group entire.

    How now? What rumour greets us here,

From mouth to mouth and ear to ear!
O ill-starred, black, disastrous night,
What baleful end you bring our plight!
The dawning day that now draws near
Unwelcome tidings holds in store;
But everywhere the cries I hear:
'The Emperor's hurt and suffers sore'.
Ah, were the presaging untrue –
Doomed, in flames, both crown and retinue.
Accurst, who tricked him and misled,
Curst the pitchy garlands spread,
The arrogant roar of singing, woe
To those who wrought this overthrow!
O youth, O youth, when will you see
That joy must measure have and season,
And you, imperious Majesty,
That power must know the reins of reason?
    Our woods are flaming 'gainst the sky
With licking, pointed tongues on high,
On raftered roof their lambent spire
Threatens a universal fire.
No measure is there to our woe,
And whence our help comes, none can know.
The morrow mourns our Emperor's might,
His pride the ash-heap of a night.

PLUTUS.

Fear has cast its shadow wide,
Some boon of help we must provide.
Strike with the hallowed wand the ground,
That the depths tremble and resound.
You airy firmament on high,
Grant cool fragrance from the sky!
Come, teeming wreaths of loaded haze,

And float upon your misty ways,
To swathe the turmoil now aflame!
Dewy, curling, cloudlets swirling,
Spread your mantling, softly drenching,
Conquering throughout and quenching;
You, with blessèd moist reprieve,
Make of this, our fiery game,
Lightning of a summer's eve.
If spirits threaten from the void,
Magic powers shall be employed.

## PLEASURE GARDEN

*It is a sunny morning.*
*The Emperor, people of his Court; Faust, Mephistopheles,*
*dressed according to the mode, discreetly and*
*inconspicuously, both kneeling.*

FAUST. For conjuring with flames, your pardon, Sire.
EMPEROR. Such artifice suits well with my desire.
It seemed, within a sphere that glimmered strange,
I thought me Pluto, by some wondrous change,
O'er embers loomed, through night, a precipice
In flickering light. To that, and the abyss,
Came flames in thousands, whirling wild,
An edifice of blaze, all vaulted, aisled,
Tonguing the highest dome in fiery play,
Nor ceased to form, nor ceased to fade away.
In vista wide, through pillars wrought of flame
The great processions of my people came,
In serried ranks their columns came in view
And offered homage, as was ever due.

And here and there were courtiers I had known,
It seemed I held the salamander's throne.

MEPHISTOPHELES.

This, Sire, was true. For elemental things
Must needs accept the majesty of Kings.
Fire you have tried, proved its docility,
Now cast yourself upon the wildest sea,
Scarce have you touched the deep and pearl-strewn
    ground,
The waters gather in a noble round;
You see the green-lit waves come rolling, swelling,
With fringe of purple for your royal dwelling,
For you alone designed. Walk at your will,
The watery palaces attend you still,
Whose very walls have life, swift-darting, teeming,
With arrowy commutation vivid gleaming.
Sea monsters, eager for the soft new sheen,
Come hurtling up: none pass the lucent screen.
Playful the gold-scaled dragon nearer draws,
Lo, the shark's gorge: you laugh in his fierce jaws.
Well may your courtiers hail you with delight,
Never did such a concourse greet your sight.
Nor from the loveliest creatures are you parted:
The curious Nereids come, all tender-hearted,
To seek your splendour in the timeless waters;
Shy, sensual as the fish, those youngest daughters,
The elder sage. Word comes to Thetis, and
A second Peleus wins her heart and hand,
With it a seat in high Olympus' court –

EMPEROR. To you, the airy space for your resort:
Full early comes the hour to mount that throne.

MEPHISTOPHELES.

And all the earth is, Sovereign Lord, your own.

EMPEROR. What happy fortune brought us your delights,
    As though you stepped from the Arabian Nights?
    Prove now Scheherazade's fruitful mind,
    And highest grace and honour shall you find.
    Stand by, in humdrum days, to serve me thus,
    When often life is vilely tedious.
LORD SENESCHAL (*entering in haste*).
    Highness, in all my days, I never thought
    To be the bearer of such glad report,
    As this which fills me with delight
    And with rejoicing in your sight:
    Debts are discharged, our turmoils cease,
    The usurer's claws are set at peace,
    From hellish debtor-pangs I'm free,
    Nor heaven itself has more felicity.
COMMANDER OF THE FORCES (*following quickly*).
    The forces find arrears are paid,
    New spirit fires them on parade,
    The trooper feels his blood revive,
    The wine-shops and the wenches thrive.
EMPEROR. A deep relief your soul has breathed,
    The furrowed face in smiles is wreathed,
    And ardour brings you here with speed.
TREASURER (*joining the others*).
    Pray, ask report from these who did the deed.
FAUST. To give account befits the Chancellor's part.
CHANCELLOR (*coming forward slowly*).
    Ay, with content that gladdens my old heart. –
    Hear and behold this leaflet rich in fate,
    That turns our woes to prosperous estate:
                (*He reads*)
    'To whom it may concern, this note of hand
    Is worth a thousand ducats on demand,

The pledge whereof and guarantee is found
In treasure buried in the Emperor's ground.
These riches, raised, are earmarked to redeem
Full payment, by authority supreme.'

EMPEROR. I fear some outrage, fraudulent and obscure.
Which of you forged the imperial signature?
Think you he goes unpunished for his crime?

LORD TREASURER.
Yourself, Sire, signed, last night at masking time.
Remember, Lord, you came as mighty Pan,
And there our Chancellor put to you the plan:
'Grant, Sire,' said he, 'a festal consummation,
Your quill's few strokes will resurrect your nation.'
You signed: as if by sleight of hand, behold,
That night provided copies thousandfold.
And, so that all might have the boon to share,
We stamped the total series then and there.
Tens, Thirties, Fifties, Hundreds, all to date,
You cannot think how people jubilate.
Your town, half dead of late and melancholic,
See, teeming now with life and lusty frolic,
Your name has blessed the world for years with graces,
But never did it win such smiling faces.
Even the alphabet we could dismiss,
For in that sign we all shall find our bliss.

EMPEROR. And do my people value this as gold,
Do court and army think these payments hold?
However much amazed, my will submits.

LORD SENESCHAL.
None now has power to stay the flying chits,
They ran as quick as lightning on their way,
And money-booths kept open night and day,
Where every single note is honoured duly

With gold and silver – though with discount, truly.
From there it flows to wine-shops, butchers, bakers,
With half the world as glutton merry-makers,
The others bent on flaunting fashion-showing,
The clothiers cutting-out, the tailors sewing.
'His Majesty!' – Toasts flow and cellar clatters,
They broil and roast, and rattle with the platters.

MEPHISTOPHELES.

Who on the lonely terrace takes a turn
A lovely, elegant woman may discern.
With peacock fan she veils her pretty wiles
And smirks at us – and on our bank-note smiles,
For, swifter far than wit or wordy powers,
That little slip makes love's rich favour ours.
No nuisance with a purse or wallet there:
A leaflet's easy next the heart to wear,
And with a billet-doux it makes a pair.
Priests keep one gravely in their Book of Prayer,
And soldiers, to manoeuvre as they please,
Lighten their belts and give their loins some ease.
Your Majesty will pardon if I seem
To touch on trifles in our lofty scheme.

FAUST. The major bulk of treasure to be found
Throughout your lands, deep hidden in the ground,
Lies yet untouched. Far fancy at its best
Would be for wealth like this a wretched chest:
Imagination in its highest flight
May strive and strain and never gauge it quite.
And yet choice spirits, fit the depths to see,
Grasp infinite faith in an infinity.

MEPHISTOPHELES.

Such paper-wealth, replacing pearls or gold,
Is practical: you know just what you hold;

No need to seek exchange or market first,
With wine, with love, you slake your noble thirst.
If coin you want, the broker is at hand,
Or, failing him, you dig a piece of land.
Goblet and chain are auctioned in your name:
Your bank-note, liquidated, puts to shame
Our scornful doubters and their pretty wit.
Folk want our scheme, they now are used to it.
In Emperor's lands henceforth, on every side,
You'll find gold, jewels, and paper, well supplied.

EMPEROR. Our realm this august blessing owes to you;
Where worth ranks high, a like reward is due.
Our Kingdom's earthy depths are yours in trust,
I name you wealth's true Wardens, as is just,
You know the well-preserved, wide-hidden hoard:
The spade shall work, but only at your word.
Now be united, Masters of our Treasure,
And seal your honours with a round of pleasure.
And thus the Nether World partakes of mirth,
Gladly at one with things above the earth.

LORD TREASURER.
No shade of strife shall come to mar our mission,
I gladly take as colleague the magician.

                                        (*Exit with Faust.*)

EMPEROR.
The court shall have my bounty, each to share,
If each has use and purpose to declare.

PAGE (*receiving the bounty*).
A merry life for me, with glad good things.

ANOTHER (*likewise*).
I'll straightway buy my darling chains and rings.

CHAMBERLAIN (*accepting*).
Your cellar's vintages shall be bewitching.

ANOTHER (*likewise*).

　Within my pocket dice have started itching.

KNIGHT BANNERET (*thoughtfully*).

　My land and castle will I free from debt.

ANOTHER (*likewise*).

　I'll store with other wealth what share I get.

EMPEROR. I hoped to hear of prowess, lofty deed;

　But him who knows you, hope will not mislead.

　Full well I see: you take the treasure's thrill,

　And what you were before, that are you still.

FOOL. Your bounty, Sire, some share on me let fall.

EMPEROR. What, come to life! You'd only drink it all.

FOOL. The magic notes, they mystify me sadly.

EMPEROR. That I believe, because you use them badly.

FOOL. What shall I do? They flutter everywhere.

EMPEROR.

　Well, pick them up, they float down as your share.

(*Exit.*)

FOOL. Five thousand crowns! A bounty unexpected!

MEPHISTOPHELES.

　You walking wine-skin, are you resurrected?

FOOL. Ay, many times, but this the best as yet.

MEPHISTOPHELES.

　Such joy is yours, it oozes out in sweat.

FOOL. But have a look: is that worth solid gold?

MEPHISTOPHELES.

　It buys as much as throat and belly hold.

FOOL. And can I buy myself a house and plot?

MEPHISTOPHELES.

　Of course! Just bid, you'll get it on the spot.

FOOL. A grange, with game-preserves, can I afford?

MEPHISTOPHELES.

　No doubt. I'll hear you yet called 'Noble Lord'.

FOOL. This night I'll be a landlord, sitting pretty. (*Exit.*)
MEPHISTOPHELES.
    Now who'll deny, our fool is wise and witty.

## A GLOOMY GALLERY

*Faust and Mephistopheles*

MEPHISTOPHELES.
    Why bring me to this antique gloomy alley?
    Is not within enough of mirth and cheer,
    And in the courtiers' close-packed motley rally
    Sufficient chance to sport and chicaneer?
FAUST. Spare me the discourse of your bygone zeal,
    That special style of yours is down-at-heel.
    And now you slink about from place to place,
    Only to shirk an answer face to face;
    While I am pinched and badgered without rest,
    At Seneschal's or Chamberlain's behest.
    The Emperor asks, with urgency forthright,
    That Helen stand with Paris in his sight;
    The loveliest type of woman and of man
    In clear dimensions will the monarch scan.
    Swiftly to work! My promise can't be broken.
MEPHISTOPHELES.
    With mad unwisdom was that promise spoken.
FAUST. Fellow, you have not truly weighed
    The fateful arts you have exerted;
    By acts of ours his wealth was made,
    And now he needs to be diverted.
MEPHISTOPHELES.
    Out of the blue you think such things appear;
    But here with steepest climbing we must reckon;

You blunder boldly in the strangest sphere,
To find at last what wrecks us and bewilders.
Think you that Helen comes because you beckon,
Much as we raised the ghostly paper-guilders?
With cretin witches, ghouls, and ghost-marauders,
Or goitrous goblins, I am at your orders;
The devil's darlings have their points, are coy,
But cannot pass for heroines of Troy.
FAUST. The same old hurdy-gurdy tune you play!
A master, you, of doubt and false deduction,
The father of all hindrance and obstruction.
For each fresh cunning you require fresh pay.
I know it only needs a muttered spell:
Scarce time to turn, and we behold her there.
MEPHISTOPHELES. The heathen race is hardly my affair,
It occupies its own particular hell.
Yet aids there are.
FAUST.                    Then quick, let these be told!
MEPHISTOPHELES.
Loth am I now high mystery to unfold:
Goddesses dwell, in solitude, sublime,
Enthroned beyond the world of place or time;
Even to speak of them dismays the bold.
These are The Mothers.
FAUST.                    Mothers?
MEPHISTOPHELES.                         Stand you daunted?
FAUST.
The Mothers! Mothers – sound with wonder haunted.
MEPHISTOPHELES.
True, goddesses unknown to mortal mind,
And named indeed with dread among our kind.
To reach them, delve below earth's deepest floors;
And that we need them, all the blame is yours.

FAUST. Where lies the way?

MEPHISTOPHELES.

There *is* none. Way to the Unreachable,
Never for treading, to those Unbeseechable,
Never besought! Is your soul then ready?
Not locks or bolts are there, no barrier crude,
But lonely drift, far, lone estrangement's eddy.
What sense have you of waste and solitude?

FAUST. You could dispense with speeches of this kind,
Which bring the Witches' Kitchen back to mind,
An echo of far distant days renewed.
Was not my fate to mix with earthly vanity,
Learn the inane, and then impart inanity?
And when I ventured what I could of sense
Dislike and protest grew the more intense.
Was I not driven, under strain and stress,
To seek for comfort in the wilderness?
And not to live foredoomed, alone, apart,
At last I have to give the devil my heart.

MEPHISTOPHELES.

And if to ocean's end your path should lead,
To look upon enormity of space,
Still would you see that waves to waves succeed,
Ay, though you have a shuddering doom to face,
You'd still see something. For in the green
Of silenced depths are gliding dolphins seen;
Still cloud will stir, and sun and moon and star;
But blank is that eternal void afar:
There eyes avail not, even your step is dumb,
No substance there, when to your rest you come.

FAUST. Like the prime mystagogue your piece you say,
The first to lead true neophytes astray;
But in reverse: into the void you send me

That greater power and cunning may attend me.
The fabled cat am I, who will not tire
To scratch your chestnuts for you from the fire.
Well, let us on! We'll plumb your deepest ground,
For in your Nothing may the All be found.

MEPHISTOPHELES.

Congratulations to you, ere we part,
I see you know the devil, Sir, by heart.
Here, take from me this key –
FAUST.                               That petty thing!
MEPHISTOPHELES. First hold it, man, not undervaluing.
FAUST. It grows, it sparkles, blazes in my hand!

MEPHISTOPHELES.

Its hidden power you soon may understand.
This key will scent the true trail from all others;
Follow it down, 'twill guide you to The Mothers.

FAUST (*shuddering*).

The Mothers – still I feel the shock of fear.
What is this Word, that I must dread to hear?

MEPHISTOPHELES.

Are you a dunce who jibs at a new word?
Or deaf, except for things already heard?
Be not perturbed, however strange it rings,
You so familiar with all wondrous things.

FAUST. And yet in torpor see I no salvation:
To feel the thrill of awe crowns man's creation.
Though feeling pays the price, by earthly law,
Stupendous things are deepest felt through awe.

MEPHISTOPHELES.

Then to the deep! – I could as well say height:
All's one. From Substance, from the Existent fleeing,
Take the free realm of Forms for your delight;
Rejoice in things that long have ceased from being;

The busy brood will weave like coiling cloud:
Wield then your key, drive back from you the crowd.

FAUST (*with ardour*).

Good! With firm grip, new strength comes surging in,
My heart leaps up: let the great task begin.

MEPHISTOPHELES.

A burning tripod bids you be aware,
The deep of deeps at last awaits you there.
And by that glow shall you behold The Mothers.
Some of them seated, some erect, while others
May chance to roam: Formation, Transformation,
Eternal Mind's eternal recreation.
Around them float all forms of entity;
You they see not, for wraiths are all they see.
Pluck up your heart, for peril here is great:
Go to the tripod well resolved, and straight
You touch it with your key.

(*Faust, with the key, assumes a resolute bearing of command.*)

MEPHISTOPHELES.          Ay, that's the style!

You it will follow, be your slave the while;
Calmly you rise, and follow Fortune's track;
Before they know it, you and your prize are back.
And once you have it here, you hold the might
To call heroic spirits from deep night,
Hero or heroine: thus are you decreed
The first achiever of this daring deed.
'Tis done: by magic power the incense-haze
Henceforth must turn to gods upon their ways.

FAUST. What's now to do?

MEPHISTOPHELES.

                 Bear down with might and main;
Stamping you sink, by stamping rise again.

     (*Faust stamps on the ground and sinks from sight.*)

MEPHISTOPHELES.

>  Now from the key some profit may he earn!
>  I wonder if he ever will return.

## STATE ROOMS

*Brightly Lit.*
*Bustle of the Court. Emperor and Princes.*

CHAMBERLAIN (*to Mephistopheles*).

>  The spirit-scene you promised to create
>  Is due. To work! Our master will not wait.

LORD SENESCHAL.

>  Just now His Highness wished this expedited;
>  Sir, dally not, lest Majesty be slighted.

MEPHISTOPHELES.

>  My colleague's gone to take this thing in hand,
>  A project he will truly understand;
>  Silent, withdrawn, he works in secret ways,
>  Must ponder the resources of the ages;
>  For he who has this lovely prize to raise
>  Needs highest Arts, the magic of the Sages.

LORD SENESCHAL.

>  As to what arts you follow, that's all one:
>  The Emperor's will is that the thing be done.

BLONDE (*to Mephistopheles*).

>  A word, Sir. This complexion that you see,
>  So pure, is changed by summer's enmity.
>  There blossom then a hundred tawny freckles,
>  A curse that loads the lily skin with speckles.
>  Your cure?

MEPHISTOPHELES. A pity such a dazzling dear

>  Should have in May a leopard's spots to wear.

Take frog-spawn, cohobate, with toad-tongues strewn,
Most carefully distilled at the full moon.
By waning moon apply with even smear,
And Spring will see the freckles disappear.

BRUNETTE. Behold the crowd, with eagerness advancing.
Sir, say the cure! A foot turned numb and lame
Inhibits both my walking and my dancing,
My very bow shows clumsiness the same.

MEPHISTOPHELES.
A cure? The impact of my foot may win it.

BRUNETTE. But surely that is called a lover's game?

MEPHISTOPHELES.
My tread, my child, has greater meaning in it.
It cures, it's like to like, when all is said.
As foot heals foot, so each limb seeks its mate.
Come on! Give heed, but don't reciprocate!

BRUNETTE. Oh, oh! It burns! That was a vicious tread,
Like horse's hoof.

MEPHISTOPHELES.
                        Cured, you have nought to dread:
Dance, girl, henceforth and revel as you please,
And true-love's foot beneath the table squeeze.

LADY (*pressing forward*).
Please let me pass. Upon my heart there preys
A torture all too great, and cruelly painful.
He, who till yesterday, adored my gaze,
Gossips with her, and turns from me disdainful.

MEPHISTOPHELES.
Now this is serious, but mark me well.
Draw softly to him with your tender ways:
This charcoal you must brush then as a spell
On shoulders, cloak, and sleeves, as best you can;
Within his heart remorse will rise and swell.

The coal at once you swallow, but no sip
Of wine or water then may touch your lip;
He'll sigh tonight before your door, your man.
LADY. No poison?
MEPHISTOPHELES (*offended*).
                    Have respect in your appeal!
For such a coal far journey would you make;
It comes from special burning at the stake,
A thing we used to kindle with more zeal.
PAGE. I am in love, but counted not full-grown.
MEPHISTOPHELES (*aside*).
I've had enough of this, if truth were known.
                    (*To the Page.*)
To find your bliss, the youngest girls avoid:
Those well in years will prize you, overjoyed.
                    (*Others come crowding up.*)
What, still they come! The fight grows thick and fast!
They'll drive me to the naked truth at last,
And that's a poor device. Hard goes the day:
Mothers, O Mothers, speed Faust on his way.
                    (*Looking around him.*)
And now within the hall the lights burn low,
The Emperor and his courtiers rise to go.
I see them move in decorous degrees
By stately stairs to distant galleries.
They gather in the old baronial hall,
A noble room, that hardly holds them all.
The lofty walls are hung with arras rich,
And burnished armour gleams from every niche.
No spell or incantation we require:
Here ghosts should gather by their own desire.

# BARONIAL HALL

*In subdued lighting.*
*(The Emperor and his Court have taken their places.)*

HERALD. My wonted task, to introduce the play,
   Is vexed by secret spirits that appear;
   One hardly dares, in any reasoned way,
   To offer to explain their wild career.
   The seats are ready, ranged in row and stall;
   The Emperor's chair will face the lofty wall,
   Where arras shows in comfort to his gaze
   The famous battles of heroic days.
   Now Emperor and Court assembled sit;
   They crowd back-benches like a theatre-pit,
   And many a sweetheart in this eventide
   Of ghostly gloom sits snug at sweetheart's side.
   And so, with all well settled in their places,
   We may begin: come, spirits, show your faces!
                    *(Fanfare.)*
ASTROLOGER. Begin the play, as by His Majesty bidden,
   Let these our walls disclose the mysteries hidden.
   Hindrance there's none, for magic is our aim,
   The arras shrivels up, as if in flame;
   The wall is cleft, folds back, and has become
   The vista of a theatre, deep, inviting,
   Embracing us in its mysterious lighting.
   And now I mount to that proscenium.
MEPHISTOPHELES *(popping up from the prompt-box).*
   My eloquence should capture every heart,
   Since prompting is the devil's special art.
                    *(To the Astrologer.)*
   You, who of starry courses keep the key,

Will take your cues quite masterly from me.

ASTROLOGER. By magic power there rises to our gaze
  A massive temple of the ancient days.
  Bearing it up, great rows of pillars soar,
  Resembling Atlas, who the heavens bore.
  This task, this granite load, for them is light,
  For two could bear a mansion with their might.

ARCHITECT. So, that's antique! I can't say I admire it:
  Top-heavy stuff, for those who may desire it,
  What's crude they noble call, what's sprawling splendid;
  For me the shaft that rises fine and swift,
  High-pointed arch, infinity suspended,
  That is the style the lofty soul to lift.

ASTROLOGER. Receive with reverence the star-sent hours,
  And let your mind be bound by magic powers,
  Unbinding in return, with impulse free,
  The glorious things of daring fantasy.
  Before your eyes your wish shall be achieved,
  That what's impossible may be believed.

     (*Faust rises on the far side of the proscenium.*)

ASTROLOGER.
  Crowned, in priest's robe, this man of wondrous might
  Has triumph of his will to bring to light.
  He bears a tripod from the cavernous deep,
  And incense-perfumes from its chalice creep.
  He girds himself, in consecration due,
  A noble work and good things must ensue.

FAUST (*majestically*).
  In your dread name, ye Mothers, where you throne
  In infinite space, eternal and alone,
  And yet at one, in presence that is rife
  With stir of lifeless images of life.
  What once has been, in light and lustre vernal,

Is there astir: it seeks to be eternal.
And ye allot its fate, in sovereign might,
To day's pavilion, or the vault of night.
And some in life's most lovely course are caught,
And others by the bold magician sought;
Sure of himself, he grants what most we prize,
Revealing the miraculous to our eyes.

ASTROLOGER.

Scarce has the glowing key approached the bowl,
When over us the misty vapours roll;
They creep and glide, as on cloud-laden air,
They spread, they bunch, they narrow, part, and pair.
Hail now a spirit-masterpiece; for, lo,
The clouds resolve in music as they go.
From airy tones flows strength that none may see,
For, as they move, all, all is melody;
It sets the pillared shafts, the triglyph ringing,
We seem to hear the whole huge temple singing.
The mist subsides and, as the veiling clears,
With rhythmic grace a splendid youth appears.
I need not name him, silence ends my duty:
Who would not know fair Paris in his beauty!

LADY.

Ah, lovely bloom, where youthful splendour reigns!

SECOND LADY. The life and blood of peaches in his veins!

THIRD LADY. The finely cut yet full, voluptuous lip!

FOURTH LADY.

A chalice where your joy would be to sip?

FIFTH LADY. Handsome he is, though not perhaps refined.

SIXTH LADY.

His step could be more graceful, to my mind.

A KNIGHT. This seems a figure of the shepherd sort,
No princely trait or manners of the court.

SECOND KNIGHT.
Well, well, half-naked he is not too bad,
But wait till we see harness on the lad.
LADY. Softly he sits, with such a gentle grace.
KNIGHT. No doubt you'd find his lap a pretty place?
ANOTHER LADY.
How handsome curves the arm above his head!
CHAMBERLAIN.
Young cub–like manners, not at all well-bred.
LADY. Trust gentlemen to point the blemish out.
CHAMBERLAIN. In Royal Presence so to lounge about!
LADY. He acts a part, and thinks himself alone.
CHAMBERLAIN.
Here even a play must have a courtly tone.
LADY. The lovely youth now sinks in slumber sweet.
CHAMBERLAIN.
And snores, no doubt, the realist complete.
YOUNG LADY (*enraptured*).
What has this incense, mingled in its scent,
That quickens all my heart with ravishment?
OLDER LADY. Truly a wave of feeling, overpowering;
It comes from him.
OLDEST LADY.　　　It is sweet youth's fine flowering:
This growth has served ambrosia to prepare,
And now is wafted to us on the air.
(*Helen enters.*)
MEPHISTOPHELES: So this is she! I'd lose no sleep for her:
Pretty, but not the kind that I prefer.
ASTROLOGER. For me the occasion brings no more to do,
This I confess as man of honour true.
Thus beauty comes; ah, had I tongues of fire!
Song, through the ages, beauty will inspire.
He who beholds her must distracted sigh,

He who possessed her won a bliss too high.

FAUST. Have I yet eyes to see? Now in my soul
  Does beauty's source reveal its rich outpouring?
  My fearful quest has reached a glorious goal.
  How sterile was my world, my blind exploring!
  This world that, since my priesthood, I behold
  Desirable, deep-based, of lasting mould!
  If ever I prove false, with sense grown cold,
  Then may life's pulse and breath forget their duty.
  That comely form enchanting once my mind,
  That mirrored magic joy of womankind,
  Was but a pale foam-phantom of such beauty.
  To you alone I vow my striving art,
  My strength, affection, life with passion twined,
  My worship, frenzy, love, my inmost heart.

MEPHISTOPHELES (*from the prompt-box*).
  Be careful, or you'll overstep your part.

OLDER LADY.
  The figure handsome, but too small the head.

YOUNG LADY.
  And what a foot! Nowhere a heavier tread!

DIPLOMAT. Princesses of this style I sometimes meet;
  Her beauty seems from head to foot complete.

COURTIER. She crosses to the sleeper, sly, demure.

LADY. How horrid, near a form so young and pure.

POET.
  He glows with light, where her sweet glance has shone.

LADY. A picture! Luna and Endymion.

POET. Ay, truly, for behold the goddess wreathe
  Her downward flight, his honeyed breath to breathe:
  A kiss – the cup is full – O envied touch!

DUENNA. To kiss in public – really, that's too much!

FAUST. A favour fatal to the boy –

MEPHISTOPHELES. Be still,
And let the phantom work out what it will.

COURTIER. She steals away, light-footed. He awakes.

LADY. I thought as much: a backward glance she takes.

COURTIER. He marvels, that this wonder should befall.

LADY. But what she sees, disturbs her not at all.

COURTIER. She turns again to him, with courtly grace.

LADY. She'll teach him things in which she is well versed,
And men are always stupid in this case;
No doubt he'll think himself to be the first.

KNIGHT. A queenly beauty! Give the girl her dues!

LADY. The trollop! Nothing can such ways excuse.

PAGE. I only wish that I were in his shoes.

COURTIER. Who'd not be brought in such a net to land?

LADY. This jewel we see has passed through many a hand,
And too much use has rubbed away the gold.

ANOTHER LADY.
A good-for-nothing girl at ten years old.

KNIGHT. A man will take at times what times provide:
With these fair remnants I'd be satisfied.

PROFESSOR. I see her clearly, but I would point out
That her identity is still in doubt.
Now, actual presence may be too exciting:
I much prefer to view a thing in writing.
I read, then, that the greybeards of all Troy
Were wont to find in her a special joy.
This proof we may accept without a qualm:
For I'm not young, and yet I feel her charm.

ASTROLOGER. A boy no longer, but a hero bold,
He seizes her, who can't resist his hold.
Now strong of arm he lifts her in the air,
And will he now abduct her?

FAUST. Fool, forbear!

Deaf to all warning! Stay! This shall you rue!

MEPHISTOPHELES.
Well, no one runs this spirit-farce but you.

ASTROLOGER.
Yet one word more: from what befell this day,
The Rape of Helen will I call the play.

FAUST. Who speaks of rape? Am I for nothing here?
Is not the key still glowing in my hand,
That led me from the solitudes so drear,
Through terror, surge, and tempest to firm land?
Here foothold is, realities abound,
Here spirit, matched with spirits, holds its ground,
And the great double spirit-realm is found.
Far though she dwelt, now is she near, divine,
Save her I will, and make her doubly mine.
Resolved! Ye Mothers, grant this, I implore!
Who knows her once must have her evermore.

ASTROLOGER.
Faust, Faust, what's this you do? With mad duress
He seizes her. Now fades her loveliness.
His key towards the stripling levelled, lo,
One touch calamitous, and all is woe!

(*There is an explosion. Faust lies stretched upon the ground.*
*The spirits fade away in vapour.*)

MEPHISTOPHELES (*taking Faust upon his shoulder*).
Well, there it is! With fools best have no truck,
Else may the devil himself be thunderstruck.

# ACT TWO

—

## A HIGH-VAULTED, NARROW GOTHIC CHAMBER

*Formerly Faust's, and unchanged.*

MEPHISTOPHELES (*stepping from behind a curtain. As he lifts the curtain and looks back, Faust is discovered, stretched out upon the antiquated bed*).

Lie there, poor wretch: seduced, you come
To bonds of love that brook no treason.
The man whom Helen has struck dumb
Gropes long ere he regains his reason.
            (*Looking about him.*)
I look around, I gaze on high,
The forms, preserved, through dust still glimmer;
The webs of spiders multiply,
And the old coloured panes seem dimmer;
The ink is dust, the pages brown,
Yet all stands as it was that day;
The very pen lies there, that Faust laid down
When to the devil he signed himself away.
Ay, deeper in the quill remains
A clot of blood I wheedled from his veins.
A curio unique as this
Would make a fine collector's piece.
The hood of fur hangs near the desk,
Reminding me of that burlesque,
That lecture for the student's heeding
On which perhaps the young man still is feeding.
Truly I itch to put you on,

Warm smoky gown and erudite,
And vaunt myself a learned don,
One always proving he is right:
This art is the professor's perquisite,
The devil long since has abandoned it.
> (*He unhooks the fur gown and shakes it; crickets,
> cockchafers, and moths fly out.*)

CHORUS OF INSECTS. Welcome, twice over,
  Our patron of old!
  We buzz and we hover,
  Sure whom we behold.
  In stillness you sowed us,
  Gave each one his form;
  Now, father, in thousands,
  We dance and we swarm.
  Of lice in the fur
  You'll sooner be rid
  Than of knaves who so snugly
  In hearts will lie hid.

MEPHISTOPHELES.

  My joy is great, as my young creatures leap,
  For as you sow, so in good time you reap.
  Once more I shake the ancient mangy fur,
  And see, the fluttering stragglers are astir.
  Fly up, with speed, and hide yourselves, my chicks,
  In many a thousand cosy cracks and nicks.
  See, where the battered boxes all await you,
  Or parchment rolls will serve to habitate you,
  In broken jars, dust-laden, you can fly,
  Or in that death's-head's dirty hollow eye.
  Where such a load of mouldy trash is spread,
  Fantastic thoughts must evermore be bred.
> (*He slips into the fur robe.*)

Now clothe my shoulders as you did before.
I'll be a Warden or Vice-Chancellor.
And yet in vain such titles advertise me:
Where are the people who will recognize me?
(*He pulls the bell, which resounds with penetrating clan-*
   *gour, so that the walls tremble and the doors fly open.*)
FAMULUS (*shuffling down the long, dark corridor*).
What a clanging and a quaking!
Staircase rocks and walls are shaking,
Leaded casements are a-quiver,
With the lightning's flash and shiver,
Floor is warped with wrack and trouble,
Pouring down comes lime and rubble.
Doors made fast with lock and bar
As by magic fly ajar.
And there, a horror manifest:
A giant in Faust's old fur is dressed.
Where his signs and glances lower
Down upon my knees I'd cower.
Shall I brave it? Shall I flee?
Alas, what will become of me?
MEPHISTOPHELES (*beckoning*).
Approach, my friend. – Your name is Nicodemus.
FAMULUS. Illustrious Sir, that is my name – *Oremus.*
MEPHISTOPHELES. Enough of that!
FAMULUS.                    I'm glad you know my name.
MEPHISTOPHELES.
I know you, greybeard, student all the same.
Thus many a moss-grown learned man, like you,
Goes studying on: that's all that he can do.
A middling house of cards is all you build;
The greatest mind sees not his task fulfilled.
Yet your prodigious master holds his ground,

The noble Doctor Wagner, much renowned,
King of the learned world, great gifts bestowing,
In fact it's he alone that keeps it going;
He sees that wisdom daily is increasing,
Omnivorous inquirer, never ceasing
To draw the listening crowds his words to sup,
Sole lustre of the professorial chair,
The realms above, below, he opens up:
It seems he has St Peter's key to bear.
And where he plies his brilliant learned trade
No name or fame is worth a mention;
Even the name of Faust is in the shade,
For knowledge is this man's invention.

FAMULUS.

Pray pardon, honoured Sir, my bold suggestion,
But this your discourse, given due digestion,
Appears to have no bearing on the question;
For modesty is his most constant part.
The great man's vanishing, his hidden fate,
Is mystery he cannot penetrate;
But hope of his return consoles his heart.
That room, Sir, as in Doctor Faustus' day,
With nothing altered since he went away,
Awaits its lord's returning from abroad.
I enter trembling here and overawed.
What planets now conjoint in power appear? –
The old foundations quake and crack,
The lintels sway, the bolts shoot back,
Or you yourself had never entered here.

MEPHISTOPHELES.

Speak, where is now your learned man's retreat?
Conduct me to him, bring him, let us meet.

FAMULUS. Calls he forbids: I hardly dare,

So strict he is, to lead you there.
Long months he burns the midnight oil,
Deep in a silent, secret toil.
And he, the nicest man of learning,
You'd think he lived by charcoal-burning.
Nose and ears all sooty-smeared,
Eyes from the bellows red and bleared,
He toils through hours with choking lungs,
His music nought but clashing tongs.

MEPHISTOPHELES.

Tell him I doubt if he'll refuse me:
His fortune's made, if he will use me.

> (*Exit Famulus. Mephistopheles takes his seat in
> solemn style.*)

Scarce do I mount the rostrum here,
I see a well-known visitor appear.
But this time, foremost in the latest group,
He'll prove an overbearing nincompoop.

BACCALAUREUS (*bustling in from the corridor*).

Opened wide, these doors and ways
Serve at last a hope to raise,
That the dry-rot no more warps
Living beings to a corpse,
Stinted things, self-mortifying,
Making life a means of dying.

In the end our walls, our ceiling,
Will be ruined, crumbling, reeling;
If no planned escape we make us
Crashing doom will overtake us.
Though I yield to none in daring,
This is more than I am sharing.

Yet, what's this? 'Twas surely here,
In a bygone anxious year,

Tongue-tied and in troubled state,
I as undergraduate
Sat and trusted grey-beards' art,
And took their gabble so to heart.
   From the crusted books in college
Lies they told, and called it knowledge,
Self-mistrusting – doubt was rife,
Robbing them and me of life.
What? There haunts in this old room
Still a figure in the gloom.
   Stepping near, I see his gown,
Strange, the same old tawny brown,
Furred as when I saw him last,
Wrapped in fleeces of the past,
Seeming wise, a mind commanding,
Passing my poor understanding.
Harder am I now to catch.
So, set to! – He'll meet his match.
If, ancient Sir, your wry neck and bald pate
Swim not in Lethe's doleful flood of fate,
Acknowledge me your pupil not unknown,
Who donnish governance has far outgrown.
I find you just as when I first began;
But I, Sir, am a very different man.

MEPHISTOPHELES.
I'm glad you came, responsive to my bell,
I rated you in those days fairly high;
For chrysalis or grub betokens well
The future brilliance of the butterfly.
Your hair in ringlets and your collar of lace
Lent you a comfortable, child-like grace.
A pig-tail, I believe, you've never worn? –
But now in Swedish crop your head is shorn.

A look of the bold resolute you show,
But, be not *absolute* when home you go.*

BACCALAUREUS.

Old gentleman, old sessions here convening,
Consider that the times have changed the while,
And spare your words of studied double meaning;
We sharpen wits in quite another style.
You chaffed a novice, true and simple-hearted,
And won without much art the game you started,
A challenge few today would dare to seek.

MEPHISTOPHELES.

If to the young the simple truth we speak,
That food offends the fledgeling's yellow beak;
But let them have a run of years wherein
They learn it shrewdly on their precious skin,
They think it by their own sweet will begot,
And then declare 'The master was a clot.'

BACCALAUREUS.

A knave, perhaps! – For say, what guide of youth,
Will really tell us, face to face, the truth?
Each will enlarge or trim with hardihood,
Now grave now gay, to keep the children good.

MEPHISTOPHELES.

Indeed there is a proper time for learning;
But now, I see, to teaching you are turning.
Through many moons, and some returns of sun,
A wealth of ripe experience you have won.

BACCALAUREUS.

Experience! Mere spindrift, you must own;
Compared with mind it makes a wretched showing.
Admit, the things through many ages known
Are safely to be called not worth the knowing.

* See Introduction, p. 17.

MEPHISTOPHELES (*after a pause*).
  I've thought as much. For I was stupid once.
  And now I feel a superficial dunce.

BACCALAUREUS.
  Hear, hear, good Sir! Why, now you're talking sense,
  The first old man to show intelligence.

MEPHISTOPHELES.
  I thought to light on wealth of hidden gold,
  And wretched charcoal lumps were all I found.

BACCALAUREUS.
  Confess then, that your cranium, bald and old,
  Equals in worth these skulls that lie around.

MEPHISTOPHELES (*good-humouredly*).
  Think you, my friend, that rudeness is your right?

BACCALAUREUS. In German only liars are polite.

MEPHISTOPHELES (*moving his chair on its castors nearer to
    the proscenium and addressing the stalls*).
  Up here they rob me of my light and air;
  I wonder if you've room for me down there.

BACCALAUREUS. I call it arrogance, to linger on
  And think to triumph when your time has gone.
  Our life depends on blood, and where, forsooth,
  Is blood astir, but in the veins of youth?
  The living blood is that which brings life's force
  To life anew, in fresh creative course.
  Then hearts will tingle, strong in word and deed,
  The weak are banned, the sturdy take the lead.
  And while our conquest of the earth was won
  What did you do? – Sat dozing, doctrines spun,
  Dreaming on plans, with theory as your creed.
  An ague is old age, in which you freeze,
  A frosty and fantastical disease.
  A man with thirty summers on his head

Has seen his best, and is as good as dead.
It would be best to have you put away.

MEPHISTOPHELES.

This leaves the devil nothing more to say.

BACCALAUREUS.

Without my will there'd be no devil at all.

MEPHISTOPHELES (*aside*).

He'll trip you yet, my lad, and see you sprawl.

BACCALAUREUS.

This is the noblest call for youthful soul!
The world was not, until I made it whole;
I raised the sun from ocean where it lay;
For me the moon began her changeful way;
The day stood forth in beauty at my feet,
The green earth blossomed my approach to greet.
A sign from me, and in that primal night
The stars unveiled the splendour of their light.
And who but me your liberation wrought
From bonds of philistines that fettered thought?
But I, a soul inspired by freedom's might,
Pursue with joy my star of inner light,
And swiftly, in the rapture of my mind,
I speed to glory, darkness left behind.          (*Exit.*)

MEPHISTOPHELES.

Go, my original, your glorious way! –
How truth would irk you, if you really sought it:
For who can think of truth or trash to say,
But someone in the ancient world has thought it?
And yet this fellow puts us in no danger,
For wait a few more years and things will mend:
The vat may hold a ferment strange and stranger,
There'll be some wine to bottle in the end.

(*To the youthful section of the pit, which declines applause.*)

My words appear to leave you cold;
Poor babes, I will not be your scolder:
Reflect, the Devil, he is old,
To understand him, best grow older.


## LABORATORY

*After the style of the Middle Ages: extensive, unwieldy
apparatus, for fantastical purposes.*

WAGNER *(at the furnace)*.
  The solemn bell shakes with its boom
  The sooty walls in dread vibration.
  Soon must uncertainty assume
  Some form, to greet long expectation.
  And now a glimmer lifts the gloom;
  The depths within the phial show
  A glint, a living ember's glow.
  Ay, as a burning jewel, the spark
  Flashes a ray to pierce the dark.
  A light emerges, white and still:
  This time an answer I implore. –
  Ah, God! Who rattles at my door?
MEPHISTOPHELES *(entering)*.
  Welcome, with the best goodwill.
WAGNER *(in anxiety)*.
  Bid welcome to the ruling star on high!
  With bated breath refrain from word or cry.
  This hour will crown a wondrous undertaking.
MEPHISTOPHELES *(softly)*.
  What, pray?
WAGNER.      A human being in the making.

MEPHISTOPHELES.
  A human being? Have you a loving pair
  Locked in your chimney, in their tender passion?
WAGNER. Now God forbid! That old style we declare
  A poor begetting in a foolish fashion.
  The tender core from which life used to surge,
  The gracious force that came from inward urge,
  Which took and gave, for self-delineation,
  Blending near traits with far in new mutation,
  To this we now deny its lordly height;
  What if the beasts still find it their delight,
  In future man, as fits his lofty mind,
  Must have a source more noble and refined.
             (*He turns to his hearth.*)
  Look! There's a gleam! – Now hope may be fulfilled,
  That hundreds of ingredients, mixed, distilled –
  And mixing is the secret – give us power
  The stuff of human nature to compound;
  If in a limbeck we now seal it round
  And cohobate with final care profound,
  The finished work may crown this silent hour.
             (*Turning again to the hearth.*)
  It works! The substance stirs, is turning clearer!
  The truth of my conviction presses nearer:
  The thing in Nature as high mystery prized,
  This has our science probed beyond a doubt;
  What Nature by slow process organized,
  That have we grasped, and crystallized it out.
MEPHISTOPHELES.
  He who lives long a host of things will know,
  The world affords him nothing new to see.
  Much have I seen, in wandering to and fro,
  Including crystallized humanity.

WAGNER (*who has not relaxed in watching the phial*).
  A flash, a mantling, and the ferment rises,
  Thus, in this moment, hope materializes.
  A mighty project may at first seem mad,
  But now we laugh, the ways of chance foreseeing:
  A thinker then, in mind's deep wonder clad,
  May give at last a thinking brain its being.
          (*He looks at the phial enraptured.*)
  Now chimes the glass, a note of sweetest strength,
  It clouds, it clears, my utmost hope it proves,
  For there my longing eyes behold at length
  A dapper form, that lives and breathes and moves.
  My mannikin! What can the world ask more?
  The mystery is brought to light of day.
  Now comes the whisper we are waiting for:
  He forms his speech, has clear-cut words to say.
HOMUNCULUS (*speaking to Wagner from the phial*).
  Well, Father, what's to do? No joke, I see.
  Come, take me to your heart, and tenderly!
  But not too tight, for fear the glass should break.
  That is the way that things are apt to take:
  The cosmos scarce will compass Nature's kind,
  But man's creations need to be confined.
          (*To* MEPHISTOPHELES.)
  And you, Sir Rascal Cousin, you here too!
  A timely call, for which my thanks are due.
  Your visit means some luck for me was brewing;
  For while I live I must be up and doing.
  I'll brace myself to work, without delay,
  And you're the man to show the shortest way.
WAGNER.
  But just one word! Till now I've been embarrassed,
  By young and old with stormy problems harassed.

For instance, in despair they have debated
How soul and body are so finely mated,
In compact such as never could be ended,
Yet each by each is constantly offended.
Well then –

MEPHISTOPHELES.

          Let be! A better question still
Would be why man and wife agree so ill;
And that's a thing, my friend, you'll never solve.
Here's much to do – with mannikin's resolve.

HOMUNCULUS. What's here to do?

MEPHISTOPHELES (*pointing to a side-door*).

                    You show your gifts within.

WAGNER (*still gazing into the phial*).

Upon my soul, a darling mannikin.

      (*The side-door opens, revealing Faust, who lies*
          *full-length upon a couch.*)

HOMUNCULUS (*in astonishment*).

Much meaning here!

  (*The phial glides from Wagner's hands and hovers over*
      *Faust, shedding a light upon him.*)

               Sweet setting! – Forest, where
The woodland nymphs unrobe by crystal waters,
The loveliest creatures, fair, and now more fair!
But one surpasses all these beauteous daughters,
Her looks descent from gods and heroes claim;
Divinely treads she the translucent gleam,
And cools the lambent beauty of her frame
In the sweet crystal clinging of the stream. –
But whence this storm, this tumult of swift wings,
That strikes the glassy pool with quiverings?
The startled nymphs have fled. Alone the queen
Remains to gaze unruffled on the scene,

Beholding now, with womanly joy and pride,
The prince of swans who nestles at her side,
On-coming tame – and now more bold, serene;
But suddenly the scarfs of mist arise,
With veil thick-woven hiding from the eyes
The loveliest of pictures ever seen.

MEPHISTOPHELES.
You surely are the lad to tell the tale,
Though small, you fable on the largest scale,
For I see nothing.

HOMUNCULUS.          No: of northern kin,
Having in misty times your origin,
In coil of priestcraft and knight-errantry,
How should you have clear eyes and vision free?
Only in murk you feel yourself at home.
                    (*He looks around him.*)
Repellent, brown-stained masonry, unclean,
With arching Gothic gimcracks, mouldering, mean! –
If this man wakes, new woes we have to bear,
For death would overtake him then and there.
His dream was all of woodland springs,
Of swans and naked forms alluring;
How could he bide this scene of cankered things,
When I, most tolerant, find it past enduring?
Go, take him hence!

MEPHISTOPHELES.     Nay, give me but the chance.

HOMUNCULUS. Command the soldier to the fight,
The girl lead forward for the dance,
And everything turns out aright.
And now – quick thought and apposite –
Comes Classical Walpurgis Night.
This is the luckiest accident;
So, bring him to his element.

MEPHISTOPHELES. This thing is news to me, I own.

HOMUNCULUS.

And how, pray, should it reach your ears?
Romantic spooks are all that you have known;
In a true ghost the classical inheres.

MEPHISTOPHELES.

Then forth! Our journey's route is clear, I trust;
I view these antique colleagues with disgust.

HOMUNCULUS.

North-west, my Satan, lies your pleasure-ground,
Whereas, this time, south-eastwards we are bound.
There lordly plains, Peneus flowing through,
A wooded stream, with lush and silent reaches;
The plain spreads green, to rocky mountain breaches,
Above it lies Pharsalus, old and new.

MEPHISTOPHELES.

No more! That privilege I gladly waive,
Of hearing about tyrant versus slave.
Those struggles bore me: scarce is riot done,
When lo, the blockheads start another one.
And none can see he is the dupe and game
Of Asmodeus, who inspires the flame.
They fight, they say, dear freedom's cause to save;
But, seen more clearly, slave is fighting slave.

HOMUNCULUS.

Leave human creatures to their fractious fate;
They have to fight and fend as best they can,
From boyhood up, and so complete the man.
The point is, how shall he recuperate,
Who now lies here. What cure you know, apply:
If none, then give me leave to try.

MEPHISTOPHELES.

Some items from the Brocken I'd essay,

But now we've heathen bolts to bar the way.
I never saw much value in these Greeks;
They set the senses free in dazzling freaks;
The sins they lure men to, have light and spark,
While ours are sombre, always in the dark.
And now, what next?

HOMUNCULUS.　　　　　Well, you were never shy;
And if I name Thessalian witches, why,
You will admit I have a handsome theme.

MEPHISTOPHELES (*with lustful relish*).
Thessalian witches, people – you are right –
Of whom I have inquired with some esteem!
To have to keep them company every night
Would hardly be a comfortable scheme;
But to drop in, to sample –

HOMUNCULUS.　　　　　Take the cloak,
And wrap the sleeping knight within its fold;
The powers of this same rag we can invoke
To carry two together, as of old.
I'll light the way.

WAGNER (*in alarm*). And what of me?

HOMUNCULUS.　　　　　　Ah, you?
You stay at home, important work to do.
Unroll the ancient parchments of your theories,
And range the elements of life in series,
Relating them together, as you ponder.
Reflect on *What*, still more on *How* and *Why*;
And while in sundry foreign parts I wander
I may unearth the dot upon the 'I'.
Then is fulfilled the mighty aim;
Renown for such high toil will not desert you:
You have your due reward, your gold, your fame,
Your wealth of knowledge and – perhaps – of virtue.

Farewell!

WAGNER (*down-cast*). Farewell! I speak it heavy-hearted,
In fear we may be now for ever parted.

MEPHISTOPHELES. Now the Peneus course we run.
Our cousin seems a likely blade.
                    (*To the Audience.*)
And we, when all is said and done,
Depend on creatures we have made.


## CLASSICAL WALPURGIS-NIGHT

### THE PHARSALIAN FIELDS

*Nocturnal gloom.*

ERICHTHO. For this night's fearful festival, as oft before,
Behold, I come, Erichtho, I, the sinister –
Though not so foul as in the wretched poet-crew's
Exaggerating slanders ... Faith, they never know
When to stop praise or blame ... All whitened seems
    the vale
With billowy tide of tents, as far as eye can see,
Like pallid phantoms of that night of care and dread.
The theme returns, how often now! And will return,
For evermore repeated ... None will empire yield
To other; none to him who won it with strong arm
And strongly rules. For every man who has not wit
To rule his inner self will be most apt to rule
His neighbour's will, according to his own proud
    whim ...
Yet here a great example in the fight was proved,
How force against a force more puissant makes a stand,
How freedom's fair and thousand-flowered wreath is
    rent,

And the stiff laurel coiled to bind the victor's brow.
Here, of the blossom-time of greatness Pompey dreamed,
There, for the tremulous, tell-tale balance Caesar
    watched,
Strength matched with strength. And well the world
    knows who prevailed.
   The watch-fires are aglow and flicker with red flame,
The soil exhales again the squandered blood in wraiths,
And, hither lured by seldom splendour of the night,
There gather now the legions of Hellenic story.
Round every fire uncertain hover, or recline
At ease, dim shapes, the fabulous forms of ages past ...
Now the moon rises, not at full yet gleaming fair,
And floods with lustrous gentle silver all the vale;
The tents as in a mirage fade, the fires burn blue.
   But o'er my head, what sudden meteor streaks its way?
It shines, and fills with shine a sphere corporeal.
I scent the stuff of life. So then, 'twill not become me
To bide the presence of the living, I their bane;
Ill fame have I from that, and me it profits nothing.
Its downward course begins. In prudence I withdraw.

(Exit.)

Travellers from the Air, above.

HOMUNCULUS. Float we in our course again
  Over flame and things of dread;
  Here the valley and the plain
  In a ghostly scene are spread.
MEPHISTOPHELES. Here I see, as in the North,
  Through my window's hoary gloom,
  Horrid, gruesome ghosts come forth,
  And I feel myself at home.
HOMUNCULUS. See, before us swiftly striding
  Goes a tall and slender shade.

MEPHISTOPHELES. Seeing us through ether gliding
　　She is anxious, seems afraid.
HOMUNCULUS. Let her go. But set the knight
　　Gently down, and you will see
　　Life return to him and light,
　　Which he seeks in legendry.
FAUST (*as he touches the ground*).
　　Where is she?
HOMUNCULUS. That we cannot say,
　　But may find answer on our way.
　　Go swiftly ere the dawn is breaking,
　　Inquire of her from flame to flame:
　　For he who to the Mothers came
　　Need fear no further undertaking.
MEPHISTOPHELES. I, too, have here a vested interest,
　　But for our project it were best
　　That each should go the round of fire
　　And seek adventure matching his desire.
　　Then, little cousin, you will reunite us
　　By sounding on your lantern as you light us.
HOMUNCULUS.
　　Thus shall it flash, and thus its chime shall ring.
　　　　　(*The glass booms and blazes with light.*)
　　And now away to many a wondrous thing.
FAUST (*alone*).
　　Where is she? – Let my questioning heart be still …
　　Perhaps no sward here to her step has sprung,
　　No wave here touched her foot with curving rill,
　　Yet 'tis the air that spoke her very tongue.
　　Here! Wondrous portent, here on Grecian land!
　　At once I felt the soil where now I stand.
　　And I, the sleeper, with new spirit fired,
　　Rise up now, like Antaeus, fresh inspired.

And even if I meet with things most strange,
This fiery labyrinth resolved I'll range.

(*He withdraws.*)

### ON THE UPPER PENEUS

MEPHISTOPHELES (*prying around*).
  Now, as I wandered through the fields of flame,
  I'd much to vex me, much to disconcert:
  Naked the lot, just here and there a shirt,
  The sphinxes brazen, griffins without shame;
  This crowd of creatures, winged and tressed, displays
  No end of back and front views to the gaze ...
  We, lewd at heart, can relish the salacious,
  But this antique's too lifelike and vivacious.
  Such doubtful points our modern wit would master,
  And smother them in style, with gloss or plaster ...
  A nasty race! But, though they seem unsightly,
  As visitor I'll speak to them politely ...
  Fair laides, hail! Greybeards, to you good cheer!
A GRIFFIN (*snarling*).
  Not grey, but Griffin! – No one likes to hear
  Himself called grey. In every word there rings
  An echo of the sense from which it springs:
  Grey, grizzled, gruesome, grim, and grave-yard – thus
  They tune in etymology, but us
  They put quite out of tune.
MEPHISTOPHELES.          Yet, all the same,
  'Grif' or 'Grip' begins your honoured name.
GRIFFIN (*as before, and so continuing*).
  Of course. This kinship has been well attested,
  With frequent blame, but most with praise invested.
  Let us then grasp for beauties, empire, gold,
  For Fortune smiles on him whose grip is bold.

ANTS (*of colossal species*).

    You speak of gold: our richest hoarding was it,

    In secret clefts we rammed a huge deposit.

    The Arimaspian people nosed it out,

    And bore it far away, and mocked our rout.

GRIFFIN. Leave it to us, we'll force them to confess.

ARIMASPIANS. But not in this free night of festival!

    We shall, by morning, have run through it all,

    And can be certain of complete success.

MEPHISTOPHELES (*who has seated himself between the Sphinxes*).

    How free and easy I acclimatize,

    For here I understand each mother's son.

SPHINX. Our spirit-tones are breathed to you in sighs,

    And then, through you, embodiment is won.

    Say who you are, not yet familiar grown.

MEPHISTOPHELES.

    Folk give me names – by many I am known.

    Are Britons here? They go abroad, feel calls

    To trace old battle-fields and look at falls,

    At musty, classic holes and crumbling walls;

    For them this place would have a special glamour.

    They'd bear me witness, since, in early drama,

    They wrote me down as Old Iniquity.

SPHINX. What reason had they?

MEPHISTOPHELES.                Blessed if I can see.

SPHINX.

    Perhaps not. Know you the map of heaven, friend,

    Or what the stellar hour may now portend?

MEPHISTOPHELES.

    Star shoots on star. The clipped moon makes fair shine,

    Within a cosy shelter I recline,

    Your fur to warm me, soft and leonine.

To climb up there were vain, a flight ill-starred;
Pray tell me some good riddle or charade.

SPHINX. Explain yourself, that's riddle enough for us.
Or try to rhyme your inmost nature, thus:
'What both the wicked and the virtuous need,
A fencing-jacket for the fierce recluse,
Companion in another's reckless deed.
And all to make the merriment of Zeus.'

FIRST GRIFFIN (*snarling*).
I like him not.

SECOND GRIFFIN (*more fiercely still*).
                    What makes the fellow here?

BOTH. A nasty brute, and this is not his sphere.

MEPHISTOPHELES (*brutally*).
Perhaps you think your visitor would pause
Before he tried his nails against your claws.
Come on, then!

SPHINX (*gently*).   Nay, you have our leave to stay,
For you yourself will drive yourself away.
In your own land you do just what you please,
But here, if I'm a judge, you're ill at ease.

MEPHISTOPHELES.
Your head and bosom make a pretty show,
What horrifies me is the beast below.

SPHINX. False wretch, you'll rue the day you came.
Our paws are sound, from vileness free:
With that shrunk fetlock you feel shame
To tread within our company.
          (*The Sirens strike up a prelude overhead.*)

MEPHISTOPHELES.
What birds are those who take their rest
Upon the river-poplars swinging?

SPHINX. Beware! The noblest and the best

Have been subjected by their singing.

SIRENS. Ah, why woo, in false conceit,
Marvels monstrous and bizarre!
Hark, our chorus from afar
Brings you notes harmonious, sweet,
As in Siren-art is meet.

SPHINXES (*mocking them in their own mode*).
Bid the darlings to descend,
For they hide in branches here
Frightful claws, like hawks', to rend
And to maul you in the end,
If you stay to give them ear.

SIRENS. Banish envy, banish hate!
Cherish we clear joys as great
As the vaulted sky has known.
Now on earth and flood be seen
Mirth of gesture and of mien,
With the warmest welcome shown.

MEPHISTOPHELES. Pretty, these charming novel things,
When from the throats or from the strings
Each sweet note has counterpart.
Trills are lost on me, I fear,
Warbling may caress my ear,
But then, it doesn't reach the heart.

SPHINXES. Your talk of heart is out of place:
A bag of leather, shrivelled, sere,
Would be the heart to match the face.

FAUST (*entering*).
Wondrous! Deep heart's content, to see these creatures,
To find, in the repellent, noble features.
Here on my way I feel propitious chance;
Where does it lead me, that most solemn glance?
                    (*Indicating the Sphinxes.*)

Once in their presence did great Oedipus stand;
    *(Of the Sirens.)*
These saw Ulysses writhe in hempen band;
    *(Of the Emmets.)*
By these a wealth of treasure once was stored;
    *(Of the Griffins.)*
And these kept faithful watch upon the hoard.
With a new spirit now I meditate:
How great the forms, the memories how great.

MEPHISTOPHELES.
Such things you've cursed away, and yet
With solace now they bid you fair;
For if the heart on love is set,
Then monsters find a welcome there.

FAUST *(to the Sphinxes)*.
Make answer, you of woman-form serene,
Has one among you the fair Helen seen?

SPHINXES. Our line was destined not to reach her reign,
By Hercules the last of us was slain.
From Chiron some fresh clue you might obtain.
In wild career, this ghostly night, he prances;
If he but stand to hear, your cause advances.

SIRENS. Hear us, and you shall not fail!
When Ulysses deigned to stay,
Turning not from us away,
He disclosed, in many a tale,
Things we would entrust to you,
If you come where, green of hue,
Ocean harbours our retreat.

SPHINX. Noble stranger, shun the cheat:
Let our counsel serve to bind
Not as was Ulysses bound;
Then, if you great Chiron find,

What I promised shall be found.
　　　　　　　　(*Faust withdraws.*)
MEPHISTOPHELES (*angrily*).
　What's this croaking, furious flight
　On rushing wings too swift for sight?
　One on another, hurtling by,
　Their speed would tire a hunter's eye.
SPHINX. Like winter's raging blast are these,
　Who keen Alcides' shafts outfly,
　These are the swift Stymphalides:
　With foot of goose and vulture's beak
　Their croakings good intentions speak;
　They'd like to join our throng, and mean
　As kindred creatures to be seen.
MEPHISTOPHELES (*pretending fear*).
　There hiss between, some things of evil will.
SPHINX. If faced with these, you have no need to quake,
　They're Hydra-heads from the Lernaean snake;
　Though cleft, they think they have their being still.
　But speak, what are your hopes, where lies your way?
　Why all this troubled gesture of dismay?
　But choose your path, and swift begone ...
　The chorus there you turn to gaze upon,
　All unconstrained approach them now apace,
　And pay your court to many a pretty face.
　These are the Lamiae, wanton girls and coy,
　Subtle in ways of giving Satyrs joy;
　With lips all smiles, they never hold aloof,
　A very triumph for a cloven hoof.
MEPHISTOPHELES.
　But you stay here, for me to come again?
SPHINX. Ay, now go mingle with that airy train.
　We are a race, as Egypt's land has known,

To stay a thousand years upon our throne.
Mark how we lie: then with respect you'll say
We rule the lunar and the solar day.
By the pyramids evermore,
High court of human race,
See we flood or peace or war,
With eternal changeless face.


## ON THE LOWER PENEUS

*Surrounded by Waters and Nymphs.*

PENEUS. Soft the sedge with murmuring stirs,
  Reeds are sister-whisperers.
  Sigh, frail willows of the river,
  Trembling poplar-branches quiver,
  Lisping through my broken dream ...
  Sense of deep foreboding shakes me,
  'Tis a drumming dread that wakes me
  From my deep and peaceful stream.
FAUST (*coming to the river*). Floats a tone, or ears deceive,
  From the thick entangled bushes,
  Where the branches interweave,
  Human voice mid reeds and rushes.
  Gossip seems the rills to please,
  Chaff and chatter fill the breeze.
NYMPHS (*to Faust*). Lie down in the shade,
  For you it were best,
  And in the cool glade
  Lay tired limbs to rest.
  At last you may cherish
  The peace that had fled;
  With lulling soft voices
  We'll sigh o'er your head.

FAUST. This is my waking. O let them rule,
  These vision forms incomparable,
  Shaped there, in my beholding eyes.
  How strange the spirit quivers through me!
  Come they as dreams or memories to me?
  Joy came before upon this wise.
  So the woodland waters slide,
  Like a deep unmurmuring tide,
  Where the boughs sway soft and slow,
  So a hundred springs unite
  In a pool, pellucid, bright,
  With bathing shallows, clear below.
  Here lissom youthful beauties pass,
  Seen two-fold in the watery glass,
  Fair limbs for gaze of pure delight.
  Here bathers make a concourse merry,
  Or swimming bold, or wading chary,
  At last, with shouts, they join in water-fight.
  Enough were here to feast the eye,
  For these should richly satisfy;
  Yet ever onward strives my mind
  To pierce the wooded verdant screen,
  Whose fronds of beauty intertwined
  Conceal the high and lovely queen.
  And wondrous fair the swans now glide
  From river-inlets curving wide,
  Swimming in cool majestic line,
  Their pride and pure content displaying,
  Self-pleased, with beak and head soft-swaying,
  In perfect consort they combine ...
  But one superb beyond the rest
  Now stems the stream with bolder breast
  And swims ahead with urgent grace;

His plumage swells above the lave,
In wave of silver answering wave,
And so he nears the hallowed place ...
The others steer their snowy gleam
Of plumage calmly on the stream,
Or suddenly, in splendid play
Of mimic war, the girls they scare,
That each forgets her duty there
In seeking safety from the fray.

NYMPHS. Sisters, pray you, lay an ear
To the green embankment's mound:
If I do not err, I hear
Horses' galloping hoofs resound.
Would I knew whose furious riding
Brings this night an urgent tiding.

FAUST. Droning seems to shake the ground,
As when hurrying horses pound.
Eager my glance!
Can the great chance
Fall so quickly to my share?
Wonder past compare!
A horseman comes in canter proud,
He seems with valiant soul endowed,
Borne high upon a gleaming milk-white steed.
I do not err, I know whom now I see,
Philyra's famous son, 'tis he! –
Stay Chiron, speak with me, stay and give heed.

CHIRON. What then? Your wish?

FAUST.                         Your furious course delay.

CHIRON. I may not stay.

FAUST.                    Then take me on your way.

CHIRON. Mount up, and I can question you at leisure.
Where lies your way? You stand here on the banks,

I'll bear you through the stream if that's your pleasure.
FAUST (*mounting*).
 Whither you will. Take evermore my thanks ...
 Great teacher, man of wisdom, might and grace,
 Whose fame it was to mould a hero-race,
 The noble company of Argonauts,
 And all who formed the world of poets' thoughts.
CHIRON. Nay, let us make no count of these.
 Pallas herself as mentor wins no bays,
 For in the end they paddle as they please,
 And go their own uneducated ways.
FAUST. The doctor who in herbals bears the palm,
 Who knows the secret of the rarest root,
 Who heals the sick, and soothes the wound with balm,
 In power of mind and body I salute.
CHIRON. Well, if a wounded hero lacked a friend,
 I'd words and means to help him to recover;
 But all my art and counsel in the end
 To priests and brewing beldams I made over.
FAUST. There speaks the man of truly noble ways,
 Who will not listen to the words of praise.
 In modesty averse, and with deaf ears,
 He acts as though the others were his peers.
CHIRON. You seem a master of dissimulation,
 Who might beguile a ruler or a nation.
FAUST. Yet of your famous times, be it confessed,
 You have beheld the greatest and the best,
 In will and deed their noblest ways have trod,
 In strenuous living, like a demigod.
 Which then the strongest, greatest do you hold
 Of all those figures of heroic mould?
CHIRON. Among the Argonauts' high company
 Each in his way had valiance of his own,

So fired with power within his soul, that he
What others lacked could well provide alone.
The Dioscuri bore away the palm
Where beauty counted most and youthful charm.
For swift resolve and deeds for others' aid
Fair tribute to the Boreads was paid.
Reflective, shrewd, in council smooth and wise,
Jason prevailed, a joy to women's eyes.
Then Orpheus would in gentle thoughts retire,
Yet conquered all if he but touched his lyre.
Lynceus, he sharp of vision, day and night
Steered through the shoals the sacred ship aright.
In comradeship is danger countered best:
Where one's high deed wins praises from the rest.

FAUST. Will you not speak of Hercules?

CHIRON. Stir not, alas, sad memories ...
Phoebus I'd never looked upon,
Nor Ares, Hermes famed of old,
When lo, before my eyes there shone
What all men for most god-like hold,
One born to be a king most royal,
A youth resplendent to the view,
His elder brother's subject loyal,
And subject to fair women, too.
His equal bears not Mother Earth,
Nor Hebe leads to heaven's throne;
Art strives in vain to sing his worth
Or wrest his likeness from the stone.

FAUST. No marble can such grace betoken,
Though sculptors claim their arts excel.
Of man's high beauty you have spoken,
Now of the loveliest woman tell!

CHIRON. Why ... woman's beauty is an idle phrase,

The arid image of a comely creature;
That being only can I praise,
Welling with life and joyous nature.
Beauty may be its own delight,
But grace has overpowering might;
Such Helen had, whom once I bore.

FAUST. Her have you borne?

CHIRON.                              As I do you.

FAUST. Was I not dazed enough before,
That I must have this honour, too?

CHIRON. Her hands like yours have grasped my hair.

FAUST. I lose myself in dream so fair.
She is my star and my desire.
Her, whence and whither did you bear?

CHIRON. Simple the answer you require:
The Dioscuri in that distant hour
Had freed their sister from the captors' power;
But these refused defeat, and resolute
Came storming on in ruthless hot pursuit,
And then the brothers found their headlong way
Was barred by swamps that round Eleusis lay.
They waded through: I plashing swam to bear her;
She sprang to shore, with thanks, ah, never fairer!
And stroked the dripping mane, so sweet, so sage,
Young, conscious of her charm, the joy of age!

FAUST. At ten years old! ...

CHIRON.                              The learned dons, I see,
In this have hoodwinked both themselves and you.
In myth the heroine is fetter-free,
And as the poet needs she comes to view.
She never comes of age, grows never old,
But still is appetizing to behold,
Abducted young, and loved when past her prime:

Enough, the poet knows no bonds of time.

FAUST. Then let not her by aught of time be bound,
  Her whom Achilles once in Pherae found,
  Beyond time's bourn. Ah, happiness how great,
  When love was won despite forbidding fate.
  And shall I not, inspired with longing's might,
  Bring back that matchless form to life and light,
  Her above death, and born of gods the peer,
  Tender as great, sublime and yet most dear?
  Your eyes once saw her, so this day have mine,
  So fair, so longed for, does her beauty shine.
  My heart, my soul her captives must abide;
  My life is null unless I reach her side.

CHIRON. In human raptures, stranger, you are caught,
  But to the spirits you must seem distraught.
  Your lucky star would seem to help you here,
  Since I, for some few moments every year,
  To Aescupalius' daughter make my way;
  She, Manto, silent lifts her hands to pray
  Her father, for his honour, so to sway
  The minds of doctors, that, enlightened, healed,
  No more they dare the doom of death to wield.
  Her hold I dearest of the Sibyls' guild,
  No gnashing fury, but a soul sweet-willed;
  Stay but awhile, you'll find her powers are sure,
  With simples she will bring you perfect cure.

FAUST. I ask no cure: grant that to baser kind.
  A mighty purpose fires my heart and mind.

CHIRON. Spurn not the healing from this noble fount.
  We come now near the place; so, quick, dismount.

FAUST.
  Now tell me where you lead, through night of dread,
  Through shingled shallows, what the land we tread?

CHIRON.

   Here Rome faced Hellas in the proudest fight,
   Olympus left, Peneus on the right.
   No greater realm gave desert sands its ghost,
   Their king in flight, triumphed the burgher host.
   Lift up your eyes, and, meaningful at hand,
   You see the timeless, moon-bathed temple stand.

MANTO (*speaking as in a dream*). The temple's sacred stair
   Resounds with horses' hooves, the air
   Trembles, for demi-gods draw near,

CHIRON. And that is true:
   Look up, eyes wide and clear.

MANTO (*waking*).
   Welcome! I see you do not fail to keep our tryst.

CHIRON.
   Well, since your temple-home does still exist!

MANTO. And still you wander tireless, unrestrained?

CHIRON. Deep peace you dwell in, self-contained,
   While mine the joy to wander wide.

MANTO. Time circles round me. I abide.
   And he?

CHIRON. In vortex sinister, this night
   Has brought him hither to your sight.
   Helen, his mind at fevered height,
   Helen this man is set on winning,
   And yet is lost for a beginning.
   Worthy your healing he may prove.

MANTO. Who longs for the impossible, I love.
        (*Chiron is already far away.*)
   Enter with hope and joy, most daring mortal!
   Behold Persephone's deep-shadowed portal.
   Where caverns at Olympus' foot now hide her,
   She hearkens for the loving word denied her.

Here, by my craft, was Orpheus once conveyed:
Go in, to better purpose, unafraid.
                    (*They go down together.*)


## AGAIN ON THE UPPER PENEUS

SIRENS. Plunge ye in Peneus' flood!
　Revel, splashing in the lave;
　Sing with many a tuneful stave,
　For the unhallowed people's good!
　Water need we for all healing.
　Seek we the Aegean sea,
　Ranked in lustrous company,
　There to find all joyous feeling.
                    (*The earth quakes.*)
Foaming back the currents sweep,
River-bed no more they keep.
Earth pulsates, the waters fume,
Shingle, banks, heave in the spume.
Swiftly all, now let us flee,
Good for none this prodigy.

　Noble, happy guests, away,
To the salt sea's pageant gay,
Where the glittering wavelets dancing
Lap the shore in rills advancing.
Luna, mirrored, swims to view,
Laving us in holy dew.
Free the life there, hearts awaking;
Here the earth in dread is quaking.
Thither fly, who wisdom know!
Here the baleful horrors grow.
SEISMOS (*growling and blustering in the depths*).
　Strive once more with might and main,

Shoulders heave and take the strain,
So the upper world we gain:
All things there must own our sway.
SPHINXES. What forbodes this dreadful shaking,
    What this dire and thundrous quaking?
    What a quivering, what a reeling,
    Swaying backwards, forwards heeling
    In the uttermost dismay!
    Yet we will not quit our posts,
    Not for hell and all its hosts.
        Now there rises up a dome
    Most wonderful. This same is he
    Who raised in hoar antiquity
    The island Delos from the foam,
    Up-heaved it from the waters wild,
    To shelter her who was with child.
    Striving, tearing, toiling, rending,
    Tense the arms, the strong back bending,
    Atlas-like he, from the surf,
    Lifts the solid ground, the turf,
    Grit and gravel, loam and sand,
    From the quiet bed of our strand.
    Crosswise thus a peaceful strip
    From the valley did he rip.
    Tireless, fierce in strength, defiant,
    He, like caryatid or giant,
    Holds on high, in earth waist-deep,
    Rocky framework, fearful, steep.
    There at last his work must stay,
    Sphinxes stand to bar the way.
SEISMOS. Alone I claim this of my making,
    My credit all at last declare;
    Had I not toiled with shock and shaking,

How could the world have been so fair?
How would the mountains range for you,
Had I not heaved against the skies,
And set them in ethereal blue,
Enchanting to the painter's eyes?
When in the sight of primal gods I came,
Of Night and Chaos, forbears of the world,
I flung, with Titans in heroic game,
Pelion and Ossa, as a ball is hurled.
Then in the riot of our youthful strength
We revelled, till the sport had lost its zest:
So, capping old Parnassus, we at length
Set wantonly both mountains on his crest ...
Apollo with his blissful Muses' choir
Had session there of glad melodious tone,
Even for Jupiter and his bolts of fire
'Twas I who lifted up the dreaded throne.
So now I win my way, with stress and strife,
I force my passage from the dark abyss,
And summon loudly, as to new-born life,
Another race to sojourn here in bliss.

SPHINXES.  This could be called indeed primeval,
    Age-old, beyond its struggling birth,
    Had we not seen the fierce upheaval,
    The pangs that bore it from the earth.
    The bosky woods now clothe the mountain face,
    Still rock on rock grinds, settling in its place;
    Not for all that we Sphinxes will retreat,
    Nor stir us from our ancient sacred seat.

GRIFFINS.  Gold in spangles, leaves, and flitters,
    In the crannies, see, it glitters!
    Let no thief such treasure win:
    Emmets, up and rake it in!

CHORUS OF EMMETS. Since they of giant race
    Upward have thrown it,
    Twinkle-feet, run apace
    Swiftly to own it!
    Nimbly now go and come,
    Picking and preening;
    Find in the smallest crumb
    Gold worth the gleaning.
    Thus the least golden grain
    Swiftly to garner,
    Run, emmets, run amain,
    Search every corner.
    Brisk in your swarms and bold,
    Wriggle away there!
    See that you bring the gold,
    The mountain can stay there!
GRIFFINS. Come on and build your golden pile!
    We'll lay our claws on it the while:
    These claws the strongest bolts excel,
    And guard the greatest treasure well.
PIGMIES. Truly here we've made our home,
    How this happened is not clear.
    Ask us not from whence we come,
    For the fact is, we are here.
    Every region yields delight,
    Life can smile in every land;
    Comes a rocky cleft in sight,
    There you'll find a dwarf at hand.
    Men and women dwarfs are there,
    Swift, industrious, and nice:
    Who knows if a better pair
    Settled once in Paradise?
    Still, we think life here is best,

Thankful for our star are we:
Mother Earth, in East or West,
Has her glad fecundity.
DACTYLS. If she in a single night
Brought these pigmies to the light,
Tiniest creatures she'll create,
Nor shall any lack a mate.
ELDERS OF THE PIGMIES.
Seize now with haste
Crannies well-placed.
Using your gift,
Strength to the swift.
Where no alarm is,
Ply the smith's trade;
Spear, mail, and blade
Forge for the armies.
Emmets forth streaming,
Swarming and teeming,
Bring metals gleaming.
Dactyls so small,
Myriads all,
Range far and wide,
Wood to provide.
Find on your ways
Charcoals to raise
Our secret blaze.
GENERALISSIMO. With arrow and bow
March on the foe:
Herons by mere,
Fish-pond, and weir,
Bring them all low,
Countless hosts nested,
Proud and high-breasted;

Straight from their doom
We will assume
Helmet and plume.

EMMETS AND DACTYLS. Rescue is none!
Iron have we won,
But they forge the chain.
Freedom to gain,
Lacks yet the hour:
Bend to their power.

THE CRANES OF IBYCUS.

Cries of death and murderous bane,
Anguished beating wings now slain!
What lament, what groans of pain
Pierce and rend our high domain!
Till at last with total slaughter
Blood incarnadines the water.
Pigmy plunder, miscreant, cruel,
Rapes the heron's fairest jewel,
Plumes that on the helmet wave
Of each fat-paunch knock-kneed knave.
Come, for vengeance, hear our call,
Ocean's heron-wanderers all,
Comrades of our armèd powers,
Come: your cause is kin to ours.
None shall spare or strength or blood,
Foes for ever of this brood.

          (*With hoarse cries they take to the air.*)

MEPHISTOPHELES (*on the plain*).

Though Northern witches I command with ease,
I'm not so sure of foreign sprites like these.
Around the Blocksberg I prefer to roam,
A place where I can feel myself at home.
*Dame Ilse* guards for us her lofty stone,

And *Heinrich's Fell* has revels of its own
The *Snorers'* snorts at *Elend* ★ greet the ears,
And this has lasted for a thousand years.
But here you step a step and never know
Whether the ground will bulge up from below ...
I saunter blithely on a level track,
And lo, a mountain rears up at my back,
And even if it's not a mountain's height,
It stands to bar my Sphinxes from my sight.
Still, down the valley, flickers many a flame
And kindles spirits to adventurous game ...
Still come with living dance, like wavering fire,
The knavish mummers of the wanton choir.
Tread softly here! Though pampered beyond reason,
One snaps at dainties in or out of season.

LAMIAE (*luring* MEPHISTOPHELES *to follow*).

Hasten away,
Swifter and fleeter,
Then make a stay
For gossip and play.
Nothing is sweeter
Than thus to win a
Hoary old sinner
His penance to pay.
Clod-foot he hobbles,
Stiff in the shanks,
Follows and wobbles
After our ranks,
Whither we stray.

MEPHISTOPHELES (*coming to a standstill*).

Here is man's curse: beguiled by idle bait,

★ The 'Snorers' was a name given to rocks near the Brocken, and Elend
(lit. ' misery') was a village on the ascent.

Since Adam's time the paltry fool of fate!
Old you grow, yes, but which of you grows wise?
Or must you greater folly still devise?
One knows full well this worthless human race,
Cramped in their corsets, and with painted face.
Their light of reason is a tallow glim;
You touch them and there's rot in every limb.
As clear as day we see their earthy type;
And yet we caper when the wretches pipe.

LAMIAE (*stopping*).
  Stay, he deliberates, and doubts, and stands,
  Engage him, or he may slip through your hands.

MEPHISTOPHELES (*striding ahead*).
  Come! You'd better not explore
  Foolish webs of doubt and cavil:
  For if the witches were no more,
  Who the deuce would be a devil?

LAMIAE (*seductively*). Round this hero weave your spell!
  Love will in his heart arise,
  Choosing one to please him well.

MEPHISTOPHELES. In the twilight's fitful gleam
  Pretty woman-folk you seem,
  Such as I would not despise.

EMPUSA (*pushing forward*).
  And such am I; your praises fit me,
  So in your company admit me.

LAMIAE. She's here too much – always the same,
  She pushes in and spoils our game.

EMPUSA (*to Mephistopheles*).
  She of your kin gives fair salute,
  Empusa, with the Ass's foot.
  One horse's hoof is yours, I see,
  But greet you, Cousin, heartily.

MEPHISTOPHELES.
  I thought to meet with strangers here,
  And find my relatives, I fear;
  But, as the ancient scriptures tell us,
  The world is kin, from Hartz to Hellas.

EMPUSA. I've many forms, in action swift,
  For transformation is my gift;
  But in your honour, be it said,
  I have put on my ass's head.

MEPHISTOPHELES. I see that kinship in this crowd
  With pregnant meaning is endowed;
  And let what will sail into view,
  The ass-head I shall still eschew.

LAMIAE. Avoid this nasty hag: she'll scare
  Whatever things are sweet and fair.
  Let things be sweet and fair before:
  She comes, and they are that no more.

MEPHISTOPHELES. These cousins, dainty, slim, cocotte,
  I view as a suspicious lot;
  And under cheeks of rosy cheer
  Strange metamorphoses I fear.

LAMIAE. Yet taste: with beauties not a few,
  Fall to, and if luck favours you
  You catch the fairest of the fair.
  Why in a lickerish prelude hover?
  You seem a miserable lover,
  For all your strutting lordly air.
  Now merging in the throng he'll glide;
  Cast one by one your masks aside,
  And lay your hideous nature bare!

MEPHISTOPHELES.
  My choice is made: this pretty dear …
  (*He embraces her.*) Alas, dry broom-sticks have I here!

(*He seizes another.*) And this one? ... Dreadful! Cursed lot!

LAMIAE. Deserve you more? Believe it not.

MEPHISTOPHELES. This little darling would I clasp ...
>     A lizard wriggles from my grasp,
>     Smooth braid of hair turned to a snake!
>     I choose another, tall and bold,
>     A thyrsus-rod is all I hold,
>     Whose head-piece doth a fir-cone make.
>     How will this end? – One plump I see,
>     In whom to find felicity.
>     So – choose once more, this will I do.
>     Soft, lush, and fleshy, such a feast
>     Commands high prices in the East ...
>     Alas, the puff-ball bursts in two.

LAMIAE. Scatter, like lightning, skim, divide,
>     Dark be your flight and swooping wide!
>     Round the intruding witch's son
>     Dreadful swirl, in dusky shivering,
>     Like the bat's wing, silent, quivering!
>     Too cheap he comes off, when all's done.

MEPHISTOPHELES.
>     No wiser I than when I first set forth.
>     Absurdity reigns here, as in the North.
>     The ghosts cavort here, just as in that waste
>     People and poets void of any taste.
>     Here's still your universal masquerade,
>     The same old play upon the senses made.
>     Thus would I catch a masquer fair and sweet,
>     But seized a thing at which I was aghast;
>     And still I would have taken on the cheat,
>     If only something could have made it last.
>                   (*He strays about, lost among the rocks.*)
>     Where am I then? Where lies my way?

What was a path is now a blurred dismay.
A smooth, clear road I hither found,
And now rough boulders ring me round.
I clamber up and down in vain,
Where are my Sphinxes to be found again?
I scarce conceived so wild a sight,
Such mountains, seen in one dread night.
That's what I'd call new witches'-ride,
And their own Blocksberg they provide.

OREAD ( *from the stronghold of natural rock* ).
My heights are old, ascend the steep
Where their primeval form they keep.
Give honour to this rugged height
Where Pindus ends his branching might.
Unshaken stood my lofty head
When o'er my heights great Pompey fled.
These forms, in which the fancies teem,
Will fade at cockcrow, like a dream.
I've looked on birth of legends much the same,
That perish swiftly, even as they came.

MEPHISTOPHELES. Honour be yours, O reverend head,
Superb with oak engarlanded.
No moon with piercing shaft of light
Can probe the gloom of your deep night.
Yet softly in the glade there goes
A light that most discreetly glows.
How strange that things can work out thus!
Bless me, it is Homunculus!
My little fellow, whither bound?

HOMUNCULUS. From point to point I float around
Longing impatiently to break my glass
And join the fullness of creation;
Only the things I've seen so far, alas,

I would not join without some trepidation.
Yet, for your confidential information,
I tracked down two philosophers, and heard
That Nature, Nature was their saving word.
And with these sages I intend to keep,
Whose knowledge of things earthly must be deep;
And so at last, I doubt not, I shall learn
Which is the best and wisest way to turn.

MEPHISTOPHELES.
To gain your end, the act must be your own.
For where your ghosts and phantoms choose to dwell
Your sage philosopher's accepted well.
His art and favour, spread for your delight,
Will bring a dozen novel ones to light.
Unless you err, naught can be truly known.
If life you want, then find it as your own.

HOMUNCULUS. Such good advice is not a thing to flout.

MEPHISTOPHELES.
Away then! We shall see how things turn out.
                    (*They separate.*)

ANAXAGORAS (*to Thales*).
Your stubborn mind will still refuse to yield.
What need of further proof to be revealed?

THALES. The wave will yield to all the winds there are,
Yet keeps from yonder beetling cliff afar.

ANAXAGORAS.
This rock was born from haze of fire and flame.

THALES. From moisture all organic living came.

HOMUNCULUS (*between the two*).
Grant me your company and words of worth,
For I myself desire to come to birth.

ANAXAGORAS. Have you, O Thales, made at any time
Within one night a mountain out of slime?

THALES. Never was Nature, with her fluid powers,
 Reduced to scale of days or nights or hours.
 Thus every form by law she will create;
 No violence she uses to be great.

ANAXAGORAS. But here she did! Plutonic, searing fire,
 Aeolian gusts, with thundrous vapours dire,
 Racked the old crust of level earth, broke through,
 And thus a new-born mountain rose to view.

THALES. And even so, what more is there to tell?
 The mountain's there, and so the tale ends well.
 You lose your time such disputes to advance,
 And only lead your patient folk a dance.

ANAXAGORAS.
 The mountain teems with myrmidons apace,
 They fill the clefts: a host begins to pour
 Of gnomes and ants and pigmies in the place,
 With many little busy creatures more.
     (*To Homunculus.*)
 You never strove for what is great,
 But lived in a cramped hermit-state;
 But I would have you crowned as king,
 If you could set your mind to governing.

HOMUNCULUS. What says my Thales?

THALES.       This I can't advise:
 When pigmies act, their deeds are pigmy-wise;
 But with great rule the small to greatness rise.
 See there! The cranes in dusky cloud
 Threaten the small folk's febrile crowd,
 And mark their king for special hate.
 They swoop with hookèd claw and beak
 The death of little folk to seek,
 All, all the air is dark with fate.
 The herons, poised by peaceful water,

Were slain in cruel and wanton slaughter;
But that same murderous arrowy rain
Breeds bloody vengeance for the slain,
And summons kindred o'er the flood
To seek the pigmies' wicked blood.
Spear, helmet, shield, what good are these?
What help has dwarf from heron's plume?
Dactyls and emmets hide from doom,
Their army wavers, breaks, and flees.

ANAXAGORAS (*after a pause, speaking with solemnity*).
Though hitherto the powers below I praised,
Behold in this my hands to heaven raised …
Ageless on high, and evermore the same,
Threefold in nature and three-fold in name,
Out of my people's woes I cry to thee,
Diana, Luna, Hecate!
Thou deep of heart, the soul's endower,
Thou outward peaceful, yet of inmost power,
Reveal thy fearful gulf, profound as night,
And, without magic, show the ancient might.
(*A pause.*)
Is my rash prayer to blame?
Has my beseeching,
Heavenwards reaching,
Shaken the peace of nature's frame?
Lo, ever mightier, candescent, clear,
With orbed throne the goddess, looming near,
Brings terror to the eyes, a portent dire,
And gulfs of gloom now redden with that fire.
Thus far, no further, globe of threatening power,
Lest we, earth, ocean, perish in this hour.
Is it thus true, Thessalian women-throng,
Trusting the wicked magic of their song,

Once lured you from your path predestinate,
And wrested from you things of fearful fate?
The fulgent shield is masked in dark,
And splits with fearful flash and spark!
What baleful hissing, roar, and rattle,
Thunder and whirlwind loosed in battle!
I, humbly prostrate, at the throne,
I call, have mercy, I alone.
      (*He casts himself down, face to the ground.*)

THALES. The things this fellow claims to see and hear!
      Our late events to me are far from clear,
      Nor can I share with him, or see his point.
      Admit, the hours are madly out of joint,
      Yet Luna keeps her ancient place on high,
      Floating in calm unchanged across the sky.

HOMUNCULUS. Look up: the Pigmies' mountain hold,
      Once round, now rears up peaked and bold.
      I felt a cataclysmal shock,
      And from the moon was rent this rock,
      Which, without pause for thought or breath,
      On friend and foe dealt crushing death.
      Yet all admiring I must praise
      An art of such creative might,
      Working above, below, to raise
      This mighty mountain in a night.

THALES. Peace, peace. This in the mind was wrought.
      Now let them go, the hateful crew:
      Well, that for King they had not you.
      Let us to ocean's festal court,
      With wondrous guests to honour brought.
                              (*They withdraw.*)

MEPHISTOPHELES (*clambering up the opposite side*).
      Here on the steep and rocky heights I stray,

And over knotted oak-roots drag my way.
Upon my Hartz the pines are redolent
With tang of pitch, and that's my favourite scent,
Excepting brimstone – but this Grecian race
Of suchlike odours yields me not a trace;
I'd like to ascertain, as worth the knowing,
On what they keep hell's flames and tortures going.

DRYAS. Your native wit at home you well may air,
But here abroad you've clearly none to spare.
Why turn your thoughts to lands of yours, when here
You have the sacred oak-trees to revere?

MEPHISTOPHELES.
Our thoughts will dwell on what is left behind:
Fond use sets paradise within the mind.
But tell me, in the cavern's doubtful light,
What thing it is that crouches threefold there.

DRYAS. The Phorkyads those: approach them if you dare,
And speak with them, if you can conquer fright.

MEPHISTOPHELES.
Why not? – I marvel, though I mark them well:
Proud as I am, I must admit
I've never seen their like as yet,
They're worse by far than hags of hell.
The foulest sins that e'er have been,
Will not they wear a milder mien
When once this triple horror's seen?
Such things our powers would not abide
In the worst hells that we provide.
Rooted in lands of Beauty's fame
This well deserves the antique name …
They stir and gibber, seem of me aware,
And squeals of vampire-bats now fill the air.

PHORKYAS. Sisters, I pray you, give me now the eye,

To see who treads our temple, who so bold.

MEPHISTOPHELES.

Most honoured dames, permit me to draw nigh,
That I may have your blessing triplefold.
I make my bow, as yet a stranger rated,
Yet, if I'm right, one distantly related.
Most venerable gods have I beheld
And bent the knee where Ops and Rhea dwelled.
Your sister Parcae, Chaos' kin, what's more,
I saw last night – or else the night before –
Yet on the likes of you I've never gazed:
Words fail me, I'm enchanted and amazed.

THE PHORKYADS.

He seems to have intelligence, this spirit.

MEPHISTOPHELES.

I marvel that no poet sings your merit –
And tell me, how and why I've never known
Your graces pictured in the chiselled stone;
The sculptor's aspiration should be you,
Not Juno, Pallas, Venus, and that crew.

THE PHORKYADS.

No thought of things like this we three assume,
Deep-sunken here in solitude and gloom.

MEPHISTOPHELES.

Indeed, how should you? From the world retired,
You see no soul, and are of none admired.
But you should make dominions your own,
Where art and splendour reign on equal throne,
Where every day, so wide is genius rife,
A hero steps from marble into life:
Where …

THE PHORKYADS.  Peace! Nor wake in us a discontent!
What gain have we in more enlightenment?

We, born benighted, kin with shades alone,
Ourselves scarce knowing, to the rest unknown?

MEPHISTOPHELES.

In such a case, no need to tax the wit,
One can one's self to other selves transmit.
You three contrive to share one eye, one tooth,
And here mythology would keep its truth,
If all were merged in two, instead of three,
While semblance of the third were lent to me,
Just for a time.

ONE OF THE PHORKYADS.

     What think you? Shall we try?

THE OTHER.

We'll venture it – except the tooth and eye.

MEPHISTOPHELES.

Withhold the best! Would you our aim defeat,
And offer the stern image incomplete?

ONE OF THE PHORKYADS.

Screw up one eye, an easy trick to do,
And let one canine tooth hang out to view;
In profile you achieve completely thus
A sisterly good counterpart of us.

MEPHISTOPHELES.

I'm honoured! Be it so!

THE PHORKYADS.   Agreed then!

MEPHISTOPHELES.      Done!

So here I stand, as Chaos' well-loved son.

THE PHORKYADS.

Daughters of Chaos we, by every right.

MEPHISTOPHELES. I blush to be declared hermaphrodite.

THE PHORKYADS.

What charms in our new sisterhood arise!
Our trio has two teeth now, and two eyes.

MEPHISTOPHELES.

> Withdrawn, with such a face, I'll hide me well,
> And scare the devils in the bog of hell.

### ROCKY INLETS OF THE AEGEAN SEA

*The Moon stays lingering in its zenith.*

SIRENS (*reclining on the cliffs around, fluting and singing*).

> If once from your realm supernal,
> By Thessalian rites nocturnal,
> Wicked witches drew you down,
> Yet look kindly from the crown
> Of your night on trembling tides,
> Where the glimmering water glides,
> Lucent, soft; and touch with light
> Multitudinous throngs of night,
> Rising from the waves to greet you,
> Gracious Luna, we entreat you.

NEREIDS AND TRITONS (*as wonders of ocean*).

> Sing aloud with thrill of singing,
> Call, across the salt-waste ringing,
> Sea-folk, fled from ocean's wrath.
> From dread vortex, tempest-wrought,
> Peace in tranquil deeps we sought,
> Noble music brings us forth.
>
>    See, we wear, with heart's delight,
> Golden gear to charm the sight,
> Blending girdle, brooch, and gem
> With the jewelled diadem.
> All this harvest now is yours:
> Plunged in shipwreck, these our treasures
> Down you lured with music's measures,
> You the daemons of our shores.

SIRENS. In the crystal stream of ocean
    Fishes glide with tranquil motion,
    Float in life that's sorrow-free;
    Yet your throngs, in splendour moving,
    Show your festal spirit, proving
    How much more than these ye be.

NEREIDS AND TRITONS.
    Ere your music hither brought us
    Of the fishes we bethought us;
    Sisters, brothers, swift as breeze,
    Haste, in lightest toil of travel,
    Soon to prove beyond all cavil
    How much more we are than these.

SIRENS. Gone are they, the lively race,
    Sped at once to Samothrace,
    Borne by following wind afar.
    What their purpose, what their gain,
    Where the great Cabiri reign?
    Gods are those, in strangest setting,
    Creatures ever self-begetting,
    Never learning what they are.

      Luna, linger in your height,
    Lovely Luna, give your light
    Graciously to ward off day,
    Lest his shafts drive us away.

THALES (*on the shore, to Homunculus*).
    I'd lead you, friend, to Nereus, ancient seer,
    And now indeed his cavern must be near;
    But stubborn temper has he got,
    The caustic, crusty picklepot.
    In fact the whole of human-kind
    Can never please this sulker's mind.
    But things to come he can foretell,

For which the world respects him well,
Honours his post and lauds his name,
And many by his aids are blessed.

HOMUNCULUS. Let's knock, and put it to the test,
It will not cost me glass and flame.

NEREUS. Are these, then, human voices I have heard?
Deep in my heart the springs of wrath are stirred.
Forms who'd resemble gods by high endeavour,
Yet doomed to go on like themselves for ever.
I could have sought, long years, a godlike rest,
But felt compelled to try to aid the best;
And when I weighed the gains for which I'd striven –
My counsel might as well have not been given.

THALES. And yet, O Seer of Ocean, all men pay
Your wisdom honour: turn us not away.
Behold this flame, though shaped like humankind,
He'll take your counsel with submissive mind.

NEREUS. Direction, wisdom, counsel of the seer!
What use to mortals, hard of heart and ear?
Men see their deeds bring self-correction sore,
And seek self-willed their follies as before.
Paris I warned, as father might a child,
Before his lust a foreign wife beguiled.
There stood he boldly on the Grecian shore,
And I, from visions, told what was in store:
Reek in the air, all lit with lurid glow,
Roof-trees ablaze, murder and death below:
Troy's day of doom, set deathlessly in rhyme,
The terror and the warning of all time.
The scoffer here saw tales to jest upon;
He sought his lust, and so fell Ilion –
A giant corpse, long writhing, still at last
For Pindus' eagles a most glad repast.

And to Ulysses, oft would I presage
Of Circe's cunning and the Cyclops' rage,
His own delays, his comrades' wanton whim,
And what not all? What gain was that to him?
Till, late enough, the favouring billows bore
That battered seaman to a friendly shore.

THALES. The man of wisdom sees such ways with pain,
But he of goodness still will try again.
A grain of thanks can be a rich repaying,
A ton of man's ingratitude outweighing.
No petty matter is our earnest plea:
This lad would know how best to come to be.

NEREUS. Come not to mar for me a mood most rare,
When projects different far must have my care.
My Dorids have I summoned to these waters,
The Graces of the Sea, my fairest daughters.
No form Olympus nor your regions bear
That moves so sweetly or that shines so fair.
From dragons of the sea, in their swift courses,
They change with lissom leap to Neptune's horses,
So kin are they with elemental Ocean,
The very foam sustains their graceful motion.
In chariot-shell of Venus, opal-hued,
Comes Galatea, loveliest of the brood,
She who, since Cypris turned from us her face,
Has reigned in Paphos, goddess of the place:
Long has her beauty held it as her own,
Heiress of temple-town and chariot-throne.

   Away, for words of blame or grudge of heart
Have in a father's hour of joy no part.
To Proteus, then! the wondrous seer in this,
The way of life and metamorphosis.
                    (*He turns and goes towards the sea.*)

THALES. To gain our hopes this step has proved unsuited:
  Proteus you find, and straight he is transmuted.
  And, if he bides your question, in conclusion
  He says strange things that set you in confusion.
  Well, it remains that counsel is your need;
  Let's try it still, and on our way proceed.
SIRENS (*above on the cliffs*).
  What are these come floating, gleaming,
  Where the tides and waves are teeming?
  As when sails of dazzling whiteness,
  Scud with the wind, so glints the brightness
  Of the shining nymphs of Ocean,
  Lovely in their gliding motion.
  Leave the cliff, and downward climbing
  Let us hear their voices' chiming.
NEREIDS AND TRITONS.
  Bear we, on the waters riding,
  That which brings you all glad tiding.
  In Chelone's giant shield,
  Shines an awful form revealed:
  These are gods that we are bringing;
  Hail them, your high anthems singing.
SIRENS. Fair these forms and slight,
  Vast in hidden might,
  Time-honoured are these gods
  Of shipwreck and of floods.
NEREIDS AND TRITONS. Great Cabiri do we bear,
  That our feast be friendly fair:
  Where their sacred powers preside
  Neptune's rage is pacified.
SIRENS. To you we must give place;
  For ships in desperate case
  Your unmatched power will save,

And snatch crews from the grave.

NEREIDS AND TRITONS.
  Three have followed where we led,
  But the fourth refused the call;
  He the rightful seer, he said,
  His to think of one and all.

SIRENS. A god may count it sport
  To set a god at naught.
  Honour the grace they bring,
  And fear their threatening.

NEREIDS AND TRITONS. Seven their full company.

SIRENS. Where, then, stay the other three?

NEREIDS AND TRITONS.
  That we know not. You were best
  On Olympus make your quest.
  There an eighth may yet be sought
  Though none ever gave him thought.
  Well inclined to us in grace,
  Not all perfect yet their race.

    Beings there beyond compare,
  Yearning, unexplainable,
  Press with hunger's pang to share
  In the unattainable.

SIRENS. Where there's a throne
  In sun or moon known,
  Prayers will we raise,
  Assured that it pays.

NEREIDS AND TRITONS. In this honoured feast sublime
  We shall not be weary.

SIRENS. Fame is dimmed of ancient time,
  Honour droops in men of old:
  Though they have the Fleece of Gold,
  Ye have the Cabiri.

(*Taken up in full chorus.*)
Though they gained the Fleece of Gold,
Ours are the Cabiri.

HOMUNCULUS. Each uncouth shape that here abides
Had earthen pot for model,
And now the sage with these collides
And breaks his stubborn noddle.

THALES. This is the faith in which they trust:
The coin grows rare because of rust.

PROTEUS (*unobserved*).
For me, old spinner of yarns, a glad effect:
Things most bizarre get all the more respect.

THALES. Where are you, Proteus?

PROTEUS (*with ventriloquial effect, now at hand, now far off*).
Here – now here!

THALES. That's your old joke, to disappear;
But spare your friend this vain confusion:
The place you speak from is illusion.

PROTEUS (*as from a distance*). Farewell!

THALES. Now he is near, so shine out bright,
He's curious as a fish: your light
Will bring him quickly hither gliding,
Lured from the form he takes for hiding.

HOMUNCULUS. My powers of light I will surpass,
Yet softly, lest I break my glass.

PROTEUS (*appearing in the form of a giant tortoise*).
What is it shines with so much grace?

THALES (*obscuring Homunculus from view*).
If such your wish – good – meet it face to face.
But take the trifling trouble for a while
To enter on two feet, in human style.
Then, by our grace and favour, what we hide
We'll show to him who would be satisfied.

PROTEUS (*appearing in a noble form*).
　The sophist's tricks remain your cunning still.
THALES. And metamorphosis your favourite skill.
　　　　　(*He reveals Homunculus.*)
PROTEUS. A lustrous dwarf! The first to greet my eyes!
THALES. He seeks to be, and needs your counsel wise.
　Most strangely made, as I have heard him say,
　For birth in his case reached but life's half-way,
　No qualities he lacks of the ideal,
　But sadly lacks the tangible and real.
　Till now the glass alone has given him weight;
　But now he longs for an embodied state.
PROTEUS. A proper spinster's son are you,
　For there you are, before you're due.
THALES (*softly*).
　One aspect of the case, I think, is critical:
　The youngster seems to me hermaphroditical.
PROTEUS. So much the better: thus the matter thrives,
　And augurs aptitude when he arrives.
　But here's no need for musing on our part;
　In the wide ocean you must make a start.
　There you begin with small things of the seas,
　Rejoicing even the tiniest to devour,
　Until you compass, growing by degrees,
　The high achievement of a loftier power.
HOMUNCULUS.
　Here float kind airs, soft, soothing to the sense;
　This gladdens me, this lush-green redolence.
PROTEUS. Well said, my dapper charming lad,
　And farther, on yon narrow beach,
　You shall find more to make you glad,
　And fragrance past the power of speech.
　See, floating hither, now quite near,

The host to carry us from here.
Come then with me.
THALES.                    I, too, will share.
HOMUNCULUS. A triune spirit-step most rare!
   *Telchines of Rhodes riding upon sea-horses and sea-dragons*
               *and bearing the trident of Neptune.*
CHORUS. The trident of Neptune we forged by our skill,
   That tames the wild surges and bids them be still.
   The Thunderer's storm-clouds will darken the sky,
   And then to the crashing comes Neptune's reply;
   And through the high vault jagged lightning may play,
   But waves up to heaven will spit the salt spray;
   And things that have striven between them for hours
   In buffeted anguish, deep ocean devours;
   Whereas, with the sceptre he lent us to sway,
   We herald the peace of our festival day.
SIRENS. You to Helios consecrated,
   Heirs of day's bright joy created,
   Greet we with great Luna's fame,
   Stirred this hour to laud her name.
TELECHINES. O loveliest Queen in star-canopied vaulting,
   Glad hearer of anthems your brother exalting,
   To Rhodes' blessed island an ear you will lend,
   Where ever his paeans of honour ascend.
   He circles, and, ending his course through the skies,
   He looks upon us with the fire of his eyes.
   Then bank-side and mountain and city and flood
   Shine peaceful and lovely, and seem to him good.
   No sea-mist enwraps us, for should it creep in,
   A beam and a breeze, and the island is clean.
   His form the high god beholds manifold there,
   A youth, a colossus, so mighty, so fair.
   For ours is the creed that first nobly began

To give the high gods the fair image of man.
PROTEUS. Let them chant their bragging themes!
  Sun's life-giving sacred beams
  Scorn dead works of folk who prate.
  Bronze they smelt with everlasting
  Boasts, and once they make a casting
  Think it must be something great.
  What is the end of all their pride?
  The great god-images they cherished,
  Recast by earthquake, long have perished,
  Broken, melted, scattered wide.
    Toils on earth, what'er they be,
  Amount to plaguey drudgery.
  The waves give life more growth and ease:
  Come now to the eternal seas
  With Dolphin-Proteus.

                    (*He transforms himself.*)
                            Forth we ride!
  Mount my back, and joys attend you,
  Thus I bear you and befriend you:
  Let the ocean be your bride.
THALES. Submit to a request so winning,
  And start to be at the beginning.
  Accept swift working of the plan:
  Then, following eternal norms,
  You move through multitudinous forms,
  To reach at last the state of man.
        (*Homunculus mounts upon the Proteus dolphin.*)
PROTEUS. In spirit seek the watery welter,
  To live in wide and living shelter,
  For boundless freedom waits you here.
  But be not lured by higher striving,
  For at the state of man arriving

Finished and damned is your career.

THALES. That all depends: it can be much
To be a man of mettle, famed as such.

PROTEUS (*to Thales*).
Meaning, no doubt, your breed, as one
Whose lease has quite a time to run;
For you I've seen about these coasts,
For centuries, with pallid ghosts.

SIRENS (*on the cliffs*).
See, the moon in cloudlets riding,
Each bright curl a lucent dove,
White in moonbeams, richly gliding,
Come from Paphos, fired with love.
Sight of these the goddess granted,
Sent her team and ardent choir;
Shines our festival enchanted,
And fulfilled is heart's desire.

NEREUS (*approaching Thales*).
Though a wanderer benighted
Call the moon-train apparition,
Spirits know far better, lighted
By a finer intuition.
Doves they are, in escort flying
With my daughter's shell-like car,
Wondrous arts their wings are plying,
Learnt in primal times afar.

THALES. What to the good is solace-giving,
That will I, too, hold for best,
If there be holy essence living
In the warm and secret nest.

PSYLLI AND MARSI (*upon bulls, heifers, and rams of the sea*).
Where rough Cyprian caves o'erspan us,
Safe from shatterings of the Ocean

And from earthquake's dreadful motion,
Where eternal breezes fan us,
Fair Cythera's watch we hold,
Tend her car since days of old,
Sure of heart, in bliss untold,
And, through whisperings of the night,
Where the wreathing waves unite,
Still unseen by human sight,
Steer we Love's fair daughter on.
Fear we then no earthly scion,
Eagle bearer, wingèd lion;
Cross nor crescent can us scare,
Though they high dominion bear,
Though they alternate in fray,
Change or triumph, flee or slay,
Cities, crops in ruin lay.
Thus to ages not begun,
Steer we Love's fair lady on.

SIRENS. Softly circling, gently gliding
Round the chariot, file on file,
Ring with ring enwreathèd riding
Serpentine through ocean's aisle;
Come, you Nereids, draw near,
Comely wild and strong in grace,
Bring, sweet Dorids, Galatea,
Lovely with her mother's face:
Grave graces of her god-like mien
Her immortality proclaim,
Yet, as in earth's fairest seen,
Charms she bears in beauty's name.

DORIDS (*as, mounted on dolphins, they glide before Nereus*).
Luna, light and shadow lending,
Bloom of youth make lucent-fair;

We, our way with bridegrooms wending,
Bring them to our sire with prayer.
> (*To Nereus.*)
Young men, these, we saved from dreaded
Rocks and breakers of the main,
Then, on reeds and mosses bedded,
Warmed to life and light again,
They, with kisses eager, true,
Now must pay thanksgiving due:
Let them your high grace obtain.

NEREUS. How blessed is this double benefit
With both compassion and delight in it.

DORIDS. Sire, your praise of our endeavour
Well may grant our joy's request:
Deathless youth be theirs, for ever
Close to an immortal breast.

NEREUS. Would you in bliss enjoy your capture,
Then mould each youth to man's estate;
But ask not me to grant the rapture
That Zeus alone can consecrate.
The wave that keeps you cradled, quickened,
On lasting love will set no store,
And should the light of love have sickened,
Then set them tenderly ashore.

DORIDS. Young cherished Sirs, our ways must part,
Though sadly we avow it;
On lasting troth was set our heart,
The gods will not allow it.

THE YOUNG MEN. Still to us sailor-lads be shown
Your former tender care;
A life so good we ne'er have known,
Nor seek we one more fair.
> (*Galatea draws near in her chariot of shell.*)

NEREUS. Dear heart, is it you?
GALATEA.                    O Sire, what delight!
  Stay, dolphins, stay, I am rapt in the sight!
NEREUS. Their wide-flung circles move away,
  And, gliding past, they soon forsake me;
  What thought for stir of heart have they?
  Ah, that their convoy yet could take me!
  Still, one glance of joy repays
  All the year of barren days.
THALES. Hail anew! Spring's burgeoning
  Leaps up within my heart, a spring
  With truth and beauty permeated –
  From the wave was all created.
  Water will all life sustain:
  Ocean, grant your endless reign!
  But for clouds of your rich lending,
  And the brooklets of your sending,
  Rivers' courses wide extending,
  Streams that reach majestic ending,
  What were our world, our mountains, and our plains?
  Your power the freshness of our life maintains.
ECHO (*as chorus of the whole assembly*).
  'Tis you from whom the life flows in our veins.
NEREUS. They wheel afar, diverge apace,
  No more the heart can seek the face.
  In circles interlinked extending,
  And in festal measure blending,
  Countless throngs now turn and veer.
  Galatea's throne of shell
  Still I see, I see it well:
  With the glitter of a star,
  Through the thronging and the teeming,
  Still the light of love is gleaming,

Even though it be so far,
Still the shimmer bright and clear
Shines for ever true and near.

HOMUNCULUS. In moist element my light
Shows to my admiring sight
Wondrous beauty all around.

PROTEUS. In this moisture-quickened sphere
Newly will your light appear
Wedded to high music's sound.

NEREUS. What mystery hovers where multitudes wheel,
New secrets to offer, new life to reveal?
What lights Galatea and glints at her feet,
Flaming up round her shell, now portentous, now
sweet,
With throb such as love in the beating pulse breeds?

THALES.
Homunculus this, whom old Proteus misleads ...
And the signs show the longing and will of their
master,
Boding the pangs and the moans of disaster;
His glass will be shivered against the bright throne;
Comes a flame and a flash, on the floods he is strown.

SIRENS.
The waves are transfigured with fire-laden wonder,
They glitter in impact, in flame leap asunder.
Here's shining and swaying, and spurting of light,
With forms all aglow in the track of the night.
And lapping of fire touches all things around:
Let Eros who wrought it be honoured and crowned!
Hail to the Ocean! Hail the wave,
The flood with holy fire to lave!
Waters hail! All hail the fire!
The strange event hail we in choir!

ALL VOICES IN CONCERT.
    Hail light airs now floating free!
    Hail earth's caves of mystery!
    Held in honour evermore
    Be the elemental four!

# ACT THREE

—

## BEFORE THE PALACE OF MENELAUS
## IN SPARTA

*(Enter Helen, with a chorus of captive Trojan women, and the Chorus-leader, Panthalis.)*

HELEN.

I, Helen, much admired, and blamed as much, am come
From yonder strand where newly we have disembarked,
Still reeling from the rolling swell of restless seas,
Waves that with strong West Wind, and favoured by
    Poseidon,
Upheaved their backs to carry us from lands afar,
From Phrygian plains, until we reached our homeland's
    bays.
Down on the beach, surrounded by his bravest men,
King Menelaus celebrates his glad return.
But here, great house, from you I seek my welcome
    home,
You whom my father near the hill-side nobly built
Whenas he, Tyndareus, returned from Pallas' hill:
While I with Clytemnestra grew in sisters' joy,
With Castor and with Pollux played glad games of
    youth,
Made he his house most fair, beyond all Spartan homes.
You too I greet, high portals, looming wings of bronze
Through these your doors, wide open, guest-inviting,
    once
It came to pass that Menelaus strode, the choice
Of many princes, shining bridegroom meet for me.

Swing back these doors again, that entering I bring
The King's command, as well befits a consort's troth.
So let me pass, and henceforth may the fateful things
Remain behind, that swept of old my path with storm.
For since the day I left this threshold, light of heart,
And sought Cythera's fame, in sacred duty bound,
Only to fall in spoiler's, in the Phrygian's hands,
Full many things have come to pass that, far and near,
The people love to tell, unwelcome talk for one
Of whom the story spread has grown to fabulous tale.

CHORUS. Without disdain, O beauteous Queen,
Assume the highest honoured estate,
For the greatest boon is your glory alone,
Renown of beauty, that passes all else.
The hero's name resounds in his path,
Lends pride to his step;
Yet bows the hardest, proudest of men,
In the sovereign presence of beauty his will.

HELEN.
Enough. I come, together with my lord, ship-borne,
And now his city must I seek, his harbinger.
But what intent his heart has, that I may not guess.
Is it as wife I come? And come I as a queen?
Or am I here a victim of my prince's pangs,
And of the evil fates long suffered by the Greeks?
I am conquered; whether captive too I may not know:
Immortal powers decreed for me a fame and fate
Ambiguous; dark escort they of beauty's form,
Who even to this threshold, keeping at my side,
Have borne me sinister company of threat and gloom.
For yet within the hollow of the ship my lord
Looked seldom on me, nor one cheerful word would
    speak,

Sat facing me as one with mischief in his mind.
But scarcely had our leading ships, with brazen prows,
Eurotas' inlets made, he spoke like one inspired:
'Here shall my warriors disembark in order due,
And, drawn up on the beach, I will review their lines;
But yours is now to mount Eurotas' sacred shores,
By groves made heavily rich with fruits your pathway
    lies,
Your horses you will rein through lush flower-spangled
    meads,
Until at last you reach the lovely upland plain,
Where Lacedaemon, once a wide-spread fertile field,
In solemn mountain close now lifts its lofty towers.
Seeking that high and princely mansion, enter in
And summon all my maids whom I departing left,
Together with my old sagacious stewardess,
And have her show you all the treasures richly stored,
Ay, those your father handed down, with more that I
In war and peace with constant increase have amassed.
Then all things will you find preserved in order: for
This is a prince's privilege, that when he comes
Again to his home he finds, in trusty keeping, all
Possessions ranged in his house, as when he went away;
For in the slave there lives no power to bring in
    change.'
CHORUS. May ever-growing, glorious wealth
Now fill with joy your eyes and your heart!
For the beauty waits of diadems rich,
And chains of gold; these suppose themselves grand;
But enter in with challenging mien,
They'll arm their array:
Ah joy, to behold when beauty contends
With the shine of pearls and of gems and of gold.

HELEN.

There followed straight a further mandate from my lord:
'When you have made survey of all, in order due,
Then take as many tripods as you think to need,
And sundry vessels, such as he will want at hand,
Who offers sacrifice, fulfilling sacred rites;
The cauldrons and the bowls, the flat-rimmed salver take,
Have purest water from the holy springs at hand
Set in high urns; and add to these dry tinder-wood,
Whence swiftly leaps the living flame; nor let me fail
To find the sacrificial keenly whetted knife;
With all that else befits, I charge your own good care.'
These things he spoke, and pressed me to depart; but naught
That draws the breath of life did he for slaughter name,
To serve his rites in honouring the Olympian Gods.
Dark omen this; but further care will I cast off,
Committing all to wait the will of Gods on high,
Who ever bring to pass what they in thought conceive,
And whether this may mean our good, or evil seems
To men, we, being mortals have it still to bear.
Full oft the priest has raised on high the weighty axe
Above the consecrated earth-bowed victim's neck,
And yet his hand has failed, prevented as it chanced
By foe at hand or intervention of a God.

CHORUS. Shapes of things to come you cannot divine.
Onward, O Queen, you may go
Strong of heart.
Blessings or evils come
Unforeseen by us mortals;
Even when warned we refuse to believe.
Gutted was Ilium; have we not seen

Death around us, death full of shame;
And are we not here
Joined with you, and glad in service,
Seeing the dazzling firmament's sunshine,
And what earth has of grace the
Fairest, you, our happiness?

HELEN.

Let come what may. 'Tis meet that I, whate'er betide,
Go up to enter undelayed the royal house,
Much longed-for home, much missed, and well-nigh forfeited,
That yet again my eyes behold, I know not how.
But I am borne no more on light and fearless feet
Up the high steps, that once, a child, I overleapt. (*Exit.*)

CHORUS. O my sisters, you
Mourning as captives here,
Cast your sorrows far from you,
Share now your Lady's joy,
Share your Helena's joy,
Who to her father's house and hearth,
Though with long delay returning
Yet with her step more resolute,
Blissful now is approaching.

Praise ye the holy ones,
Fortune-restoring ones,
The gods granting homing.
Soars the delivered one
As upon pinions
Over fate's harshness, though forlorn
Pines the prisoner longingly,
And with his outstretching arms
Reaches in vain from the battlements.

Nay, but a God has seized

Her the exiled;
And from the wreckage of Troy
Hither has borne her again
Into her father's newly garnished
Home of old,
After blisses and
Sorrows past telling
Here to ponder on
Freshened dreams of her childhood.

PANTHALIS (*as leader of the chorus*).

Leave now the joy-embowered and festal path of song,
And turn your gaze towards the lofty portal-folds.
What, sisters, do I see? Is it not the Queen returning
With agitated steps? Is it not she, much moved?
O mighty Queen, what thing is this, that in your halls,
Your home, you find, instead of smiling hail,
Soul-shattering encounter? This you may not hide
For there's abhorrence written plain upon your brow,
A noble anger, yet contending with surprise.

HELEN (*she has left the folding-portal open, and she is deeply
moved*).

Ignoble fear would ill become the child of Zeus,
And her the flitting hand of panic cannot touch;
But there's a horror gliding from the womb of night
Since time primeval, taking many forms, as clouds
Will shape them, glowing from the crater's fiery gorge
In spiral dread: this even shakes a hero's heart.
And thus today the Stygian Gods have cruelly set
Such mark upon my father's doors that all my wish
Is from the often-trod long yearned-for threshold soon,
Soon to depart, as a mere guest might turn and go.
Yet no! I yielded only to regain the light:
No further shall you drive me, Powers, whoe'er you be.

Atoning rites be mine, to cleanse the hearth, so may
The mistress, as the lord, be welcomed with pure flame.

LEADER OF THE CHORUS.

My noble Lady, to your handmaids here disclose,
To us who honour you, what thing has come to pass.

HELEN.

What I have seen shall you with your own eyes behold,
If only ancient night has not engulfed those forms
Once more within her depths, her wonder-teeming
    womb.
And yet, that you may know, I tell it you in words:
As with grave steps I reached the royal inner court,
Treading that solemn place with thoughts on duty bent,
I paused dumbfounded at the silent corridors.
Blank solitude, no busy servant's step to hear,
Nothing to see of swift officious household stir,
And not a maid appeared, no stewardess or dame,
Whose duty once received the stranger smilingly.
But when I neared the big embrasure of the hearth,
There saw I in the dying embers' sullen glow
A huge veiled woman crouching down upon the ground,
With aspect not of sleeping but of brooding deep.
With voice of firm command I bade her to her work,
Supposing her the stewardess, one whom perhaps
My husband, in his care, had left with duty charged;
But cloaked she sits, a muffled creature motionless;
Until, upon my threats, her right arm she lifts up,
As with a sign to send me from my hearth and hall.
Forthwith I turn from her in wrath and swiftly move
Towards the steps where stands on high the Thalamos,
Richly adorned, and there, hard by, the treasure-house;
Then on a sudden springs the monster from the floor,
Imperiously to bar my way, reveals itself

Of haggard height, its deep-set eyes bedimmed with
    blood,
A shape most strange, confounding to the heart and eye.
I speak this to the winds; for words must strive in vain
To build and body forth creatively such forms.
See, now she comes herself, braving the light of day!
But we are masters here, till comes our Lord and King.
The ghastly broods of Night are chased by Phoebus,
    friend
Of beauty, back to their caverns, or he quells their spite.
    (*Phorkyas steps forth on the threshold, between the
        door-posts.*)

CHORUS. Much have I lived through, what if the tresses
    Youthfully cluster, hiding my temples.
    Many the fearful things I have witnessed,
    Desolate warfare, nightfall of Troy,
    When it crashed.
        Through the beclouded, dust-ridden tumult
    Crowded with warriors, heard I the awful
    Call of Immortals, listened while brazen
    Clashing of discord, loud in the field,
    Smote the walls.
        Ah, still standing were Ilium's
    Ramparts then, but the licking flames
    Shot from neighbour to neighbour's house,
    Ever spreading from this to that
    With their own tempestuous sweep
    Over the night-ridden city.
        Saw I in flight through smoke and blaze,
    Through the flickering tongues of flame,
    Dreadful presence of wrathful gods,
    Stalking figures of wonder
    Looming giant-like moved, and through

Fire-reddened pillars of reek passed.
   Saw I this? Or was it a
Fabric spun by fear-laden mind's
Fevered invention? I ne'er shall know;
Here, though, is horror assured,
Terribly clear before my eyes,
This is a thing most certain;
Now could I grasp it with my hands,
Did not fear from the perilous
Creature ever withhold me.
   Speak then, of Phorkyas'
Daughters, which are you,
Since I must take you for
One of their kindred?
One of the fearful gray-born come you,
One sole eye having, and one tooth,
Sharing these alternately?
Are you one of the Graiae?
   Dare you, Monster,
Here beside beauty
Come to the critical
Judgement of Phoebus?
Step then none the less boldly forward,
Since what's ugly escapes his sight,
Even as his holy gaze
Never turned to the shadows.
   But us mortals, alas, condemns
Ever tragic our star-crossed fate,
Binds us to anguish of soul and eye,
Which the abhorrent, the doom of unblessedness,
Wakes in the lovers of beauty's might.
   Nay then, hearken, if brazen-faced
You encounter us: hear the ban,

Hear the threatening doom of blame,
Curses invoked by the lips of the happy ones
Who are fashioned by Gods on high.

PHORKYAS.

Old is the saying, yet the sense is high and true,
That Shame and Beauty never yet went hand in hand
In consort on the highway of the verdant earth.
Deep-rooted in them both there dwells of old such hate,
That wheresoever one should cross the other's path
Each of them on her rival turns at once her back;
Then speed they on their courses, each more vehement,
Shame much cast down, but Beauty much emboldened, till
At length the hollow night of Orcus wraps her round,
Save she be chastened by old age before that time.
    But you, you froward hussies, come from foreign shores,
And flown with insolence, I count you as the cranes,
Whose hoarse and clamorous train, flying above our heads,
An elongated cloud, send down their screeching noise,
Causing the lonely silent wanderer to turn
His gaze aloft; yet still they pass upon their way,
While he goes his; and thus it will befall with us.
    Who may you be, that round the King's high palace rave
In maenad frenzies, like a tipsy revelling crew?
Who may you be, that round the royal stewardess
Will howl and bay as does a pack of hounds the moon?
Think you 'tis hid from me, to what race you belong?
A brood begot by war, your youth on battle fed,
Man-mad, lascivious you, seducing and seduced,
Unnerving both the soldier's and the citizen's strength.

To see your clustering crowd, a locust-swarm I think
Has swooped from heaven above and covered the green
    corn:
Destroyers nipping thrift and promise in the bud,
You loot of war, cried on the market, bartered wares.

HELEN.

Who chides the waiting maids before their lady's face
Lays an audacious hand upon her household right;
For hers alone it is to give the praise deserved,
Even as she alone reproves where they have failed.
What's more, the services have left me well content
That these have given while proud Ilium's might yet
    stood
Beleaguered round, then fell, lay wrecked; nor less their
    worth
Enduring change and peril on the troubled seas,
Grim toil, and moments when men think first of them-
    selves.
And here I wait like service from their lively throng.
Lords ask not what the servant is, but how he serves.
You, therefore, hold your peace, nor give them further
    snarls,
If you have so far tended well your sovereign's house,
As warden for his lady, that shall bring you praise;
But she herself now comes, which means you keep your
    place,
Lest you receive rebuke in place of tribute earned.

PHORKYAS. To threaten the domestics still remains a
    right
That fits the noble consort of our heaven-blest king,
Well-earned by years of that high lady's governance.
Since, Madam, you, now recognized, assume again
Your former privilege of chatelaine and queen,

Then take in hand the reins long lying slack, to rule
And have the treasures in possession, us with them.
But most of all protect me, shield my reverend years,
From this young brood, who by the swan your beauty
    is
Seem naught to me but coarsely feathered cackling geese.

LEADER OF THE CHORUS.

How ugly, seen near beauty's pride, is ugliness.

PHORKYAS.

How foolish, seen at wisdom's side, is foolishness.

(*From here on, retort is made by Choretids stepping out
        singly from the Chorus.*)

CHORETID I.

Of father Erebus tell, tell us of Mother Night.

PHORKYAS.

Speak you of Scylla then, first cousin of your blood.

CHORETID II.

No lack of monsters have you in your pedigree.

PHORKYAS.

Go you to Hades: call upon your kindred there.

CHORETID III.

But much too young for you are hell's inhabitants.

PHORKYAS. Go, try on old Tiresias your amorous charms.

CHORETID IV.

Doubtless Orion's nurse great-grandchild was to you.

PHORKYAS.

The Harpies were, I think, your wet-nurses in filth.

CHORETID V.

What nourishment may feed your choice and skinny
    frame?

PHORKYAS. Not blood, the object of your over-hot desire.

CHORETID VI.

For corpses do you crave, a loathsome corpse yourself.

PHORKYAS.

The teeth of vampires glisten in your insolent chaps.

LEADER OF THE CHORUS.

Yours could I quickly stop, by telling who you are.

PHORKYAS.

First you can name yourself: the riddle then is out.

HELEN.

With naught of wrath, nay sorrowful I intervene,
Forbidding to-and-fro of quarrelling hubbub here,
For no harm greater can assail the sovereign's state
Than trusted servants' strife, in secret pledge of feud.
Then echo of his mandate comes to him no more
In pleasing accent of the swiftly finished deed;
No, swelling wild around him, in a wilful storm,
It finds him self-distraught, his chiding all in vain.
Nor is this all. You have, in rough, unseemly wrath,
Evoked the frightful forms of images unblest,
Which hem me in, with fear lest Orcus and the shades
Snatch me away, in mockery of the fields of home.
Looms this from some past life? Or am I seized and
    crazed?
Was all this me? Is still? And ever shall I be
The phantom scare of them that lay proud cities waste?
My maids now shudder, but the eldest, you alone
Stand there unmoved: then give me words of truth and
    sense.

PHORKYAS.

Whoever calls to mind the chequered fates of years
Will see at last the Gods' high favour as a dream.
But you, so highly favoured, past all measure blest,
Saw nothing in life's scene but souls inflamed with love,
And swiftly fired to any hazard or exploit.
First Theseus bore you off, he goaded by desire,

As strong as Heracles, one glorious to behold.
HELEN. Abducted me by force, a ten-year slender roe,
To keep me in Aphidnus' tower, in Attica.

PHORKYAS.
But soon, by Castor and by Pollux set at large,
You knew the wooings of a chosen hero-band.

HELEN. Yet secret silent favour, willingly I own,
Patroclus won, who was Pelides' second self.

PHORKYAS. Yet wed to Menelaus by your father's will,
Bold rover of the sea and pillar of his home.

HELEN.
He gave his daughter, gave with her his realm to rule,
And from our wedded life came forth Hermione.

PHORKYAS.
But while he strove afar, for heritage of Crete,
To you in loneliness came all too fair a guest.

HELEN.
Why do you call to mind that well-nigh widowed state
And how there grew from it my havoc and my doom?

PHORKYAS.
And that same venture brought for me, a Cretan born,
Captivity, ay, slavery for life it meant.

HELEN.
He brought you here forthwith, appointed stewardess
With trust of citadel and treasure bravely won.

PHORKYAS.
All which you left, your heart inclined to towered Troy
And the delights, the never-ended joys of love.

HELEN.
Speak not of joys, for tides of bitterness and rue
Came flooding in, ceaselessly whelming head and heart.

PHORKYAS.
Yet rumour has it, you assume a two-fold shape,

 Seen both in Ilium and in Egypt's lands.

HELEN. Spare the confusion in the sad distracted mind.

 Even here, the truth of what I am, I do not know.

PHORKYAS.

 Again 'tis said that from the hollow realm of shades

 Achilles rose in burning passion for your sake,

 You whom he loved of old, despite the voice of fate.

HELEN.

 Then was I but a wraith, and with a wraith was joined.

 It was a dream, the very words declare this true.

 And now – I swoon, becoming to myself a wraith.

  (*The Semi-chorus take her swooning in their arms.*)

CHORUS. Hold your peace, you

 Evil-eyed creature, who speak what is false.

 From that horrible single-toothed

 Mouth, what comes but foulest

 Breathings fetched from a hateful maw?

  For the malevolent, charity posturing

 Rabid wolf in sheep's clothing soft fleeced

 More do I dread even than jaws of the

 Three-headed gnashing hell-hound.

 Sick at heart we listen here:

 When? How? Only say, where breaks

 Forth the deeply

 Lurking malice of this thing of hell?

  You now, instead of a word rich in kindness,

 Lethe's calm to give, gentle with comfort,

 Summon the past, fraught with calamity,

 Smothering good by evil,

 Bringing darkness at a swoop

 Both on the present gleams of light

 And the future's

 Softly gleaming dawn of hope.

Stand you silent,
That the soul of fair Helen,
Ready but now to take flight,
Still may dwell in, and dwell fast in
Loveliest form of all forms
Ever the golden sun-rays have touched.
(*Helen has come to herself and once more
stands in their midst.*)

PHORKYAS.

Comes now, from the cloud-wrack striding, noble sun-
shine of this day,
Sun, that even veiled rejoiced us, now in dazzling splen-
dour reigns.
As the world unfolds before you, lives your own be-
holding grace.
Though as hideous they revile me, yet I know true
beauty well.

HELEN.

Come with trembling feet from darkness, which my
swooning wrapped me in,
Quiet rest is all my longing, I so weary in my limbs:
Yet for queens it is befitting, as for all of human-kind,
Well to nerve themselves with courage, whatsoever
threats may rise.

PHORKYAS.

Now you rise up in your greatness, in your beauty stand
you there,
With commanding eyes most regal: what your will is,
tell us now.

HELEN.

Then make good by swift amendment these your brawl-
ing base delays.
Go, a sacrifice make ready, following my lord's behest.

PHORKYAS.

All within the house stands ready, bowl and tripod,
        sharpened axe,
  Font for sprinkling, spice for incense: let the victim now
        be named.

HELEN. Unrevealed, the King has left this.

PHORKYAS.               Left unspoken? What dread word!

HELEN. What means this dismay and pallor?

PHORKYAS.               O my Queen, the victim you.

HELEN. I?

PHORKYAS. These, too.

HELEN.               Ah, woe and mourning!

PHORKYAS.               By the axe to meet your doom.

HELEN. Dreadful! Yet – poor me! – foreshadowed.

PHORKYAS.               Doom, it seems, beyond recall.

CHORUS. Woe to us! What will befall us?

PHORKYAS.               Hers will be a noble death.

  But for you: among the gables, high on the roof-tree's
        sturdy beam,
  Shall you dangle, as when fowlers hang dead thrushes in
        a row.

(*Helen and the Chorus stand in grouping carefully produced,
        to signify fear and amazement.*)

PHORKYAS.

  Poor spectres! ... There like creatures turned to stone
        you stand,
  Aghast to part from day, that nothing is of yours.
  So mortals, ghosts in common, phantom things like
        you,
  Are ever loth to leave the august light of the sun;
  Yet none can intercede or save them from that end;
  All know this well, but hardly any does it please.
  Enough, you all are doomed: so, speedily to work!

(*She claps her hands, whereupon masked, dwarfish figures appear at the gate, ready to carry out with alacrity commands as soon as they are uttered.*)

Come then, you bullet-shapes of dark monstrosity.
Come trundle up, here's glut of mischief waiting you.
Set up the altar here, the handable, gold-tipped,
Give place, the axe shall glitter at the silver rim,
Fill now the ewers full, for rinsing must be done,
Laving away the hateful stain of blackening blood.
Now spread luxurious rich carpets on the dust,
So may this royal victim kneel majestical;
And, swathed forthwith, enshrouded, even with severed
    head,
Revered and honoured shall she then be laid to rest.

LEADER OF THE CHORUS.

The Queen now stands aloof, in contemplation wrapt,
Her women droop and sicken, like meadow grass when
    mown;
But me, the eldest, sacred devotion moves to seek
Some closer speech with you, primeval Spirit of Age.
With all your lore of life, it seems you meant us well,
Wise, though this brainless throng misjudged you and
    reviled.
Speak, therefore, of deliverance, if hope there be.

PHORKYAS.

Soon said: upon the Queen alone the fate depends
To save herself and, in the bargain, you her maids.
But firm resolve is needed, and of swiftest kind.

CHOIR.

Honoured most among the Parcae, wisest of the sibyls
    you,
Stay the golden shears from closing, grant us life and
    light of day;

For our tender limbs already feel a fluttering unjoyous,
Writhing, reeling, we whose arms are used to seek the
    joys of dancing,
Then the peace of lover's breast.

HELEN.

To them their trembling! Sorrow is mine, but naught of
    fear.
Yet, know you means of help, I'll hear with grateful
    thanks.
Often through wisdom, with far-seeing eyes, indeed
Things seeming out of reach will come to hand. Say on!

CHORUS.

Speak and tell us, tell us quickly: how may we escape the
    gruesome
Evil coil that clinging threatens, noose that like a hateful
    necklace
Twines about our neck with terror? This already we poor
    wretches
Feel with strangling suffocation, comes not Rhea in her
    mercy,
Mighty mother of Gods, to save us.

PHORKYAS.

Have you then patience, all the long-drawn tale to hear
In peace and quiet? Many things would I unfold.

CHORUS.

Patience enough! For while we listen we have life.

PHORKYAS.

He that still clings to home, and noble treasure guards,
With skill to grout and point his lofty mansion's stones,
Cementing walls and roof against the lashing rain,
That man will find great comfort, all his life-long
    days:
But he that gads about, and mocks his austere house

Profanely crossing the threshold on wanton errands
    bound,
Will find some day when coming back to that old place
That all its face is changed, or even desolate.

HELEN.

Why do you now dispense your well-worn maxims
    here?
A tale you had to tell: then leave offensive themes.

PHORKYAS.

This turns on history, and nowise means reproach.
A buccaneer did Menelaus cruise from bay to bay,
Coasting the seaboard and the islands under arms,
Much booty bringing home, that still he's heaped
    within.
Before the walls of Troy he served for ten long years;
Of moons required for passage home I cannot tell.
But lo, the house of Tyndareus, how stands it now,
That noble house, and in what state the realm around?

HELEN. Is then reproach so firmly planted in your bones,
That never can you stir your lips without some blame?

PHORKYAS.

So many years the mountain-slope waits desolate,
That north from Sparta reaches up towards the sky,
Behind Taygetus, where as yet a lively brook
Eurotas babbles down, then, rolling through our vale,
Broad-spreading by the sedges, bears and feeds your
    swans.
Behind there, in the mountain dale, a hardy race
Has settled, pushing in from the Cimmerian dusk,
With towers impregnable have made their stronghold
    there,
From whence they harry land and folk at their sweet
    will.

HELEN.

And this they have achieved? Scarce credible it seems.

PHORKYAS.

They had the time: it may be well on twenty years.

HELEN.

Have they one lord? Or many brigands are they,
    leagued?

PHORKYAS.

No brigands they, but one of them commands as lord.

I blame him not, though raids of his have reached us
    here:

He could have taken all, yet made himself content

With trifles, that he called not tribute but free gifts.

HELEN. What sort of man?

PHORKYAS.                  Nothing amiss. I like him well.

A man well-favoured is he, dashing, debonair,

As few among the Greeks he shows discerning mind.

Barbarians we call this race, yet none I think

So cruel as many the heroes seen at Ilium,

Slaughterers whose joy was in devouring men.

This man has greatness I respect: I'd trust in him.

His citadel you must with your own eyes behold!

Quite other is it than the clumsy piles of stone,

The walls your ancestors at random raised aloft,

In Cyclopean style, like Cyclops hurling stone

On stone unhewn; whereas the castle there, ah there,

Is all a symmetry, fine craft of lead and line.

Look on it from without: it soars to very heaven,

So proud, in perfect lines, and mirror-smooth like steel.

To climb this height – nay, thought itself will shrink and
    quail.

Within are spacious courts, where, ranged by builders'
    art

Stands lofty masonry of every kind and use.
There you have columns, shafts, pilasters, archlet, arch,
Balconies, and galleries, for gazing in and out,
And scutcheons.

HELEN.            What are scutcheons?

PHORKYAS.                        Such did Ajax bear:
Upon his shield a serpent, coiled, yourselves have seen.
The Seven against Thebes have carried figured forms,
Each one, upon his buckler, rich and meaningful.
There you saw moon and stars, on the dark dome of
    heaven,
And goddess, too, or hero, ladder, torch, or sword,
And all that threatens goodly towns with grim advance.
Such figuration now our band of heroes bears,
Emblems from sires of old in splendour handed down.
Thus you see lions, eagles, beak, and talon too,
Device of buffalo-horns, wings, roses, peacock-fan,
Bars also, gold and sable, argent, azure, gules:
The like hang high in state-rooms, ranging row on
    row,
In halls that have no end, a world of spaciousness:
There could you dance.

CHORUS.            What, partners for the dance are there?

PHORKYAS.
None better! Dashing, golden-headed troops of lads,
All redolent of youth. So only Paris breathed,
As once too closely to the Queen he drew.

HELEN.                        Enough.
You speak what stands not in your part: say your last
    words.

PHORKYAS.
Last word is yours: let me but hear an earnest 'yes',
And I will close you safely in those castle walls.

CHORUS.

O speak the simple word, to save yourself and us.

HELEN.

What, must I fear that Menelaus, King and lord,
In ruthless cruel transgression means my hurt and doom?

PHORKYAS.

Have you forgotten how he your Deiphobus,
Brother of fallen Paris, mangled shamefully,
Him who laid stubborn hands upon your widowhood,
And won you for his bed? Both nose and ears he
    cropped,
With more of mutilation, ghastly to behold.

HELEN.

Thus served he him, and all for love, on my account.

PHORKYAS.

On his account he now will do the like to you.
Beauty is not for sharing; he who has mastered her
Would rather slay her, with a curse on love that's
    shared.

(*Trumpets are heard in the distance. The Chorus
        starts in terror.*)

How sharp the trumpet's shattering tone, that rends the
    ear
And grips the very entrails. So will jealousy
Rend with her claws the heart of man, that ne'er forgets
What once was his, now lost, and gone for evermore.

CHORUS.

Hark, the sound of horns, do you hear them? See you not
    the glint of arms?

PHORKYAS.

Welcome to my King and Master: reckoning I gladly
    make.

CHORUS. What of us?

PHORKYAS.
 Full well you know it: stands her death before your eyes,
 And your own awaits within there; nay, for you there is
  no help.
HELEN. My mind is ready with the step that I shall dare.
 A hostile Demon are you, that I well perceive,
 And fear your work is ever turning good to ill.
 But first to yonder castle I will go with you;
 The rest I know; but things a queen may have in mind,
 In secret places of her heart's deep sanctuary,
 May none have access to. Old crone, you may lead on.
CHORUS. Thither, ah, gladly we go,
 Fleetfooted, swiftly;
 Death follows near,
 While before us there
 Rises a stronghold
 With impregnable ramparts.
 Shelter they offer, as once
 Safely did Ilium's wall,
 Which, when ruin came,
 Only fell to the basest guile.
  (*Mists spread around, veiling the background and the
              foreground too, at will.*)
 What can this be?
 Sisters, see what comes!
 Had we not jocund bright day?
 Mists are rising, mounting in scarfs,
 From Eurotas' sacred stream;
 Dim is now the beautiful
 Reeded shore, as it fades from our sight;
 Fade the free, dainty-proud,
 Smooth and silvery floating
 Swans in company swimming,

Lost, alas, from my sight.
  None-the-less, still
Float strange tones from them,
Far-off tones, sounding so hoarse,
Death-betokening notes, men say;
These, ah, may they not for us
Mock deliverance promised fair,
With the knell of doom at last:
Us, so swan-like and pale,
Slender-throated ones, doom with
Her, our swan-begotten.
Woe to us, ah woe!
  Thicker now is the pall,
All is shrouded in mist,
Scarcely we see each other now!
Can this be? Tread we still?
Hover we now,
Touching with thistledown steps the earth?
See you naught? Floats not Hermes there,
Even the God? Gleams not his wand of gold
Bidding, commanding us, that we return
To the cheerlessness of the gray-glimmering
Filled with beings insubstantial
Peopled thick yet ever empty Hades?
Ay, the dusk falls at a swoop now, mist rolls by with
    deadened lustre,
Murky grey, and dun as brickwork. Wall on wall now
    meets the sight,
Rigid barrier to vision. Court-yard is it, or deep quarry?
Which it be, it is appalling. Sisters, ah, we are im-
    prisoned,
Captive now as ne'er before.

# INNER COURTYARD OF A CASTLE

*Surrounded with ornate fantastic buildings of the Middle Ages.*

LEADER OF THE CHORUS.

Foolishly forward, you true types of womankind,
The passing moment's puppets, puff-balls to the breath
Of trouble or of luck; and neither schooled to bear
With equanimity. This one gainsays the rest
With vehemence, and they will cross-wise contradict;
In joy or pain, your voices use the same shrill note,
To laugh or howl. Now hold your peace and mark what
   way
Our sovereign's noble mind may choose for her and us.

HELEN.

Where lurk you, Pythonissa? Whatsoe'er your name,
Step from the vaulted chambers of this castle's gloom.
If you have gone to seek this wondrous hero-lord,
To herald my approach, and welcome fit ensure,
Then take my thanks and swiftly lead to where he waits:
Let these my wanderings cease. I only long for rest.

LEADER OF THE CHORUS.

O Queen, you lift in vain your gaze on every side:
The hateful form has vanished, or perhaps yet dwells
Within the mist, from whose grey bosom come we here,
I know not how, with swift yet scarcely stirring tread.
Or she may stray confused in labyrinthine ways
Of this strange castle, made from many into one,
To ask a high and noble welcome from its lord.
But see, up there, already stirs a multitude
Of serving-people, passing swiftly to and fro
In galleries, by casements, and at stately doors,

Betokening ceremonial welcome of a guest.
CHORUS. Rise up then, my heart! O, do but behold
    How in measure and state comes the brilliant throng,
    And moves in a train of comeliest youth,
    Ruled by modesty's grace. Whose, then, was the behest
    Bringing, marshalled so soon in a splendid array,
    Young pride of manhood, a glorious race?
    What admire I here most? Is it poise in their step,
    Or the head's crisp curls round the dazzling brow,
    Or the bloom of the cheeks, with the colour of peach,
    And velvet as peach with the tenderest down?
    With zest would I bite, yet shuddering shrink,
    For I know, in like venture, the mouth only filled –
    The thought of it loathsome – with ashes.
    Handsomest these now
    Who hitherward come;
    What things do they bear?
    Steps for a throne,
    Carpet and dais,
    Canopy-like
    Tapestry rich:
    Forming o'erflowing
    Garlands like cloudlets
    Over the head of our Queen,
    For, graciously bidden,
    Now she ascends the sumptuous throne.
    Draw you all near,
    Mounting each step to a
    Solemn array.
    Honoured, O honoured, threefold honoured,
    Such high welcome we consecrate now.
        (*The things described by the Chorus are fulfilled order
                        in due.*)

(*Faust, after the long train of squires and pages has come down, appears at the head of the stairs in the court costume of a medieval knight. He descends with grave dignity.*)

LEADER OF THE CHORUS (*with steadfast gaze*).

If these be no ephemeral gifts the Gods bestow,
After their wont, upon this man, his wondrous form,
His firm nobility, his winning presence mean
That triumph waits him wheresoe'er he turns his hand,
Whether his virile power be tried on battlefields,
Or in the miniature of war with women's hearts.
Indeed his worth surpasses hosts of those whom I
With these same eyes have seen most honourably famed.
Gravely, with reverent steps and dignity composed,
So comes this Prince: O Queen, now deign to turn!

FAUST (*advancing, with one in fetters at his side*).

Instead of ceremony's fitting grace,
Instead of reverent welcome, lo, I bring
A servant, shackled fast in welded chains,
Whose duty slighted made me turn from mine.
Before this noble lady kneel you now,
And make confession of your wretched guilt.
Before your Royal Highness stands the man
Who, for his piercing vision, had the trust
To scan from the high tower the spreading lands,
Watching the very sky-line for a sign
Of anything astir upon the hills,
Or through the vale, towards the castle walls,
Whether a billowy herd astray, or men
In hostile march; the one we will protect,
The other meet in arms. Today, alas,
What dereliction! Blind to your approach,
No word he gave; the honour due, to guest
So noble, now is lost. His life is forfeit

For this shame, already would he lie
    In blood of well-earned death; but you alone
    Shall punish or show mercy, at your will.

HELEN. Great as is the dignity which you bestow,
    As I were judge or sovereign here, or great
    The test which, as I think, you make of me,
    I now assume a judge's foremost duty,
    To give due hearing to the accused: speak on.

LYNCEUS (*Warden of the Tower*).

Let me kneel, let me gaze,
Let me live, or let me die,
Pledged to her are all my days,
Her come down from Gods on high.

    Waiting for the morning's gladness,
Scanning East for dawning light,
Saw I sunrise, thought it madness,
In the South, a wondrous sight.

    Sought my eyes the well-known places,
Valley, gorge, the heights of old;
Blind to earth or skyey spaces,
Only her did I behold.

    Piercing vision I was granted,
Sharp as lynx, a gift supreme,
Yet I struggled, I enchanted,
From the darkness of a dream.

    How to turn, or find my way then?
What were tower and gate to me?
Rolling mists withdraw their sway, then
Radiant comes this deity.

    Eye and heart in full surrender
Drank the softly shining light;
She whose beauty blinds with splendour,
She bereft me of my sight.

    All forgotten was my duty,
  Warden's oath and trusted horn;
  Though your threats destroy me, Beauty
  Stronger is than wrath or scorn.

HELEN. The evil that I caused, I may not punish.
  Ah me, what woe, what unrelenting fate
  Pursues me, working havoc in men's hearts,
  That so infatuate they lose all care
  Or of themselves, or of what honour bids.
  Thus, bent on plunder, fight, seducers' raids,
  Gods, heroes, demigods, nay demons too,
  Have led me much bewildered to and fro.
  Singly I shook the world, my double form
  Still more; now three-fold, four-fold bring I bane.
  Remove this innocent man and set him free.
  Nor set disgrace on whom the Gods beguile.

FAUST. In wonder lost, O Queen, I both behold,
  Her the sure archer, him the stricken mark.
  I see the bow from whence the arrow sped,
  And him now wounded; but with shaft on shaft
  Myself am struck. With sense of criss-cross flight
  I feel, through castle and court, the feathered whir.
  What is become of me? One glance from you,
  And henchmen turn to rebels, while my walls
  Lose their resistance. So my troops, I fear,
  Will hail the conquering unconquered Queen.
  What then remains, except to yield myself
  And all I fancied mine, now yours alone?
  In loyal truth now let me, at your feet,
  Acknowledge as Liege-Lady none but you;
  Who but appeared, and throne and power were yours.

LYNCEUS (*with a casket, and men following with other coffers*).
  O Queen, behold me at your feet.

Your glance the rich man must entreat,
And feel, in what that one look brings,
A beggar with the wealth of kings.

    What am I now? Or what of late?
What's now to do? What aim, what fate?
What hope in eyes the keenest known,
When baffled by your beauty's throne?

    We wandered from the Rising Sun,
And soon the West was over-run.
So great the trail of folk that passed,
The first knew nothing of the last.

    The foremost fell, the next could stand,
The third was ready, lance in hand;
Each took new strength a hundred-fold,
The slain lay heaped, unmarked, untold.

    We forged along, we stormed along,
In every place victorious, strong;
And where I lorded it today
The morrow's thief would rob and prey.

    We gave one glance, a glance of haste;
One seized a beauty to his taste,
And one the oxen from the stall;
Where horses were, we took them all.

    But all my joy was to espy
The rarest treasures of the eye,
And what the other might amass
Was naught to me but withered grass.

    To trace this wealth was my delight,
Trusting alone my power of sight.
No wallet missed I in my quest,
Transparent then was every chest.

    And gold, and many a precious stone,
With splendid blaze, were mine: alone

The emerald in lustrous sheen
Is fit to grace your heart, O Queen.
　　Hang trembling now twixt mouth and ear
Pearls from the depths of ocean: near
Such beauty even jewels pale
And fires of burning rubies fail.
　　Thus all my mighty hoard I place
Before the presence of your grace,
And bring in homage here the yield
Of many a fierce and bloody field.
　　Though all these coffers bring rich store,
My treasure-chests of iron are more:
Grant I be near you: I will fill
The vaults with riches, serving still.
　　For scarce enthroned you take your crown
Than all do homage and bow down,
All reason, wealth and thought and power,
Before your beauty's matchless flower.
　　This wealth I guarded as my own,
That now is lavished at your throne,
I thought high value to possess,
And now I see its nothingness.
　　So my possessions fade and pass,
Like mown and withered swathes of grass.
Give one sweet look, from Beauty's reign,
And all that worth will live again.

FAUST. This burden boldly won, take quickly hence,
　　Without reward or praise, though free from blame.
　　All that the castle holds within its depths
　　Is hers already: special gift to make
　　Is useless. Treasure upon treasure heap
　　In fair array. Splendour unseen bring forth,
　　A picture of high pomp. And let our vaults

Be sparkling skies. Compose a Paradise,
Still-life where lifeless things are born anew.
Fly you before her, flowered carpets lay,
And set soft pile on pile: so for her tread
The ground be gentle; so shall rest her gaze,
Blinding to all but gods, on naught but beauty.

LYNCEUS. All is easy to obey,
Where the service turns to play.
Wealth and heart's blood rules this Queen
By her proud and lovely mien.
Lo, our armies quiet and tamed,
Sword and sword-hand blunt and lamed;
Sunlight, near her form divine,
Dwindles, cools, and loses shine;
All is hollow, void of grace,
Near the glory of her face.                    (*Exit.*)

HELEN (*to Faust*).
Some speech, Sir, would I have with you, but come
Where I am here enthroned. The empty place
Invites its prince, and so assures me mine.

FAUST. First, on my knees, most noble Lady, may
My true allegiance please you: give me leave
To kiss the hand that bids me come to you.
Invest me as co-regent of your realm,
That knows no bounds: so win you to your side
A servant, guard, and worshipper in one.

HELEN. Many the wonders that I hear and see;
Amazement holds me, much I long to ask.
And first, this man, how comes it that his speech
Chimed strangely in my ears, so strange, yet kind,
Each tone in full accord with what came next?
No sooner has a word well pleased the ear,
Than comes another, as with a caress.

FAUST. If in mere speech our people charm your ear,
  O then most surely will their song enchant,
  And satisfy the hearing's inmost sense.
  But best it is we practise now this art,
  Alternate speech will call and coax it forth.
HELEN. For words so lovely, how the gift impart?
FAUST. Soon said: it must come welling from the heart;
  And, overflows heart's bliss without alloy,
  We lift our eyes and ask –
HELEN.                          Who shares the joy?
FAUST. Then not to past or future turns the mind,
  And only in the present –
HELEN.                        Bliss we find.
FAUST. And this as pledge of wealth we understand:
  Who sets the seal, confirms the gain?
HELEN.                                    My hand.
CHORUS. Who would now reproach our princess,
  Though she grant this castle's lord
  Token of her liking?
  For, admit, we one and all are
  Captive here, as we have been often
  Since the Trojan inglorious
  Overthrow, and the fearful
  Labyrinthine journey's woes.

    Women, used to love of menfolk,
  Not the choosers look to be,
  But the cunning judges.
  Even gold-cluster-curled shepherds,
  Or the fauns, dark with their beardings,
  As may happen the chance and hour,
  These do they stablish in equal
  Claim on beauty of lissom limbs.

    Near, still nearer throned they now sit,

Shoulder leaning on shoulder,
Knee beside knee, they sway and keep,
Hand in hand, measure and pulse
Over the throne's
High luxurious pillowed pomp.
Not for majesty to deny
Joys that are sweet,
Yet in wilfulness broadcast,
Plain before the eyes of the people.

HELEN. So far away I feel, and yet so near,
And most I long to say 'Here am I, here!'

FAUST. I tremble, scarcely breathe, my words have fled;
Space, time, all gone, I live a dream instead.

HELEN. I feel my life fordone, yet live anew,
In you inwoven, to the unknown true.

FAUST. Brood not, rare truth of destiny to trace,
Being is duty, were it a moment's space.

PHORKYAS (*entering brusquely*).
Lisp your lovers' alphabet then,
Coo, caress in love's duet then,
Brood and toy and wanton yet then,
Though here's not the time or place.
Trumpet clangour recognizing,
Feel you not dark tempest rising?
Ruin comes, and comes apace.
See, in hard pursuit, arms gleaming,
Hosts of Menelaus teeming,
Arm for battle's grim embrace.
By the victor-throng defeated,
Like Deiphobus maltreated,
You shall pay for consort grace.
For the trash the hangman's halter;
She full soon upon the altar

Has the whetted axe to face.

FAUST. Bold trespass! Hatefully it forces entrance in;
    Not even in danger will I brook insensate broil.
    And be the envoy fair, ill news disfigures him,
    While you, most foul, take joy in evil news alone.
    This time you fail. Your idle breath can shake the air
    With shattering mouthings. Danger is there none to us;
    And were there danger, I would count it empty threat.
    (*Alarms. Explosions from the towers, bugles and trumpets,*
      *martial music, the passing of powerful armed forces.*)

FAUST. Nay, heroes shall you see, none braver,
    Whose phalanx yields to no alarm.
    He only earns a woman's favour
    Who shields her with his strong right arm.
    (*To the leaders of the forces, as they leave the columns and*
                    *advance towards him.*)

    With governed strength, and bridled wrath,
    Sure of the victory in your power,
    Go, flowering manhood of the North,
    Go, Eastern men of fire and flower.

      Clad all in steel, where lightnings shiver,
    The host that realm on realm subdued,
    They come, the trembling earth must quiver,
    They pass, and thunder is renewed.

      At Pylos did we make our landing,
    Where ancient Nestor was no more,
    And petty kings together banding
    Our free force quelled on Hellas' shore.

      Drive from these walls, with no delaying,
    King Menelaus back to sea,
    To lurk with piracy and slaying
    As is his choice and destiny.

      I hail you with the ducal title,

Thus bids the Queen from Sparta's throne.
Valleys and hills in glad requital
Lay at her feet, her wealth your own.
  Yours, German, be the force defending,
As shield and rampart, Corinth's coasts;
Achaia's hundred vales extending
Commit I, Goths, to your fierce hosts.
  With Frankish arms to Elis veering,
Saxons, Messene falls to you;
You, Normans, seas of pirates clearing,
Shall stablish Argolis anew.
  There, each in settled habitation,
Fire, strength to outward foes make known;
But Sparta, ruling every nation,
Be still our Queen's time-honoured throne.
  There, in your single powers residing,
Rejoice in wealth, as in her sight;
And, at her feet, seek faith-abiding
Authority and law and light.

CHORUS. Who would make the fairest his own,
  First in his wisdom let him
  Cast for his weapons carefully round.
  What if smooth words won the prize,
  Brought him earth's highest beauty,
  Yet to keep it in peace he fails:
  Fawners softly may lure her away,
  Robbers snatch her by force from his sight;
  How he shall counter this, let him give heed.
    Lo, in this our Prince I praise,
  Rank him high above others,
  Him, for so joined he wisdom and strength,
  That the heroes stand and obey,
  All with heed for his gesture.

Faithfully now his will they do,
Each for his own behoof and weal,
As for bountiful thanks from his lord,
And for the noble renown of them both.

    For who shall sunder her now
From her great lord and master?
His she is, bestowed on him alone,
His with joy from us, whom he
Rescued with her, sheltered within by his ramparts,
Guarded without by his mighty host.

FAUST. Gifts now have these of wealth and blessing –
    Bestowed on each a fruitful land –
    Let them march on, their realms possessing,
    While in the midst we take our stand.

    So serve they, rivals in defending
This sea-girt land from all alarm,
Coasts linked, mid dancing waves extending,
With Europe's last long mountain-arm.

    Land rich in sun, and happy-fated,
Be blessed light to every race,
Won for my Queen and dedicated,
The first that looked upon her face,

    When, mid Eurotas' reedy sighing,
She left the shell, in gentle blaze,
And mother, kin, such beauty eyeing,
Were blinded by her lovely gaze.

    This land will give its flower, loyal
To you, all other names above;
Though all the world shall call you royal,
Give yet your fatherland your love.

    What though on aery ridges sun is glinting
Like frosty arrows through the jagged peaks,
The cliffs are green with verdure, no more stinting

The scanty nibbled meal the wild goat seeks.
  There gush the springs, the brooks leap downwards merging,
Already gorges, slopes, and meads are green;
And far, upon a hundred hills diverging,
The fleecy flocks at pasturage are seen.
  Divided, moving slow, with measured paces,
To the dread brink the hornèd cattle feed;
Yet all have refuge: in a hundred places
The rocks form vaulted shelter for their need.
  There Pan protects them, and the nymphs of fountains,
Who haunt the bosky, dew-drenched dells and leas,
From which there rise, as yearning towards the mountains,
The crowded ranks and billows of the trees.
  These timeless woods! The mighty oak tenacious
Rears stubborn crooks, in regal, stiff array;
The gentle maple, full of sap and gracious,
Lifts clear and fine its load as if in play.
  And mother-bounty, in the peaceful shadows,
Gives soft the flowing milk for lamb and child;
Fruit is at hand, the mellow fare of meadows,
And hollow trunks drip honey in the wild.
  Here is bliss as birthright reigning,
Here cheeks and lips aglow are found;
Each in his place immortal life attaining,
Content and blessed health abound.
  Here, in pure light, to father-strength is growing
The lovely child with glory shod.
We tax our hearts with wonder, hardly knowing
If man we call this race, or god.
  So like the herds Apollo was in feature,
That self-same grace their fairest could command;

For where the orbit rules of perfect Nature,
Worlds else divided merge and blend.
                    (*He takes his seat beside her.*)
    Behold, my fate and yours by joy attended;
Now let the pennons of the past be furled,
O, feel yourself from God supreme descended,
For yours it is to claim the primal world.

    No walls can circle you or capture,
In flower of youth for us abide,
As lovely realms of lasting rapture,
Arcadia and Sparta side by side.

    Tempted to sanctuary in that hour,
You found the brightest destiny:
Let throne be changed to leafy bower,
Arcadian be our bliss, and free.

    (*The scene is entirely transformed. Ranged against rocky
caverns are seen a number of closed arbours. Faust and Helen
are no longer seen. The Chorus, scattered here and there, lies
sleeping.*)

PHORKYAS.

How long these girls lie sleeping here, I cannot tell;
Or whether they have dreamed the things that stark and
    clear
Were mine to see, that also is to me unknown.
I'll wake them; and these youthful things shall stand
    amazed;
You bearded gentry, too, who wait down there, agog
To find the key of marvels credible at last.
Awake, arise, and quickly shake your sleepy locks,
Dash sleep from your eyes, your blinkings cease, and hear
    me speak.

CHORUS. Speak, say on, and tell us quickly any wonders
    that have happened.

Most of all our ears will welcome things that we can
    scarce believe in,
For our hearts and minds are weary, gazing all this time
    at cliffs.

PHORKYAS.

What, young people, scarce awake yet, and you talk of
    being tired?
Hearken then, within these grottoes, in these caves and
    in these bowers,
Screen and arbour is afforded, as to loving pair
    idyllic,
Namely to our lord and lady.

CHORUS.                    What, within there?

PHORKYAS.                              Sweetly sundered
From the world, they called me only, me to give a silent
    service.
Honoured did I stand in waiting, yet, as well becomes
    one trusted,
Bent my care on other duties, turning hither, looking
    thither,
Seeking roots and barks and simples, versed in all their
    special virtues,
So that they remained alone.

CHORUS.

Why, you prate as if within there stretched a world of
    spacious prospect.
Forest, pasture, lakes, and rivers; what fantastic tale is
    this?

PHORKYAS.

This is sure, unknowing creatures, these are secret depths
    unfathomed:
Court on court and all the state-rooms, these I traced
    with musing mind.

But a sudden note of laughter echoes through the lofty
　　vaulting;
As I gaze a boy leaps lightly from his mother to his father,
From his sire to lap of mother; now is banter and
　　caressing
Which with sound of love's fond teasing, merry shouts,
　　and jubilant laughter,
Mingling, almost deafen me.
Naked leaps the wingless genius, like a faun with no
　　brute-nature,
Springs on firm-set earth, which straightway counters
　　with a strange resilience,
Speeds his flight in airy arches, till at second bound or
　　third he
Soars to touch the vaulted roof.
With misgiving calls the mother: 'Leap and leap, to
　　heart's contentment,
Only have a care of flying; not for you free scope of
　　flight.'
Warning speaks the trusty father: 'In the earth the vital
　　spring is,
Which is yours in upward leaping; touch the earth but
　　with your toe-tips,
Like the son of Earth, Antaeus, you will straight have
　　strength renewed.'
Whereupon he scales the cliff-face, skims from rocks to
　　dizzy ledges,
Light returning, hither, thither, like a shrewdly stricken
　　ball.
　Suddenly a frowning cavern in its rugged maw
　　engulfs him,
And we think no more to see him. Mother weeps and
　　sire gives comfort,

While I shrug in my misgiving. Yet, again, behold a
  vision!
Are there treasures hidden yonder? Flowered he stands
  in broidered raiment
Worn with grace and majesty.
Tassels swing from his fair shoulders, at his bosom rib-
  bons flutter,
In his hand the golden lyre, boyish image of Apollo,
Strides he on the beetling cliff-top, blithely to the brink;
  we marvel,
And in thankful joy the parents turn to seek each other's
  arms.
What strange glory gilds his forehead? Scarce we dare
  to name that gleaming,
Is it jewelled gold, or is it fire of genius nobly gifted?
Thus his bearing and his gesture, even as a boy, proclaim
  him
Future master of all beauty, one in whom eternal music
Stirs in every limb with rapture; even thus you all shall
  hear him,
Thus it is that you shall see him, with a wonder never
  equalled.
CHORUS. Call you a wonder this,
  Offspring of Creta?
  Poetry's formative word
  Never has reached your hearing?
  Never heard Ionia's legends,
  Nor the stories of Hellas,
  Tales handed down through ages,
  Wealth bequeathed of gods and heroes?
    All that can come to pass
  Now in our era,
  Pitiful echo is,

Borne from ancestral splendour;
No compare your story brings us
With what halcyon fiction,
Winning belief more than truth can,
Sang about the son of Maia.

   Him so pretty and sturdy, though
Yet a newly born nurseling,
Straight have his garrulous nurses
Swaddled in bands of the softest fleece,
Wrapped in a vestment rich and rare,
Thus did these in their folly.
Sturdy and graceful soon the rogue
Lifts his limbs with a subtlety,
Limbs so flexible, lissom,
Forth from the clothes, now leaving the
Cramping, purple-bright sheathing
Empty, peacefully in its place;
As when perfect the butterfly
From the crusted chrysalid
Freeing its wings most adroitly slips
Forth in its pinioned freedom bold,
And floats in the sun–drenched ether.

   So he, lord of dexterity,
That to thieves and scoundrels,
To self-seekers and pickers all,
Ever the favouring god he be,
Well he testified then and there
By the deftest devices:
Stole the trident from Ocean's King
Quick as thought; from Ares, too, with guile
Filched the sword from the scabbard;
Purloined the bow of Phoebus then,
And the smith's tongs of Hephaestus;

Even the bolts of Father Zeus
He'd take, did not the fire scare him;
Eros though he overthrew
In a leg-tripping wrestling-match;
From Venus then a stolen embrace,
And the zone from her bosom.

(*There comes from the cavern exquisite pure music of
string-players. All listen attentively and soon seem deeply
moved. From here onwards, to the marked pause, there is a
fully-scored accompaniment of music.*)

PHORKYAS. Hear the music, sweetly sounding.
Break from musty tales at last!
Gods in hierarchy abounding,
Let them go, their day is past.

Yours, an age none grasps, is going,
Nobler themes we must impart:
Only from a heart o'erflowing
Comes the power upon the heart.
(*She withdraws to the cliff.*)

CHORUS. If, dread Shape, the music stealing
Brings a solace to your ears,
We, in new-won health, are feeling
All the gentle joy of tears.

Let the sunshine fail in heaven,
So the soul be bathed in light:
What the world has never given,
Find we in our hearts aright.

(*Helen, Faust; with Euphorion dressed as described above.*)

EUPHORION. Hear you songs of children's singing,
Joys your own they manifest;
See you me in measure springing,
Joy leaps in the parent breast.

HELEN. For the bliss of human feeling,

Love will join a noble pair;
But, the joy of gods revealing,
Love creates three spirits rare.

FAUST. All is now achieved and righted,
I am yours and you are mine,
Each in each fulfilled, united,
If but love for ever shine.

CHORUS. Thus shall flow, through years of pleasure,
Gentle radiance from the boy,
Crowning love in bounteous measure;
Ah, how moving is their joy.

EUPHORION. Let me be springing,
Let me be leaping,
Pressing on, mounting,
Through the clouds sweeping,
Strong these desires
In my thoughts run.

FAUST. Gently, ah gently,
Be not too daring,
Lest in disaster
All of us sharing
See our great sorrow
Come from our son.

EUPHORION. No more as earthbound
Will I be stranded;
Let go my tresses,
Leave me free-handed,
Let go my garments,
All mine alone.

HELEN. Think, think whose you are,
To whom belonging,
How you would wound us,
Wrecking and wronging

All the joy won now,
His, mine, your own.

CHORUS. Soon, as I fear,
Is love overthrown.

HELEN and FAUST. Curb now, ah curb,
At parents' desire,
Over-impetuous
Projects of fire!
Peacefully rural
Grace you the plain.

EUPHORION. Only to please you,
Flight I restrain.

(*He winds his way among the Chorus, drawing them to
join in the dance.*)

Round the glad throngs I see,
Gentler my flight.
Is this the melody,
And is the movement right?

HELEN. That is well done, indeed;
Beauty in dance to lead,
Graceful the art.

FAUST. Fearing what fate may bring
Ever such capering
Saddens my heart.

(*Euphorion and the Chorus join, with song,
in the interweaving figures of the dance.*)

CHORUS. Lifting your arms so fair,
Gracefully swaying,
Shaking your shining hair,
Where lights are playing,
When with a foot so light
Scarce touching earth, you skim,
And in alternate flight

Hovers each lovely limb,
Then have you reached your goal,
Beautiful youth:
All of us then in truth
Yours heart and soul.

EUPHORION. Your troop advance then,
Light-footed does,
On with the dance then,
So the game goes:
I am the hunter,
You are the chase.

CHORUS. If you will catch us,
Gentle the tasking:
When you outmatch us,
All we are asking,
Picture of beauty,
Is your embrace.

EUPHORION. On through the wood, then!
By field and flood, then!
Hateful I find the spoil
Taken with ease;
Only when won with toil
Will quarry please.

HELEN and FAUST. Ah, what passion! Ah, what riot!
Hope of sweet restraint is banished.
Through the vale and woodland quiet
Peals like hunters' horn resound:
What a tumult, what mad cries!

CHORUS (*entering quickly, one after another*).
In a scornful, bitter chevvy,
He outran us at a bound
And the wildest of our bevy
Hither drags as hunter's prize.

EUPHORION (*bearing in a young girl*).
  Here I drag the little courser,
  And to joy of mine will force her;
  Now with rapture and with zest
  Press I her unwilling breast,
  Kiss her rebel mouth, that so
  She my will and strength may know.
GIRL. Let me go! This frame so fragile
  Keeps its strength and spirit still;
  Ours is force and mind too agile
  To be subject to your will.
  Think you to have me in a corner,
  Strength of arm as your resort?
  Hold me fast and I, your scorner,
  Soon will singe you, fool, for sport.
     (*She bursts into flame, and soars flaring on high.*)
  Follow me in airy spaces,
  Follow in deep craggy places,
  Till your vanished prize be caught.
EUPHORION (*shaking off the last flames*).
  Barrier cliffs are here,
  Forest growth among.
  What are the odds I fear,
  Since I am fresh and young?
  Storm winds may rage and roar,
  Tempests may lash the shore,
  These though afar I hear,
  Glad were I to be near.
     (*He leaps even higher up the cliff.*)
HELEN, FAUST, and CHORUS.
  Would you ibex-like aspire,
  Danger fills us with dismay.
EUPHORION. Still will I leap ever higher,

Still a wider world survey.
Now perceive I where I stand,
In the midst of Pelops' land,
In the island by the firth,
Kin with ocean and with earth.

CHORUS.
Tarry, where wood and height
Peacefully shine.
Seek we for your delight
Fruit of the vine,
Grapes from the mountain-side,
Figs, apple-gold;
Ah, in this land abide
With joy untold.

EUPHORION. Dream you of peaceful day?
That dream let dream who may.
War! Send the password round,
Victory the answering sound.

CHORUS. In peace whoever
Wishes war back again
Does himself sever
From hope's glad reign.

EUPHORION. All whom this land has bred,
Ever on peril fed,
Free their own blood to spend
In courage without end –
    In whom unquenched remain
High thoughts for evermore,
May these from toils of war
Have noble gain.

CHORUS. Distant, yet not smaller seeming,
See, he mounts, to what a height!
Victor-like, in armour gleaming,

Bronze and steel glint not more bright.

EUPHORION. On no wall or dyke relying,
  Armour of self-trust is best;
  Citadel all shocks defying
  Is the man of iron breast.
      Will you proudly spurn the yoke, then
  Forth to fight, light-armed and free!
  Amazons your women-folk then,
  Every child a hero be!

CHORUS. Mounting to heaven, see
  Blest soul of Poesie!
  Shine out, you fairest star,
  Far, ay, and ever far.
  Sweet voices reach us still,
  Those tones of poet's skill
  Our solace are.

EUPHORION. Nay, not as child was I appearing,
  But an armed youth before your eyes,
  Joined with the strongest, free, unfearing,
  In spirit with their deeds he vies.
  Onwards I dare,
  For there
  The way to fame and honour lies.

HELEN and FAUST. Scarce you reach the joy of morning,
  Scarce life's threshold do you know,
  And you yearn, the summits scorning,
  For the fields of pain and woe.
  We so fond,
  Is our bond
  Naught but dream or empty show?

EUPHORION. Hear you not thunder on the ocean,
  And echoed thunder, vale on vale?
  In dust and foam comes war's commotion,

With storm and stress and clash of mail.
The agony
Is death's decree;
So it runs, and who shall quail?

HELEN, FAUST, and CHORUS.
Ah, what horror! Death as master
Will you hail? Ah, what despair!

EUPHORION. Shall I view from far disaster?
Nay, their bitter woes I'll share.

HELEN, FAUST, and CHORUS.
Rashness in danger brings
Deadly despite!

EUPHORION. I must! And here are wings
Spreading for flight.
Give way! Fate wills it thus.
I must rise up.

(*He casts himself into the air. For a moment his robes bear him up. His head is radiant, and a trail of light follows him.*)

CHORUS. Icarus! Icarus!
Full is the cup.

(*A beautiful youth falls headlong at the feet of his parents. We think to recognize in the dead a well-known form; but what is corporeal fades away at once, the aureole rising meteor-like to heaven. Robe, mantle, and lyre are left upon the ground.*)

HELEN and FAUST. Brief joy must be our lot,
That woes overwhelm.

THE VOICE OF EUPHORION (*rising from the deep*).
Mother, forsake me not
In the dark realm.

CHORUS (*lament*). Not forsaken: for abiding,
Yet to us one seen and known,
Take our hearts, to darkness gliding,
And you shall not be alone.

So we mourn, yet scarce repining,
Sing with envy of your fate,
For in clouded days or shining
Lovely was your song and great.

   High in lineage and power,
Born for every earthly boon,
Snatched away in youthful flower
Lost to self and love so soon.
Eyes the world so sharply proving,
Insight that all woes beheld,
Heart for woman's ardent loving,
And a song unparalleled.

   Headlong yet your way pursuing
In the mesh that blinds the will,
Moral code and law eschewing,
You would ride a rebel still;
But at last a high aspiring
Gave pure courage worth and weight,
Glorious things all your desiring
Still, alas, denied by fate.

   Whose the gain then? – Question dreary
Mocked by fate in hooded guise,
When, in days of grief grown weary
Nations bleed, and none replies.
Yet droop not, nor dirges render,
Flow of poesie renew,
For old earth will songs engender,
As she has the ages through.

   (*There is a full pause. The music comes to an end.*)

HELEN (*to* FAUST).

   An ancient word, alas, is now fulfilled in me,
   That happiness and beauty are not mated long.
   The link of life is wrenched apart, like that of love;

Mourning them both, with aching heart I say farewell,
And cast myself this last sad time upon your breast.
Persephone, I come, take now the child and me.
            (*She embraces Faust; her bodily form vanishes,
                her robe and veil are left in his arms.*)

PHORKYAS (*to* FAUST).

What things remain from all you had, hold fast.
The robe, release it not! Already demons
Begin to pluck it by the hems, in zeal
To drag it to the shadow-realm. Hold fast!
True, this is not the Goddess you have lost,
But god-like is it. Take the priceless gift
To serve the flight in which you soar aloft;
'Twill bear you swiftly up above all dross,
On through the ether, if you can endure.
We meet again, far, very far from here.
    (*The garments of Helen dissolve into clouds; enveloping
    Faust they lift him on high and bear him from the scene.*)

PHORKYAS (*gathering up Euphorion's robe, mantle, and lyre
    from the ground, she steps forward to the proscenium, holds
    up the spoils, and speaks*).

This find I call a happy ending!
What if the flame is done, past mending,
It's not a world to weep about.
Enough is left for poet's consecration,
To stir up envy in their guilds devout;
And if I can't provide the inspiration,
At least I'll lend the wardrobe out.
        (*She comes down to the proscenium and sits at the
                foot of a pillar.*)

PENTHALIS.

Come, girls, be swift. At last we shake the magic off
With which the old Thessalian hag would bind the soul,

Freed from the strumming, too, of heady wreathing tones
The ear bewildering, and still worse the inward sense.
Descend we then to Hades; for our Queen went down
With swift and solemn bearing, and her faithful maids
Should plant their steps in hers; so shall we surely find
Our Lady near the throne of the Inscrutable.

CHORUS.

They that are queens indeed find solace everywhere,
Ranking high, even in realms below.
Proudly holding court with their peers,
Sharing closely Persephone's trust;
But for us, who haunt the background,
Deep in asphodel, companions
Of the straggling poplars,
Where they with unfruitful willows range,
What have we by way of pastime?
What but a bat-like squeaking,
A spectral and calamitous twitter?

PENTHALIS.

Who no fair name has won, nor strives for noble things,
Belongs but to the elements: so get you gone!
My heart longs for my Queen: in merit not alone
But in our loyalties we keep our personal life.

ALL. Restored again are we, back to light of day,
Persons, indeed, no more.
This feel we, and know it true.
Nonetheless never return we to Hades.
Nature eternal asserts
Claim on us spirits,
As on her we call with full warrant.

PART OF THE CHORUS.

We in myriad trembling branches breathe the whispers,
    charm the softly

Cradled rustling, luring gently from the roots the flow-
ing pulses

To the twigs; and now with leafage, now with riot of
fair blossom,

Will we deck these streaming tresses for their spreading
joy of growth.

Falls the fruit, then come the lusty herds and country-
folk, hearts gladdened,

For the harvest merry, eager, busy crowding, gathering,
tasting,

Bending one and all around us, as before the world's first
gods.

ANOTHER PART.

Where the walls of rock are mirrored, spreading far their
glassy image,

We in gliding waves will nestle, soothingly to ride and
rest;

There for every note to listen, song of bird or reedy
fluting,

Hoarse the voice of Pan uplifted – quickly floats the
answer back;

Murmur we with murmur answer, thunder with our
rolling thunder

In a deep reverberation, double, treble, tenfold crash.

A THIRD PART.

Sisters, we of fleeter spirit race with ever running brook-
lets;

For the hills that charm the distance tempt us with their
load of beauty.

Downwards, ever deeper falling, in meandering flow we
water

Now the meadow, now the pastures, soon the garden
round the house.

There stand out the spires of cypress, rising slender to-
    wards the ether

From the landscape's watery mirror, from the darkening
    line of shore.

A FOURTH PART. Range you others at your fancy, we
    encircle with sweet rustling

Terraced hill-sides richly planted, where is propped the
    ripening vine;

There the vintager so zealous shows us every hour in
    fervour

How a doubtful consummation waits upon his loving
    care.

Now with hoe and now with mattock, now in trench-
    ing, pruning, binding,

Prays he all the gods to help him, and the sun-god most
    of all.

Small concern the pampered Bacchus has for this his
    honest servant,

Takes his ease in caves and arbours, trifling with the
    youngest faun.

All he needs for tipsy dreaming, for the half-light of his
    musing,

Stands around in jars and wine-skins, near at hand in
    butts and pitchers,

Left and right the cool recesses offer immemorial store.

But when gods have granted breezes, Helios the warmth
    has given,

Dews and glowing sun maturing grapes in horn of plenty
    heaped,

Where they dressed the vines in silence, on a sudden
    all is bustle,

Swish of leaves on every trellis, rustling heard from stock
    to stock.

Baskets creak and buckets clatter, laden hods now groan
   along,
All towards the mighty wine-press, for the treaders'
   lusty dance;
So the wealth of blessed bounty, grapes in bloom and
   luscious beauty,
Trodden ruthlessly and foaming, spurting, mingles
   foully crushed.
Now the timbrels smite the ear and cymbals with their
   brazen clashing,
For the wine-god Dionysos comes revealed from
   mysteries,
Comes with train of goat-foot satyrs, reeling nymphs,
   they too goat-footed,
And mid all, unruly, strident, brays Silenus' long-eared
   beast.
Naught is spared! All decent custom cloven hoofs now
   trample under,
All the senses swirl and stagger, ears are stunned with
   fearful din.
Drunken grope they for the goblet, surfeit swills in heads
   and paunches,
Here and there is some misgiving, but the tumult waxes
   wilder,
Since, to garner this year's vintage, drain they all the
   wine-skins dry.

   (*The curtain falls. Phorkyas, in the proscenium, rears her-
self to giant stature, but steps down from the buskins and, re-
moving mask and veil, reveals herself as Mephistopheles, as
though to provide such epilogue as might seem necessary.*)

# ACT FOUR

—

## MOUNTAIN HEIGHTS

*A mighty summit of jagged rocks. A cloud draws near,*
*clinging to the peak, and settling on an overhanging ledge.*
*The cloud parts and Faust steps forth.*

FAUST. Downgazing here I view the deepest solitude,
   Treading with pensive step the lofty mountain-ridge,
   My chariot of cloud relinquished, that so soft
   Bore me through shining days serene by land and sea.
   In cloud unscattered, floating slow, it draws away,
   And eastward strives compacted in a mass clear-curled,
   Where eyes must strive to follow, in deep wonder lost.
   In moving wave it sunders, changeful as it glides,
   Yet form assuming. Nay, no trick of vision this!
   In pillowed splendour couched, soft-gilded by the sun,
   Behold, a giant and yet a god-like woman-form,
   And well I see, like Juno, Leda, Helen – so
   In lovely majesty it glides before my sight.
   Ah, now it breaks and widens, towering loses form,
   And settling in the East, like distant snow-capped peaks,
   Reflects the deep significance of fleeting days.
   Yet still about my brow and breast a wreath of mist
   Clings lightly with a gentle cheer and cool caress.
   Now soft it mounts, and hovering high and higher still
   Shapes its own image. – Am I bewitched by pictured
         form,
   A glimpse of tender youth's high bliss I long had lost?
   The earliest treasures of the heart come welling up:
   Aurora's love, that means for me light-soaring wings,

The first, so swiftly felt, scarce comprehended glance,
Which, claimed and held, all other treasure could out-
    shine.
Now like the soul's pure beauty mounts the lovely
    form,
Nor suffers change, but floats to ether far on high,
And all that's best within my soul it bears away.

    (*A seven-league boot lurches on to the stage; another
follows immediately. Mephistopheles alights. The boots
swiftly stride away.*)

MEPHISTOPHELES. Now that I reckon's travelling in style!
Yet tell me what on earth you mean,
By landing in a place so bleak and vile,
Bare crag and precipice, a ghastly scene.
Though somewhat changed in site, I know it well;
This was, indeed, the very floor of Hell.

FAUST. In foolish legends you were never lacking,
And here you come again your store unpacking.

MEPHISTOPHELES (*in a serious tone*).
When the Lord God – and well do I know why –
To depths abysmal hurled us from the sky,
To central lurid glow of realms infernal,
Encompassed there with fire and flame eternal,
We found ourselves within that glaring waste
Much crowded and most miserably placed.
Then all the devil folk began to cough,
And fell to belching and to blowing off:
All Hell was swollen with sulphur-stench and fuming,
A filthy gas, prodigious strength assuming,
So that earth's level crust, so strong at first,
Cracking, upheaved its mighty floor and burst.
So now we claim another rule as best,
With deep abyss transposed to mountain crest;

What's more, they found their doctrine on this base,
And give to lowest things the highest place;
Free from the thraldom of the fiery pit,
We take the air with lordship infinite,
A mystery manifest, for long concealed,
And to the peoples but of late revealed.     (Ephes. 6. 12)

FAUST. The nobly silent hills loom up on high
In peace that stills my question whence or why.
When Nature was in her own image founded
To earth she gave proportion pure and rounded,
And in the peaks and gorges took delight,
Ranged cliff on cliff and height on mountain-height.
Then hills she formed in gentle beauty blending,
In softened lines to valleys mild descending.
There verdure teems, a growth that for its gladness
Needs nothing from your tale of seething madness.

MEPHISTOPHELES.
Ay, clear as day, to hear you state the case!
But he knows best who saw the thing take place.
I was at hand when burst the flaming shock,
And molten fury from the depths upsprung,
When Moloch's hammer wrought upon the rock,
And mountain-ruin far and wide was flung.
The earth has still these massive loads to bear,
That hurling-power has left us all astounded.
The thing is your philosopher's despair:
There lies the rock, and we must leave it there,
We've taxed our brains, to own our wits confounded.
Only the simple common folk are sure,
And nothing ever shakes them in their story,
Their wisdom's ripe and old and will endure:
A marvel this, and Satan gets the glory.
My pilgrim, with faith's crutch and privilege,

Thus limps to Devil's Rock and Devil's Bridge.

FAUST. Most interesting, in this pleasant wrangle,
    To look at Nature from the devil's angle.

MEPHISTOPHELES.
    Be Nature what she will, why should I care?
    My honour's touched: I say the Devil was there.
    We are the folk to bring off great designs,
    With tumult, madness, force – behold the signs.
    But now, to speak at last with meaning clear,
    Did nothing charm you in our upper sphere?
    For there you saw, in pageant wide unfurled,
    The glory of the Kingdoms of the World.        (Matt. 4)
    For you, with your insatiate mind,
    Was there no tempting joy to find?

FAUST. Why, yes. A great plan won my heart.
    Guess what!

MEPHISTOPHELES. Soon done. To make a start.
    I'd choose some mighty capital,
    It's core the folk's foul feeding-stall,
    All gabled alleys, crooked, stale,
    Cramped stalls of garlic, turnips, kale,
    Meat-shambles, where the blow-flies fatten
    And on fat joints in clusters batten.
    There any hour you'll find, I think,
    Business activity and stink.
    Then come wide streets and many a square,
    To arrogate a lordly air;
    And lastly, past the town's redoubt,
    The endless suburbs straggle out,
    There, in the city's loud approach,
    I'd take my pleasure in my coach,
    Amused to see the ceaseless flow
    Of human ants run to and fro.

And when I walked or drove abroad,
I'd be the person to applaud,
The cynosure of veneration.

FAUST. Not this would set my mind at peace.
One's glad to see the folk increase
And thrive, each in his style and station;
Their knowledge grows, their manners mend –
Yet rebels breed we in the end.

MEPHISTOPHELES.
Then would I build in style, with conscious grace,
A pleasure-palace in a pleasant place,
With hill and forest, field and glade,
Into a noble garden made;
With velvet lawns, clipped verdant walls,
Paths true to line, trim shadows, waterfalls
From rock to rock cascading, well designed,
And fountain-play of every kind,
The centre soaring to majestic height,
The sides in squirting miniature delight.
To house the fairest women then I'd make
Small cosy villas, for seclusion's sake.
And there I'd spend the hours unfettered, free,
In the most charming social privacy.
Women, I say: to give the fair their due
I always have preferred a plural view.

FAUST. Sardanapalus: vice that's old – and new!

MEPHISTOPHELES.
May one but know your lofty scheming?
Sublime, no doubt, the things you dare.
Towards the moon you hovered dreaming,
Perhaps your quest would take you there?

FAUST. Not in the least. This homely earth
Invites heroic deeds and bearing.

I feel a strength that leads to daring,
To marvels of a wondrous worth.

MEPHISTOPHELES. And there your lust for fame begins:
One sees you've been with heroines.

FAUST. So realm and rule to me will fall;
The glory's nought, the deed is all.

MEPHISTOPHELES. Yet unborn poets will proclaim
To all posterity your fame,
More fools with folly to inflame.

FAUST. Shut out from life, you have no part
In things that stir the human heart.
Your bitter mind, where envy breeds,
What can it know of human needs?

MEPHISTOPHELES.
Then, yielding to your will, let be what must.
The compass of your whims to me entrust.

FAUST. My eyes were turned towards the open sea:
Its towering swell against the heaven it bore,
Then, shaking out its waves exultantly,
Came charging up the level stretch of shore.
This grieved me, that a haughty arrogant flood
Can cast free spirit, prizing every right,
Through passion of the wildly kindled blood,
Into a trough of feeling's vexed despite.
Lest this were chance, sharp watch I would renew:
The surge hung back, the towering wave withdrew,
Rolling afar from goal so proudly won;
The hour returns, again the game's begun.

MEPHISTOPHELES (*ad Spectatores*).
This brings no novel tidings to my ears,
I've known it well these hundred thousand years.

FAUST (*continuing passionately*).
So in a thousand channels creeps the sea,

Sterile itself, it spreads sterility.
It seethes and swells and streaming far and wide
Takes desolate regions in its rolling tide.
There wave on wave, by hidden power heaved,
Reigns and recedes, and nothing is achieved.
This thing can sadden me to desperation,
Wild elements in aimless perturbation!
To soar beyond itself aspired my soul:
Here would I strive, and this would I control.
    And this is possible. – The fullest tide
Will skirt the hill and nestle at its side;
Despite the threat and tumult it may waken,
A little height will face it proud, unshaken,
While little hollows suck it down, you'll find.
Thus plan on plan developed in my mind:
Grasp then the priceless triumph, evermore
To hold the lordly ocean from the shore,
To set the watery waste new boundary lines,
And bid it wallow in its own confines.
My plan I could expound, as step by step I made it;
My wish I have declared, and you must dare to aid it.
    (*Drums and martial music are heard in the distance,*
         *to the right, behind the spectators.*)

MEPHISTOPHELES.
    Easy, no doubt! – Hear you those drums afar?
FAUST. War once again – and wise men frown on war.
MEPHISTOPHELES.
    Come war, come peace, your wisdom will be shown
    In raking off some profit of your own.
    You wait, sharp-eyed, a watcher none can oust.
    Here comes the chance: grab it at once, my Faust.
FAUST. Say briefly what's to do. Upon my soul,
    You tire me with your riddling rigmarole.

MEPHISTOPHELES. Upon my journey I became aware
  That our good Emperor floats on floods of care.
  You know him well: with revels we supplied him,
  And when we'd bogus riches to provide him
  He thought he'd buy the world up for his own;
  For young he was when coming to the throne,
  And in a fallacy he took delight;
  Two functions would he pleasantly combine,
  In fact he thought his notion very fine:
  To govern, and indulge one's appetite.
FAUST. A woeful error. He who has to hold
  Command of men must have a leader's mind,
  Joy in authority, lofty will and bold,
  A will not by the common herd divined.
  To trusted ears he tells his quiet intent,
  And this is done – to nations' wonderment.
  So stands he high, supreme, and so obeyed,
  The noblest still. Indulgence must degrade.
MEPHISTOPHELES.
  But not this one! He spared no joys, not he!
  So all his realm collapsed in anarchy,
  With men both high and low enmeshed in feud,
  Brother by brother murderously pursued.
  Castle fought castle, town invaded town,
  And guilds had plots to pull the nobles down,
  Chapter and flock against the bishop rose,
  And nowhere could men meet, except as foes.
  In church they stabbed to kill, before the gate
  The travelling merchant met a bloody fate.
  Bold, ruffian force gave no alternative,
  So they went on: defend yourself to live.
FAUST. Went on, limped on, fell, rose again perhaps,
  Then, losing balance, lurched to a collapse.

MEPHISTOPHELES.

    And this condition none should really blame.

    Each saw his chance and each would stake his claim.

    The smallest boor then aped the greater folk,

    Until the best men found it past a joke.

    The sturdy ones of worth then rose in strength,

    And said: He's lord who brings us peace at length.

    Our Emperor can't or won't: then let us choose

    A new lord who the realm renews

    By setting all upon their feet,

    In a fresh world, made safe and sweet,

    And peace with righteousness imbues.

FAUST. That sounds like priest-craft.

MEPHISTOPHELES.                    Ay, the priests were there,

    And made the well-fed paunch their foremost care.

    They, more than other men, were implicated:

    Revolt arose, revolt was consecrated;

    The monarch we contrived to entertain

    Comes on to fight – perhaps his last campaign.

FAUST. I pity him, so good, devoid of guile.

MEPHISTOPHELES.

    Well, while there's life there's hope. We'll watch
        awhile:

    If he escape the pass by our device,

    Once saved is saved a thousand times. The dice

    Can no-one reckon up before they're played.

    If luck is his, come vassals to his aid.

      (*They cross over the middle mountain-range and view the
    disposition of the army in the valley below, from which come
    the sounds of drums and martial music.*)

MEPHISTOPHELES.

    Their ground, I see, is chosen with some skill;

    We'll join, and set the seal on victory still.

FAUST. What hopes are here, I'd like to know?
Delusion, devilment, a hollow show.

MEPHISTOPHELES. Say battle-cunning, set to win!
So, with a mind intrenched, begin
By thinking on your lofty aim:
The Emperor we save, his lands, his hosts,
So shall you proudly kneel to claim
The lordship of unbounded coasts.

FAUST. So many things you've tried and done,
Just see the battle here is won.

MEPHISTOPHELES. No, that shall you: I plan, in brief,
That you shall hold command-in-chief.

FAUST.
O grand promotion! What could please me more
Than high command all ignorant of war?

MEPHISTOPHELES. That is the General Staff's affair;
The General's covered, free from care.
War's witlessness suspecting long,
I've fashioned a war-council strong
In men and mountains' primal might;
Lucky is he, for whom those powers unite.

FAUST. What band is this, in arms appears?
Have you stirred up the mountaineers?

MEPHISTOPHELES. No, but as Peter Quince would do,
Of all the bag a chosen few.

       (*Enter three men of might.*) (2 Sam. 23. 8)
Ah, now my pretty lads are here,
In years and garb of sundry sort;
Though age and armour odd appear,
You'll not do ill with their support.

                  (*Ad Spectatores.*)
Now every child delights to see
The warrior knights in armour cased;

And allegories though my rascals be,
So much the more they'll suit the public taste.

SMITE-ALL (*young, lightly armed, and in gay garments*).
Is there a man that looks me in the eyes,
I up with my fist and smash him in the face;
Or if a dastard cowardly turns and flies
I grab his pigtail, and so end the chase.

GRAB-ALL (*with virile air, fully armed, and richly clad*).
An empty business, tricks like this,
You waste your chance and spoil your day;
Go grab and get, and nothing miss,
And afterwards let come what may.

KEEP-ALL (*stricken in years, heavily armed, lacking a robe*).
You've not much gain there at the finish;
The biggest fortunes soon diminish,
Lost in life's stream, and gone astray.
To get is good, but keeping it is better,
So follow greybeard's counsel to the letter,
And no one takes your stuff away.

       (*They go down the mountain-side together.*)


## ON A MOUNTAIN SPUR

(*Drums and martial music from below. The Emperor's tent
is being pitched.*)
    *Emperor, Commander-in-Chief, Life-Guardsmen.*

COMMANDER-IN-CHIEF.
It still appears the best-advised of courses
To choose this valley's favourable ground,
And here withdraw and mass our total forces,
A move I hope to see with victory crowned.

EMPEROR. That hope awaits the issue of the day;

I hate this part-retreat, this giving way.

COMMANDER-IN-CHIEF.

See there, my Liege, our left flank, on that slope,
For better ground no strategist could hope:
Hills not too steep, yet not one easy gap,
For us a gift, and for the foe a trap;
By rolling ground our lines are half concealed,
Forbidding cavalry to take the field.

EMPEROR. I praise your plan and think it best;
Now strength and courage bide the test.

COMMANDER-IN-CHIEF.

Here, where the mid-plain levels come in sight
You see the phalanx eager for the fight.
In early sun the halberds catch the rays
And glint and glimmer through the morning haze.
In sombre mass, how stirs the mighty square,
Where thousands are on fire to do and dare.
The strength of our main troops you well perceive,
And them I trust the enemy strength to cleave.

EMPEROR. The first time this, I have so fair a view,
Where such an army has the strength of two.

COMMANDER-IN-CHIEF.

About our left is nothing to be told,
That rugged cliff heroic stalwarts hold.
Yon rocky height, where glint of arms is seen,
Protects the vital neck of the ravine:
Here, blundering on a strength they don't suspect,
Will enemy hopes most bloodily be wrecked.

EMPEROR. And so my treacherous kinsmen take the field,
Who, late as uncles, cousins, brothers known,
Encroached, with growing trespass unconcealed,
To steal the sceptre's might and flout the throne;
They now, ill-joined, the realm in arms have led,

And threatening me they raise rebellious head.
The masses hover, doubtful-minded sway,
Then join the stream which sweeps them on its way.

COMMANDER-IN-CHIEF.
A trusty man, sent out to spy the land,
Comes down in haste: good news may be at hand.

FIRST SCOUT. We have done the task awaited,
Craft we have, nor courage lack,
Everywhere we penetrated,
But we bring cold comfort back.
Many shun disloyal faction,
Swearing troth, with oaths of weight,
But pretend their own inaction
Saves from civil strife the state.

EMPEROR. Thus self will ever teach men self-protection,
Not thanks or honour, duty or affection.
Will you not think, when comes the reckoning hour,
Your neighbour's fire may well your house devour?

COMMANDER-IN-CHIEF.
A second clambers down, far-spent and grim,
Slowly he comes, and shakes in every limb.

SECOND SCOUT. First with comfort we detected
Chaos in their riotous course;
Rapid then and unexpected
Came a new emperor in force.
Now the hosts in ordered manner
March to plan, advancing far,
Following his lying banner,
Like the silly sheep they are.

EMPEROR. A rival emperor brings our cause this gain:
That I in truth am emperor is plain.
Simply as soldier I put on the mail,
But now, thus armed, a higher cause I hail.

On all my state-occasions shining bright,
While nothing lacked, no danger was in sight.
When tilting at the ring was all you chose,
Longing for jousts of peril in me rose;
Warfare you deprecated, else the fame
Of deeds heroic would make bright my name.
Yet to new fortitude did I aspire
When ringed and mirrored in the realm of fire.
Then leapt on me a fury dire to see,
A phantom show, but one of majesty.
Thus have I dreamt of victory and fame,
And will redeem things forfeit to my shame.

    (*Heralds are dispatched to challenge the rival Emperor.*)
    (*Enter Faust, in armour, with half-closed visor. With him are the three Mighty Men, armed and clad as already described.*)

FAUST.

We come with hope, and blameless would proceed,
Foresight commending, though there be no need.
You know, that mountain-miners think and brood,
And Nature's runic lore they have pursued.
The spirits that in lowlands cease to roam
Have ever more made craggy heights their home.
Silent they work, through intricate crevasses,
In rich metallic fumes of precious gases;
To sift and test and blend is all their thought,
Whereby some new discovery may be sought.
With the soft touch of spirit-power they build
Translucent forms, in crystal they are skilled,
And see in that eternal silent glass
The things that in the upper world may pass.

EMPEROR.

This I have heard, and think it true, but how,

My gallant man, can this concern us now?

FAUST. The Sabine sage, the Norcian necromancer,
   Your true devoted servant, gives the answer.
   How stood he doomed upon the dreadful pyre,
   Mid crackling brushwood, leaping tongues of fire!
   Piled up around him were dry faggots packed,
   Mingled with pitch and brimstone they were stacked;
   When help of man, god, devil, had been vain,
   Your Majesty struck off the fiery chain.
   This was in Rome; and still he serves you there,
   Making your path of life his constant care.
   That hour all thoughts of self he set aside,
   For you he seeks the stars, the depths as guide.
   He charged us, made the urgent duty ours,
   To bring you aid. Great are the mountain's powers;
   There Nature works with might, majestic, free,
   What stupid priesthood blames as sorcery.

EMPEROR. On festal days, when we receive our guests
   Who come with joy, and follow joy's behests,
   Each makes us glad, and in the crowded hall,
   In dwindling space, we welcome one and all.
   But doubly welcome is the stalwart friend
   Who comes an ally's forceful aid to lend,
   As breaks the day on which dread issues wait,
   For dawn brings in the quivering scales of fate.
   Yet bide, in this high hour, what fates afford,
   Staying the strong hand on the willing sword,
   Honour the moment when to battle move
   Thousands who now my friends or foes will prove.
   Man's self is man! Who claims a throne, a crown,
   Must show himself as worthy of renown.
   Now may this phantom challenging our reign,
   This self-styled emperor of our domain,

Field-Marshal-Duke and Liege Lord of our earls,
Be hurled to death, and mine the hand that hurls.

FAUST. You do not well, howe'er your cause advance,
To set your royal head upon the chance.
Is not the helmet crowned with plume and crest?
It shields the head that gives our courage zest.
Without the head, what could the limbs avail?
For if that slumbers, all will droop and fail.
If it is hurt, the wound afflicts the rest,
And all revive if cure is swift and blest.
The arm is quick and privileged to wield,
As shelter for the head, its massive shield;
Aware of duty, sword-hand, nothing slow,
Parries with vigour and returns the blow.
The sturdy foot then seals the victory granted,
Upon the neck of slaughtered foeman planted.

EMPEROR. Such is my wrath, the proud head so to treat,
And make of it a footstool for my feet.

HERALDS (*returning*). Little honour, scanty hearing,
Had we from their bold array;
Stately challenge took they jeering,
As it were a mummers' play.
'Gone is all your Emperor's glory,
Dim the echo of his prime.
Gone from mind, except as story
Starting – Once upon a time.'

FAUST.
Thus come to pass those things the best men planned,
Who here beside you in true service stand.
The foe comes on, your troops will never quail;
Sound the attack, and fortune shall prevail.

EMPEROR (*to the Commander-in-Chief*).
In the command I here resign my lead;

Yours solely, Prince, this duty is decreed.

COMMANDER-IN-CHIEF.

Then let our right advance and take the field.
The foe's left wing, now mounting up the height,
Will meet young trusted stalwarts of our right
And there, before their march is done, will yield.

FAUST. Accept then in your ranks this man of might,
A tough and lively hero for the fight;
Let him be closely trusted on your side,
And show his own true mettle thus allied.

(*He points to the right.*)

SMITE-ALL (*stepping forward*).

No man who faces up to me withdraws
Before I smash his cheek-bones and his jaws;
Who turns his back, one slash below the crest
Sends head, neck, top-knot dribbling down his chest.
If yours strike home with sword and mace
While I in fury rage ahead,
The slaughter then will grow apace,
Foes drown in their own blood that's shed.          (*Exit.*)

COMMANDER-IN-CHIEF.

Let then our centre-phalanx join the line
And in a secret sharp attack combine;
There, on the right, some enemy posts are taken,
And by our zeal their battle-plan is shaken.

FAUST (*pointing to the middle one of the three*):

Let this blade follow where your word ordains:
He's nimble, quiet, and bears off sweeping gains.

GRAB-ALL (*coming forward*).

The royal host's heroic pride,
Should march with plunder-thirst allied;
And be the goal of this intent
The rival Emperor's splendid tent.

To boast his throne, his days are running out,
And I will lead the phalanx in this bout.

SPEEDY LOOT (*a sutler-woman. She nestles up to him*).
What if we two were never wed,
He's the best lover for my bed.
And now what profits will accrue!
Woman is fierce when she falls to,
In looting leaves remorse to fools,
Goes out to win, and devil take the rules!
                    (*They go off together.*)

COMMANDER-IN-CHIEF.
Their right attacks our left, as was foreseen,
Charging in force. Our troops, as fierce and keen,
To the last man this onslaught will repel,
And keep the narrow pass beneath the fell.

FAUST (*pointing to the left*).
Consider, sire, this gallant at your side,
No harm is done when strength is fortified.

KEEP-ALL (*coming forward*).
About the left, no need for care!
To keep possession's my affair.
An ancient's strength in this behold:
No lightning splits the thing I hold.                    (*Exit.*)

MEPHISTOPHELES (*coming down from above*).
And now to rearward give a glance,
You'll see a host in arms advance:
It comes from rocky depths, and fills
The narrow roadway through the hills;
With helm and harness, shield and spear,
It forms a rampart in our rear,
Waiting the sign for bloody task.
          (*Aside, to those in the know.*)
And whence it comes, you'd best not ask.

Frankly, I've scoured the country-side
For what the armouries could provide;
Both foot and horse in pride and worth,
Stood there like lords of all the earth;
These once were kaisers, kings, and knights in mail,
That now are empty shells left by the snail.
The ghosts dress up in armour for the strife,
The Middle Ages get new lease of life.
No matter then what devils lurk inside,
This serves our turn, and all are edified.

(Aloud.)

Hark, how they start to rage in anger,
With clashing and with brassy clangour!
And now the banners' fluttering strips one sees,
That longed impatiently for freshening breeze.
Lo, ready now in arms, an ancient race,
But in new conflict keen to take its place.

(There is a shattering flourish of trumpets from above;<br>and a noticeable wavering in the enemy host.)

FAUST. The skyline darkens, day grows dimmer,
With here and there a warning shimmer
Where red rays portentous dart;
On the weapons gleams the blood now,
Atmosphere and rock and wood now,
With the whole heaven, bear their part.

MEPHISTOPHELES. The right wing struggles on defiant,
But, towering in their ranks the while,
I see our Smite-All, nimble giant,
Most active in his own sweet style.

EMPEROR.
Where first one sword-arm flashed upheaving,
Now do I see a dozen cleaving;
No natural forces have we here.

FAUST. You never heard of mists that cover
    Sicily's coasts, and wreath-like hover?
    There, floating free in daylight clear,
    Uplifted to the middle air,
    Mirrored in exhalation rare,
    Most wondrous visions will appear;
    For towns will hover into sight
    And gardens undulating bright,
    As forms break through the atmosphere.

EMPEROR. Yet comes a portent fraught with fear:
    Behold, the glint of many a spear;
    But, through the phalanx, on each lance
    I see a nimble flamelet dance,
    A spectral, all too dread a sight.

FAUST. Your pardon, sire, but those are traces
    Of ghostly long-forgotten races,
    Wraiths of the Dioscuri pair
    By whom the seamen used to swear;
    They gather here in final might.

EMPEROR. To whom, then, is this service owing,
    That Nature should, her bounty showing,
    For us her secret powers unite?

MEPHISTOPHELES.
    To whom, then, but to that high master
    Who makes your fortune all his care,
    Who, when your foes intend disaster,
    Has deep anxieties to bear?
    His thankful thoughts your safety cherish,
    Willing to rescue, though himself should perish.

EMPEROR.
    With cheers they bore me, with proud pomp invested;
    Coming to power, I wished to have it tested,
    And found it good, without a further thought,

To rusticate the greybeards from my court;
To thwart the clergy my next stratagem,
For which I frankly got no love from them.
And now shall I, when all these years have gone,
Reap harvest from a thing so gaily done?

FAUST. Free-hearted help brings rich return.
Look up: I think his art has sent us
An omen that may be portentous;
Its meaning we may soon discern.

EMPEROR. An eagle hovers in the heaven's space.
A griffin follows, fierce in menacing chase.

FAUST. Give heed: propitious seems the sign.
The griffin is a beast of fabulous line;
How comes it that he dares to match his flight
Against the true, the royal eagle's might?

EMPEROR. Now circling widely for attack they float.
Now closer swoop – and even as we lift
Our gaze, in impact terrible and swift
Each strives to rend the other's breast and throat.

FAUST. Now see the villain griffin quail:
Torn, battered, and with blows distressed,
He, shrinking and with drooping lion-tail,
Plunges from sight upon the wooded crest.

EMPEROR. Then as the sign, so be the event!
I bow to fate in wonderment.

MEPHISTOPHELES (*towards the right*):
Pressed by strong assaults repeated,
The enemy must yield, defeated,
And even now in dubious fight
They move in hordes towards their right,
Which shift of troops confused in numbers
The main force of their left encumbers.
Our phalanx then, with strength and dash,

Veers to the right, and in a flash
Attacks them where their front is shaken. –
Now, as the storms at sea awaken,
Equal powers, with shock and surging,
In the double clash are merging.
Never were more glorious hours,
And the victory is ours.

EMPEROR (*on the left, to Faust*).
Yonder, see a danger rises
And the front line jeopardises.
Ours have ceased their rocks to throw
And have lost the ridge below,
While the hill-posts seem forsaken.
Now the foe, his mass unshaken,
Presses on in steady flow,
And perchance the pass is taken:
Such an end has impious striving,
Vain your arts and your contriving.

(*Pause.*)

MEPHISTOPHELES. Lo, hither come my raven-pair,
What sort of message may they bear?
Ours is, I fear, a sorry plight.

EMPEROR. What mean these evil birds of dread,
That stretching their black sails have sped
Straight from the furious mountain-fight?

MEPHISTOPHELES (*to the ravens*).
Perch snugly, children, by my ears.
Whom you protect is saved from fears,
For shrewd you are and counsel right.

FAUST (*to the Emperor*).
The ways of pigeons have you known,
That for their brood and food have flown,
Returned from many a distant coast.

Though altered here, the need remains:
The pigeons serve where peace obtains,
But war requires a raven-post.

MEPHISTOPHELES. Their tidings threaten a disaster.
See, how the enemy may master
Our heroes' hard-fought rocky post.
The neighbouring heights are over-run,
And if the pass itself is won
Poor hope of standing has our host.

EMPEROR. And so at last you have betrayed me.
Already had your snares dismayed me,
And now you have me in your net.

MEPHISTOPHELES.
Take courage! We're not beaten yet.
Keep a cool head, to the last ditch;
Strain often waits the final stand;
I've adjutants in wisdom rich;
Command that I may take command.

COMMANDER-IN-CHIEF.
These were the allies of your choosing,
A grief to me, my plans confusing,
For conjuring breeds no good, alack!
War's fortune fails, I cannot mend it;
As they began, so let them end it.
Thus, Sire, I give my baton back.

EMPEROR. Yet keep your staff for better fate
That fortune still may have in store.
This evil fellow's arts I hate,
And all his trust in raven-lore.

(*To* MEPHISTOPHELES.)

No staff I grant, though doomed you see us,
I count you not the proper man;
But if command of yours can free us,

So be it, do what things you can.
(*He withdraws with the Commander-in-Chief to his tent.*)
MEPHISTOPHELES. Him may his stupid baton shield!
   It's not the thing for us to wield:
   There stood a sort of cross thereon.
FAUST. What's next to do?
MEPHISTOPHELES.                    Why, all is done.
   Come, swarthy cousins, prompt and fleet,
   By the great mountain-lake the Undines greet,
   Borrow the semblant that their flood enfolds,
   For they, through strange elusive feminine art,
   Can set the seeming from the real apart,
   And holding this each swears the real he holds.
                         (*Pause.*)
FAUST. Well does our ravens' flattery succeed
   In coaxing water-nymphs to give us heed,
   For lo, the first free-flowing rills descend;
   Where barren rock lay baking in the sun
   The swift abundant torrents have begun;
   Those fellows' victory is at an end.
MEPHISTOPHELES.
   That's wonderful, a welcome unsurpassed,
   Bold mountaineers among them are aghast.
FAUST.
   Stream rushes to join stream, down gushing, leaping,
   In double might through mountain gulley sweeping,
   Now in a grand out-curving arch they flow,
   Now fill the level bed of living rock
   On every hand with smooth and foaming shock,
   Plunging in steps and falls to vales below.
   What serves it, that the bravest hearts resist?
   Bearing them down, the mighty floods persist,
   Such wildness fills my own heart with alarm.

MEPHISTOPHELES.

Naught do I see of all these watery lies:
The cheat has power alone on human eyes;
For me the strange event can have its charm.
Headlong they quit the field in fear profound.
Poor fools, they all imagine they'll be drowned,
With desperate snorting, though all safe and sound,
They run with swimming gestures on dry ground,
And laughable confusion spread around.

(*The ravens return.*)

To the high Master will I praise your merit;
But if yourselves would show a master spirit,
Turn to the glowing forge your courses fleet,
Where dwarf-folk sparks from stone and metal beat;
Coax them with gossip that they lend a fire
Of special gleam and crackle, flame and heat,
Such as the highest fancy could desire.
Sheet-lightning, truly, in the sky afar,
With sudden shooting of the loftiest star,
May happen any clear midsummer night;
But lightning caught up in the tangled bushes
And stars that hiss their way among the rushes
Present themselves more rarely to the sight.
Therefore, to save much trouble in your quest,
You first entreat, then make a firm behest.

(*Exeunt the ravens. Everything takes place
as described above.*)

MEPHISTOPHELES.

For foes, thick shrouding gloom is spreading,
Dark, doubtful ways let them be treading,
False fire to flicker and ensnare,
Then suddenly a blinding flare!
All very fine; but let us hear

Some sounds that strike the soul with fear.
FAUST. The hollow arms from musty rooms of state
　　Here sniff the breezes that reanimate;
　　Yonder the clashing, clattering knocks redound,
　　A prodigy of false and frightful sound.
MEPHISTOPHELES.
　　Ay, now unchecked the tumult grows,
　　The hills resound with chivalrous blows,
　　As in the noble times of old.
　　Brassards and greaves in strength appear,
　　For Guelfs and Ghibellines are here,
　　In swift undying feud and bold;
　　Each firm in his ancestral style,
　　That none can ever reconcile,
　　They spread this clangour uncontrolled.
　　In short, where devils celebrate,
　　What helps them most is party-hate,
　　Till the last horror ends the tale;
　　Hideous notes of rage and panic
　　Shot with wildness shrill-satanic
　　Shatter the air throughout the vale.
　　(*Clash of war is heard in a tumult of music, the orchestra
　　　　settling at last into bright martial themes.*)


## THE RIVAL EMPEROR'S TENT

*Throne, in sumptuous setting.*
SPEEDY LOOT *and* GRAB-ALL.

SPEEDY LOOT. We come in first, we take the lead.
GRAB-ALL. No raven equals us in speed.
SPEEDY LOOT. Ah, here is wealth, in piles heaped up!
　　Where to begin, and where to stop?

GRAB-ALL. The room is loaded fit to burst,
  I hardly know what I'll grab first.

SPEEDY LOOT. This carpet here would suit my taste,
  For bedding I am badly placed.

GRAB-ALL. Here's a star-mace, in fine steel wrought,
  A thing these many years I've sought.

SPEEDY LOOT. This scarlet robe with golden seams
  Is what I've longed for in my dreams.

GRAB-ALL (*taking the weapon*).
  With this the job is quickly done:
  You strike him dead, and then pass on.
  But you, you load yourself with swag,
  And yet have rubbish in the bag.
  Put down such loot and let it stay,
  And choose yon chest to take away,
  One that has army-pay to hold,
  One with a belly made of gold.

SPEEDY LOOT. A murderous weight, for this I may
  Nor lift nor carry it away.

GRAB-ALL. Be quick, duck down to take the pack,
  I'll hoist it on your sturdy back.

SPEEDY LOOT. I'm done for! Quick, for mercy's sake,
  Under this weight my back will break!
              (*The coffer falls and bursts open.*)

GRAB-ALL. There's the red gold in masses strown,
  Fall to, and make the heaps your own.

SPEEDY LOOT (*crouching down*).
  Quick, fill my lap, and forth with speed!
  There's plenty here to serve our need.

GRAB-ALL. Away! We've taken tidy toll –
  But in your apron there's a hole:
  A spendthrift, when you move around
  You scatter treasure on the ground.

LIFE-GUARDS OF THE REAL EMPEROR.
> What, near the throne will you make free,
> And ransack in the treasury?

GRAB-ALL. We risked our lives for little pay,
> And here we take our spoil away.
> All hostile tents as booty fall,
> And we are soldiers, after all.

GUARDS. The men who answer to our drum
> Are soldiers, not a thieving scum;
> Whoso will serve our Emperor, he
> Must have a soldier's honesty.

GRAB-ALL. Your honesty's a well-known thing,
> You call it Requisitioning,
> You're all the same, your bright brigade,
> 'Hand over' is the pass-word of your trade.
> > *(To* SPEEDY LOOT.*)*
> Take all you can and disappear;
> As guests we are not welcome here.          *(Exeunt.)*

FIRST GUARDSMAN. Say, why not finish with this lout,
> And fetch his cheeky face a clout?

SECOND. I don't know how, but strength forsook me,
> A sense of spectres overtook me.

THIRD. There came a cloud across my sight,
> Then flashes; I saw nothing right.

FOURTH. So strange it is, I can't well say:
> We'd such a heat throughout the day,
> So sultry, clammy, like a spell,
> And here one stood and there one fell.
> So fought we groping for the foe,
> And brought one down at every blow;
> Before our eyes a gauze of mist,
> While in our ears it hummed and hissed;
> So it went on, and here are we,

But how it happened none can see.
              (*Enter the Emperor with four Princes.*
                  *The Life-Guards withdraw.*)
EMPEROR.
   Let him fare as he may, the hostile force is shattered,
   Across the level plain their flying rout is scattered.
   Here stands the vacant throne, whose tapestries abound,
   In traitorous treasure crowding, lumbering the ground.
   We, well defended by our life-guards, now await
   The people's envoys, here in our imperial state.
   For tidings full of joy come in from every side;
   And, gladly loyal to us, the realm is pacified.
   Black arts indeed were sometime in our battle known,
   But in the end we fought and won our war alone.
   For men who toil in battle chance may work for
          good:
   A meteor falls and foes are drenched in rain of blood.
   From rocky caves strange notes of wondrous power
          resound
   Which raise our hearts on high, the enemy's confound.
   The vanquished fell, condemned to earn renewed des-
          pising;
   The victor sings God's special grace in paean uprising;
   And, needing no command, the masses blend their
          notes,
   'We praise thee, Lord our God!' comes from a million
          throats.
   Yet as the highest praise, too rarely manifest,
   With piety I turn and search within my breast.
   A gay and youthful prince glad days may dissipate,
   But with the years he learns the moment's worth and
          weight.
   Therefore immediate close alliance I have planned

With you four trusty Lords, for house and court and
  land.

(*To the First.*)

The expert building of the forces, Prince, was left to
  you;
In crisis yours the bold command that brought us
  through.
In harmony of peace work now with full accord,
Invested with High Marshal's noble rank and sword.

HIGH MARSHAL.

Your army, Sire, engaged till now in civil war alone,
Shall at the frontiers guard your person and your throne.
Yet, when a banquet's splendour throngs your ancestral
  hall
Grant that the pride of arms may grace the festival:
A burnished sword's salute would pledge defence as
  bright,
To noblest majesty a guard of lasting might.

EMPEROR (*to the Second*).

Here's one who strong in courage makes courtesy as
  sure.
You I proclaim High Chamberlain, and grant no sine-
  cure;
For highest power is yours in all my retinue,
Whose inner enmities discord in service brew;
Honouring you, they'll seek the things of good report,
And learn what pleases most their lord and all his court.

HIGH CHAMBERLAIN.

A grace is won in serving a majestic will,
To aid the good, nor be too harsh should men do ill,
Give frankness free from guile, be calm without deceit.
If, Sire, you know my heart, then is my joy complete.
Imagining state banquet, may my thought be bold?

At festal board I offer then the ewer of gold,
Receive and hold your rings, what time your hands
     delight
In fragrant freshness, as my mind does in your sight.

EMPEROR.

My mood, Sirs, is too grave on festive things to dwell,
Yet be it so – a glad beginning augurs well.
               (*To the Third.*)
The office of High Steward is yours with honour due:
Mews, chase, and royal farms are subject all to you;
Each month shall furnish me the season's choicest fare,
My favourite viands, rich and varied by your care.

HIGH STEWARD.

My grateful duty shall be that of rigid fast,
Until my service offers, Sire, a choice repast.
And they who serve your kitchens shall collaborate,
To bring from far, and seasons to anticipate.
True, viands rare, forced fruits, by which some boards
     are graced,
Are naught to you, who have a strong and simple taste.

EMPEROR (*to the Fourth*).

Since festivals remain our one engrossing theme,
Transformed, young hero, be you Cupbearer supreme,
And, tending well your charge, make it your constant
     will
That wealth of choicest wines the royal cellars fill.
Be moderate yourself, lest court occasions gay
Become a tempting lure in which you go astray.

HIGH CUPBEARER.

The flower of youth, my Liege, if trust in it be shown,
Is found, ere one's aware, to man's full stature grown.
Already in my mind I tend the festive day,
And deck the serving-table with a royal array,

With lordly vessels rich, of gold and silver wrought,
And first for you the rarest goblet shall be sought:
A lucent Venice-glass in which deep solace waits,
Where vintage gains in strength yet not inebriates.
To treasure such as this too freely men may yield,
But noble moderation, Sire, is still your shield.

EMPEROR.

What I, this solemn day, have compassed for your good,
That have you as from lips authentic understood.
Great is the Emperor's word, investing gift with trust,
Yet, ratified in state, this needs a hand august,
A signature. The writ to draw, and duly scan,
Here comes authority, the moment brings the man.

(*Enter the Archbishop, who is also Lord High Chancellor.*)

EMPEROR.

When to the key-stone the great arch is wed secure,
Then against times to come the building's life is sure.
Four Princes here behold: even now we have observed
How royal house and court's stability is served.
And now to Princes five we here commit the state,
To govern all it holds in fullest strength and weight.
These shall outshine all men, in wealth of lands more
    splendid;
Therefore the bounds of their demesnes I have extended
With added lands of those deserting us of late.
To you, the faithful, grant I many a fine estate,
With lordly right of greater growth, as chance may rise,
By purchase or exchange, reversion or demise;
What sovereign rights soe'er to lordship may pertain,
These shall you wield unquestioned in your own domain.
Your final judgement in High Court shall all esteem,
There shall be no appeal against your power supreme.
Then yours be tax and tribute, tollage, rent, and fines,

With royalties on mintage, passport, salt, and mines.
For I, that full and strong my gratitude be shown,
Have raised your rank as highest next the Imperial
    throne.

ARCHBISHOP.

I offer deepest thanks, in which we all unite:
You stablish us in power, and strengthen thus your
    might.

EMPEROR. Lo, to you five I have still higher trust to give.
I live yet for my realm, and thus am glad to live;
But even in active toil a chain I contemplate
Of high ancestral past, and read the hand of fate.
I too must wait the call that takes me from my friends;
The choice then of successor on your care depends.
Crowned at the sacred altar raise his royal form,
Fulfilling then in peace things here begun in storm.

HIGH CHANCELLOR.

With deep pride in their hearts, and yet with humble
    bearing,
Great princes bow to you, earth's highest honours
    sharing.
As long as blood shall stir within our loyal veins,
The body we, o'er which your will serenely reigns.

EMPEROR.

Then, to conclude, let all we have declared in sum
Be signed and sealed, to stand for ages yet to come.
Possession, Sirs, is yours, as free as it is wide,
With one proviso: not to share it or divide.
And all that you may add to lands from us possessed
Shall be your eldest son's by unimpaired bequest.

HIGH CHANCELLOR.

Right gladly I'll commit to parchment, for your seal,
This statute, blessing us and all the commonweal.

The documents our busy Chancery shall draw,
And place the seal: your scared hand will make it law.

EMPEROR.

So I dismiss you all, that each may go his way;
Let all in conclave ponder the auspicious day.
(*The Lords Temporal withdraw. The Archbishop remains,
and speaks with much feeling.*)

ARCHBISHOP.

The Chancellor is gone, the Bishop has remained:
A father's anxious care at heart, he is constrained
In solemn warning audience with his Liege to seek.

EMPEROR.

In such an hour of joy, why these misgivings? Speak!

ARCHBISHOP.

What bitter grief to me to find, in such an hour,
Your consecrated head conjoined with Satan's power.
Securely throned it seems you claim your royal right,
But this, alas, in God's and in the Pope's despite.
His Holiness, apprised, such sin will overwhelm,
With sacred fire of swift destruction on your realm.
Nor is that time forgotten in the Holy See
When, newly crowned, you chose to set a sorcerer free.
Your diadem's first gleam brought Christendom to
      shame,
Lighting with grace a head accursed in evil fame.
Yet beat upon your breast, your wicked gain forswear,
Repaying to our holy Church some modest share:
The noble sweep of hills that saw your tent erected,
Where evil spirits joined, that you might be protected,
Where to the Prince of Lies a docile ear you lent,
These lands devote, with faith, to sacred high intent;
With mountains and dense woods, howe'er their
      bounds extend,

With verdant heights, whose slopes to pastures rich
    descend,
Clear lakes that teem with fish, and countless brooks
    that flow
In swift and sinuous tumult to the vale below,
Then the wide vale itself, with meadow, combe, and
    dale:
Speak your contrition thus, and mercy shall not fail.

EMPEROR.

So heavy lies my grievous fault upon my soul,
I leave all bounds of penance to your own control.

ARCHBISHOP.

Then first, where sin was rank, that place contaminated,
Devote to the Most High in service consecrated.
Swiftly the spirit sees the lofty walls aspire,
And shafts of morning sun already gild the choir.
The fabric rises, spreads, in cruciform the whole,
The nave looms up, with joy for each believing soul;
Floating o'er hill and vale comes now the call of bells,
And through the mighty doors the throng to worship
    swells.
The heaven-aspiring towers ring out above the fane,
The penitent draws near, in spirit born again,
On consecration day – and may we see it soon –
Your presence, Sire, will be the highest grace and boon.

EMPEROR.

In this great work may now my pious will be shown,
To render praise to God, and for my fault atone.
Enough! I feel my spirits rise, new hopes aspire.

ARCHBISHOP.

As Chancellor your covenant I must require.

EMPEROR.

Submit a deed, conveying to the Church this land,

With joy it shall be given by my seal and hand.

ARCHBISHOP (*He takes his leave, then turns at the threshold*).

Then grant the growing work, by this same testament,
All income from the lands, of tollage, tithe, and rent,
In perpetuity: strong funds the upkeep needs,
And no good governance without high cost proceeds.
To speedy building, in a solitude remote,
Some gold from plundered treasure doubtless you'll
    devote.
Moreover, we shall need, as cannot be denied,
Timber and lime and slate, from distant parts supplied.
This toil, from pulpit taught, a willing folk will bear:
The Church still blesses him who makes her tasks his
    care.                                            (*Exit.*)

EMPEROR.

Now stand I loaded with my guilt and troubled sore,
With harm from evil sorcerers that I deplore.

ARCHBISHOP (*returning once more, he makes profound
    obeisance*):

Your pardon, Sire, you granted to that infamous man
Some rights upon our coasts: on them shall fall the ban,
Unless the bounty from your penitence accrues,
Endowing there the Church with rents and revenues.

EMPEROR (*with ill-humour*).

That land is not yet there, beneath the foam it lies.

ARCHBISHOP.

His day will come, who holds his rights in patience
    wise.
For us, your promised word shall be our hope and stay.
                                                    (*Exit.*)

EMPEROR. If this goes on, I soon shall sign my realm away.

## ACT FIVE

—

## OPEN COUNTRY

WAYFARER. Ay, 'tis they, dark linden-trees,
Standing yonder, old and strong.
Ah, to come again to these
After pilgrimage so long!
These the dunes that gave me shelter,
In the hut upon the lea,
When the waves in stormy welter
Hurled me shoreward from the sea.
And my hosts, with love I'd greet them,
Them so kind, so staunch a pair,
Hoping against hope to meet them,
Who already aged were.
Shall I call? – Sweet folk, godfearing –
Ho, I greet you, call you blest,
If you still, with ways endearing,
Give good comfort to a guest.

BAUCIS (*a little old dame*).
Softly, stranger, lest you spoil
For my man his resting hours:
Age must sleep, to gather powers
For the waking-times of toil.

WAYFARER. Tell me, mother, are you even
She to whom my thanks I bear
For the life a lad was given,
By her goodman's and her care?
Are you Baucis, who devoutly
Half-dead lips to death denied?

*(The husband enters.)*

You Philemon, who so stoutly
Snatched my treasure from the tide?
Changed was all the menace dire
Of adventure that befell,
By the kindling of your fire,
And your silver-sounding bell.
Let me mount the dunes and, gazing
Out upon the boundless sea,
Let me pray, these hands upraising,
Till the burdened heart be free.

*(He steps up on to the dunes.)*

PHILEMON *(to Baucis)*. Quickly, set the table under
Blossomed branches of our trees.
Let him stride and stop, in wonder,
Scarce believing what he sees.

*(Joining the Wayfarer.)*

Where the cruel surge was booming,
Whelming you in grim despair,
See, we have a garden blooming;
Paradise was not more fair.
Ageing, I had grown less eager,
Lacking zeal of younger blood,
But, as ebbed my strength so meagre,
Gone was all the stormy flood.
Hardy knaves, with masters clever,
Delved the dykes, the ground to gain,
Foreshore from the sea to sever,
Making it their own domain.
See, the woods and verdant meadows,
Gardens, homes with paddocks blest. –
Come, before the creeping shadows
Show the sun has gone to rest. –

Sails afar will glide from light,
Seeking port with star-lit prow,
Like the birds in homing flight,
Harbour will they find there now.
See the distant ocean gleaming,
Where the blue rim stretches wide;
Left and right, in fertile teeming,
Homesteads fill the country-side.


## IN THE LITTLE GARDEN

*The three at table.*

BAUCIS. Not a word? No morsel raising,
   That your famished mouth may eat?
PHILEMON. He would hear of things amazing:
   Tell, what gladly you repeat.
BAUCIS. Ay, amazing is the word, Sir,
   Things that haunt me to this day;
   And the marvels that occurred, Sir,
   Happened in no honest way.
PHILEMON. Who will Majesty accuse?
   'Twas the Emperor gave the shore:
   Herald's trumpet brought the news,
   Sounding as he passed our door.
   Stroke of tools then struck our hearing,
   Near our dune the start was made:
   Huts and tents, then high uprearing
   Stood a palace in the glade.
BAUCIS. Day-work failed, though never quitting
   Pick and spade men toiled away;
   But where fires at night were flitting
   Stood a finished dyke next day.

Nightly rose a wailing sorrow,
Sacrifice of human blood;
Trim canal was seen the morrow,
Where had ebbed the fiery flood.
He is godless, long has lusted
To possess our home and glade;
Claims to be a neighbour trusted,
Yet by us will be obeyed.

PHILEMON. But in friendship did he proffer
Homestead fair, in his new ground.

BAUCIS. That's a doubtful marsh to offer;
Keep our knoll, we're safe and sound.

PHILEMON. Now to church let us be going;
Let the vesper chimes be tolled:
We'll kneel and pray, in sunset's glowing,
God revering, as of old.


# PALACE

*Spacious Pleasure-garden.*
*A grand Canal, wide and straight-cut.*
*Faust, in extreme old age, is walking to and fro*
*in meditation.*

LYNCEUS, *the Keeper of the Watch Tower (speaking through*
*an amplifier).*
Sundown, and a sound of cheering
As the last ships make the port;
Closer, a big vessel steering,
In the canal to moorings brought.
Her pennons gay the light wind raises,
Her masts and yards are trim and taut;
The happy seaman sings your praises,

And fortune's crown for you is wrought.
> (*The bell starts to ring, from the dunes.*)

FAUST (*with a start*). Accursèd chime, all solace ending,
　It strikes and wounds with treacherous aim;
　Before my eyes whole realms extending,
　And at my back affront and shame.
　The bell condemns as incomplete
　My high estate: the cottage brown,
　The crumbling church, the lindens sweet,
　Are things I cannot call my own.
　And should I think to rest me there,
　Another's shade must be my dread:
　Would I were far from regions where
　My thoughts are thorns, and thorns I tread.

THE KEEPER OF THE WATCH TOWER (*speaking as before*).
　Glad sight, with freshened evening breeze,
　The gallant vessel inward sails,
　Comes towering proudly through the leas,
　Deck-laden high with chests and bales.
> (*A splendid ship comes in with rich and colourful cargo from foreign lands.*)
> *Mephistopheles. The Three Mighty Fellows.*

CHORUS. And so we land,
　See us arrive.
　Good luck to the Master,
　May he thrive!
> (*They disembark, and the goods are brought ashore.*)

MEPHISTOPHELES.
　We've proved our worth in this event,
　If Master's pleased we're well content.
　With but two ships we left his shore,
　And back in port we bring a score.

As to our exploits' mighty scale,
We let the cargo tell the tale.
The open sea sets free the mind,
Compunction then is left behind.
What matters there is speedy grip,
You catch good fish or catch a ship:
If mastery of three you seize,
You'll hook a fourth one in with ease;
The fifth then is in perilous plight,
Since might is yours, you'll have the right.
You ask not *How* but *What* is done.
If I know aught of life at sea,
War, trade, and piracy are one,
An indivisible trinity.

THE THREE MIGHTY FELLOWS. No look to greet,
No smile to thank!
You'd think we'd brought him
Stuff that stank.
A rueful face
The Master makes;
In regal wealth
No joy he takes.

MEPHISTOPHELES. You need not look
For better pay;
You took your own
Good share away.

THE THREE. With idle hours
And time to spare,
We all expect
An equal share.

MEPHISTOPHELES. First range and garnish
Hall on hall,
To show the treasures

One and all.
And if he views
The rich display,
And makes more accurate
Survey,
Not beggarly
He will us treat,
But royally entertain
The fleet.
Tomorrow come birds gay and rare,
Best leave what's needed to my care.

(*The cargo is borne away.*)

MEPHISTOPHELES (*to Faust*).

With cloudy mien and furrowed brows
You take the riches fate allows.
Your wisdom's worth is crowned and prized,
And sea and shore are harmonized.
From moorings deep the ships apace
Move out to ocean's glad embrace.
One word, then, from your regal seat
Reveals your world-control complete.
From this same spot your power was spread,
Here stood the first rude wooden shed.
Here first a ditch was cut on shore,
Where now they ply the splashing oar.
Your people's zeal, your noble aim,
The prize of land and sea can claim.
From here –

FAUST.        Accursèd is that *here*!
To me a burden grim and drear,
To you so shrewd I must declare,
My heart has stabbings of distress,
New thrustings, more than I can bear,

I speak with shame as I confess.
Yon aged couple ought to yield,
The lindens still I have to gain,
The clustering trees above the weald
Mock and destroy my wide domain.
There would I build from bough to bough
A framework, vista to allow;
A spacious view were thus conceived,
To look on all that I've achieved,
And with one glance behold defined
The triumph of the human mind,
That carried out fair wisdom's plan,
And added living-space for man.

Thus 'tis a pang of deadly stealth
To feel what's missing in our wealth.
The chime, the scent of linden-bloom,
Confines me as in aisle or tomb.
The flights of my all-powerful will
Are broken on this sandy hill:
How shall I drive this chagrin forth?
I hear the bell, and burn with wrath.

MEPHISTOPHELES. Why certainly, one prime distress
Embitters all your happiness.
Who doubts? For any noble ear
This clanging is a grief to hear.
And this accursed ding-dong bell
Clouds the sweet evening with its knell,
Intrudes on every act, will boom
On babe's first bath and on the tomb,
Contrives that mortal life should seem
Twixt ding and dong an empty dream.

FAUST. Recalcitrance and wilfulness
Can mar the most superb success,

Till, to our painful, deep disgust
We tire of trying to be just.

MEPHISTOPHELES.

Then why on scruples choose to dwell,
Since colonizing's served you well?

FAUST. You know the pretty homestead there
I chose to give the aged pair –
Go move them out, make this your care.

MEPHISTOPHELES.

We'll see them gone, and well transferred,
Before they know it has occurred.
When folk have violence to endure,
A restful stay will work the cure.

        *(He gives an ear-splitting whistle.)*
           *The Three appear.*

MEPHISTOPHELES. Come, and obey the Master's call,
Tomorrow Sailors' feasts for all.

THE THREE. The old 'un gave us welcome scant,
To sail into the feast is what we want.

MEPHISTOPHELES (*ad Spectatores*).

What happened once, again takes place,
For Naboth's Vineyard is a well-known case.


## DEEP NIGHT

LYNCEUS, *the* KEEPER OF THE TOWER (*singing from his
    watch-post*).
A look-out born,
Employed for my sight,
To tower-service sworn,
The world's my delight.
I see what is far,

I see what is near,
Moon, planet, and star,
The wood with its deer,
In all things perceiving
The charms that endure,
And, joy thus achieving,
My own joy is sure.
Dear eyes, you so happy,
Whatever you've seen,
No matter its nature,
So fair has it been!

(*Pause.*)

Not for simple pleasure-taking
Keep I watch upon this height:
Darkened earth sends horror-making
Threat of woe to shock the sight.
Fire I see, sparks wildly raising
Through the midnight linden-trees,
Ever stronger grows the blazing,
Fanned to fury by the breeze.
Ah, the hut within is flaming,
Mossgrown, cool it used to stand,
Now its need of help proclaiming,
Where no rescue is at hand.
Good old man and kindly mother,
Keeping long their careful fire,
Perish in the reek and smother,
Doomed to misadventure dire.
Tongues of fire now glow and quiver,
Round the hut with menace fell;
Ah, what power can deliver
That good pair from blaze of hell?
Flames leap out, like forks of lightning,

Leaves and linden-branches brightening;
Wrapped in fire, the dry boughs burning
Plunge amid the embers' glow;
Must these eyes, this far discerning,
Look upon such sights of woe?
Now, with shock of timber crashing,
Yields the chapel to the fire;
Wreathing upward, leaping, flashing,
To the tree-tops flames aspire.
Charred and hollowed in the blazing,
Trunks and roots now crimson glow. –
          (*Long pause. Sound of singing.*)
All that won the fondest gazing
Gone, with ages long ago.

FAUST (*on his balcony, overlooking the dunes*).
  Whence this strain of lamentation?
  Word and tune too late I heed.
  My warden mourns; for me vexation
  Rises from the hasty deed.
  Yet, though lime-grove devastated
  Makes charred horror in this place,
  Soon is coign of view created,
  Outlook clear on boundless space.
  There, the aged folk beholding,
  A new homestead now I raise,
  That they feel my grace enfolding
  All the sunset of their days.

MEPHISTOPHELES AND THE THREE (*below*).
  Here we come, in speed pell mell.
  Your pardon! Things have not gone well.
  We knocked and knocked, renewed the din,
  And no one came to let us in;
  We rattled, rapped, and knocked the more,

And levelled soon the rotten door;
We called aloud, with many a threat,
But little hearing did we get.
In such a case the truth is clear:
None deaf as those that will not hear.
But, in your orders nothing lacking,
We quickly sent the couple packing;
They, with a suffering brief and slight,
Gave up the ghost and died of fright.
A stranger lurking thereabout
Showed signs of fight. We laid him out.
In struggle lasting little space
The coals were knocked about the place,
And caught the straw: up leaps the fire
And makes all three a funeral pyre.

FAUST. Deaf to commands you seem to be!
Exchange I meant, not robbery.
My curse on this exploit of woe!
Now take your share of curse and go!

CHORUS. The proverb keeps its meaning still:
You serve the mighty with a will;
Let you be brave where knocks are brisk
And house, and home and life you risk.    (*Exeunt.*)

FAUST (*on the balcony*).
The shine and glance of stars is veiled,
The flames are dwarfed, the fire has paled;
A creeping wind the embers lifts
And brings me smoke and reek in drifts.
Command too rash, too soon obeyed! –
What means this shape of hovering shade?

# MIDNIGHT

*Enter four Grey Hags.*

FIRST HAG. My name, it is *Want*.

SECOND HAG. *Guilt*, the name that I bear.

THIRD HAG. Men know me as *Need*.

FOURTH HAG. They know me as *Care*.

THE FIRST THREE.

The door is fast-bolted, we cannot get in,

Here lives a rich man, we come not within.

WANT. Then I'll become shadow.

GUILT. I'll merge into space.

NEED. The pampered avoid me with indolent face.

CARE. Nay, Sisters, you cannot and should not go in,

But Care has a way through the key-hole to win.

*(Care disappears.)*

WANT. Ah, Sisters, grey Sisters, afar let us glide.

GUILT. I go with you, Sister, to walk at your side.

NEED.

Comes Need on the heels of her kin, Guilt and Shame.

THE THREE.

The clouds weave their shrouding on star-light and star.

From the void and beyond, from afar, from afar

Our brother draws nearer – and Death is his name.

FAUST (*in the Palace*).

There came here four, but only three went hence;

I heard their speech, but scarce could grasp the sense.

A word like *Need* I heard, with bated breath,

And chiming with it * came the sound of *Death*,

A hollow, muted note of spectral night.

I'm left to struggle still towards the light:

* In German the two words rhyme, '*Not*' and '*Tod*'.

Could I but break the spell, all magic spurning,
And clear my path, all sorceries unlearning,
Free then, in Nature's sight, from evil ban,
I'd know at last the worth of being man.

　Such was I once, before dark ways I sought
And with fell words a curse on living wrought.
Now teems the air with many a spectral shape,
So thick that none can shun them or escape.
What if a day with light of reason beams,
Night weaves around us webs of ghostly dreams.
Homewards, from meadows, ours the joy of life:
Then croaks a bird. What croaks he? Evil rife.
'Tis superstition shrouds us, soon and late,
It looms, it warns us, lies for us in wait.
Bewildered thus we stand alone with fear. –
Now creaks the door ... will no one, then, appear?
(With a shudder.)
　Is someone there?

CARE. 　　　　　　　　　　　The question calls for 'yea'.

FAUST. And you, then, who are you?

CARE. 　　　　　　　　　　　　　　I come, I stay.

FAUST. Go off from me!

CARE. 　　　　　　　　　　　It suits me here to dwell.

FAUST (*first wrathful, then more gently, to himself*).
　Take heed, and speak no word of magic spell.

CARE. Outward ear will never hear me,
　Yet the listening heart will fear me;
　And, in forms that ever change,
　Powerful, grim, through life I range.
　On the road and on the sea
　Men have my dread company,
　Never asked, appearing first,
　Coaxed and flattered, and accursed.

Is, then, black Care unknown to you?

FAUST.

My way has been to scour the whole world through.
Where was delight, I seized it by the hair;
If it fell short, I simply left it there,
If it escaped me, I just let it go.
I stormed through life, through joys in endless train,
Desire, fulfilment, then desire again;
Lordly at first I fared, in power and speed,
But now I walk with wisdom's deeper heed.
Full well I know the earthly round of men,
And what's beyond is barred from human ken;
Fool, fool is he who blinks at clouds on high,
Inventing his own image in the sky.
Let him look round, feet planted firm on earth:
This world will not be mute to him of worth.
Why haunt eternity with dim surmise?
Things he perceives are his to realize.
So may he wander through his earthly day;
If spirits gibber, let him go his way;
In forward-striving pain and bliss abide,
He finds them who is never satisfied.

CARE. He finds, once within my power,
His world is useless, from that hour,
Eternal gloom before his eyes,
For him no sunset nor sunrise.
Though in his outward senses whole,
He harbours darkness in his soul;
No matter what the treasure is,
He lacks the power to make it his.
Pleasures or ills mock him, forlorn,
He starves in sight of plenty's horn;
Faced with bliss or faced with sorrow,

He defers it to the morrow,
Always on the future waiting,
Nothing ever consummating.

FAUST. No more! You get no hold on me,
I spurn the folly that you say.
Get hence! Your wretched litany
Might lead the shrewdest man astray.

CARE. Come or go? Or in, or out?
His resolve is lost in doubt.
Mid-way on the beaten trail
He will grope and halting fail;
Ever straying, ever thwarted,
He beholds a world distorted,
Burdens others with his yoke,
Gasps for breath, and then will choke;
Chokes he not, of life repining,
Not despairing, not resigning,
Swept along in pained let-live,
Shunning an imperative,
His round of durance and release,
Its hazy sleep, its troubled peace,
Brings him down and pins him well,
And prepares his soul for hell.

FAUST. Unhallowed spectres, plague of mortal flesh,
Thus have you led mankind to age-long error;
And even innocent days you will enmesh
In tangled torment, foul with pain and terror.
'Tis hard, I know, of daemons to be rid,
The spirit-bond is difficult to sever;
But you, O Care, in stealing action hid,
Creep with a power I will acknowledge never.

CARE. That power more potent you may find
As with a curse I go my ways;

For mortal men through all their life are blind,
Which you, my Faust, shall be to end your days.
(*She breathes upon him.*)

FAUST (*blinded*).

Deep falls the night, in gloom precipitate;
What then? Clear light within my mind shines still;
Only the master's word gives action weight,
And what I framed in thought I will fulfil.
Ho, you my people, quickly come from rest:
Let the world see the fruit of bold behest.
Man all the tools, spade, shovel, as is due,
The work marked out must straight be carried through.
Quick diligence, firm discipline,
With these the noblest heights we win.
To end the greatest work designed,
A thousand hands need but one mind.


# THE GREAT OUTER-COURT OF THE PALACE

## *Torch-light.*

MEPHISTOPHELES (*taking the lead as overseer*).

Come on, you Lemures, come, begin,
You with loose limbs and dismal features,
Cobbled from sinew, bone, and skin,
You patched-up, shambling, demi-creatures.

LEMURES (*in chorus*). Quickly for you we are at hand,
And, what we're partly guessing,
The business is a spacious land
That we should be possessing.

Long chains for measuring are there
And stakes of sharpened timber;

But why we're called to take a share,
Is more than we remember.

MEPHISTOPHELES. This is no case for subtle art;
Measure your lines in your own style:
Full-length the tallest lays him, for a start,
Round him the others raise the turf the while.
Cut a deep oblong, straight, and true,
As for our sires they used to do.
Out from the palace to this narrow home,
The end must be this sorry bed of loam.

LEMURES (*with mocking gestures, as they dig*).
In youth when I did live and love
Methought 'twas very sweet,
To go where song and frolic was,
And thither ran my feet.
    But age, with his stealing steps,
Has clawed me with his crutch;
There the grave's door: I stumbled in,
'Twas open overmuch.

FAUST (*coming from the palace, groping by the door-posts*).
What joy the clash of spades now brings to me!
Thus toil my people for me without cease;
They make, that earth may find itself at peace,
A frontier for the billows of the sea,
Committing ocean to a settled zone.

MEPHISTOPHELES (*aside*). And yet you work for us alone:
Your dykes and quays prepare a revel
For Neptune, the old water-devil,
His pleasure do you serve, my friend.
Now, damned and lost, hope leaves your side –
We are with elements allied,
And ruin waits you in the end.

FAUST. Overseer!

MEPHISTOPHELES. Sir!

FAUST.                    Use every means, and strive
    To get more workers, shift on shift enrol,
    With comforts spur them on, and good control.
    Pay them, cajole them, use a press-gang drive.
    A fresh report you'll bring me daily, showing
    How my projected locks and dykes are growing.

MEPHISTOPHELES (*sotto voce*).
    What news I have, from all reports they gave,
    Concerns not dyke nor graving dock but grave.

FAUST. A marshland flanks the mountain-side,
    Infecting all that we have gained;
    Our gain would reach its greatest pride
    If all this noisome bog were drained.
    I work that millions may possess this space,
    If not secure, a free and active race.
    Here man and beast, in green and fertile fields,
    Will know the joys that new-won region yields,
    Will settle on the firm slopes of a hill
    Raised by a bold and zealous people's skill.
    A paradise our closed-in land provides,
    Though to its margin rage the blustering tides;
    When they eat through, in fierce devouring flood,
    All swiftly join to make the damage good.
    Ay, in this thought I pledge my faith unswerving,
    Here wisdom speaks its final word and true,
    None is of freedom or of life deserving
    Unless he daily conquers it anew.
    With dangers thus begirt, defying fears,
    Childhood, youth, age shall strive through strenuous
        years.
    Such busy, teeming throngs I long to see,
    Standing on freedom's soil, a people free.

Then to the moment could I say:
Linger you now, you are so fair!
Now records of my earthly day
No flight of aeons can impair –
Foreknowledge comes, and fills me with such bliss,
I take my joy, my highest moment this.

(*Faust sinks back into the arms of the Lemures, who lay
him upon the ground.*)

MEPHISTOPHELES.

Him would no joys content, no fortune please,
And thus he wooed his changing fantasies.
This wretched, empty moment at the last
He sought, poor wretch, to grasp and hold it fast.
Me he would sturdily withstand:
Time wins, with Greybeard stretched out on the sand.
The clock stands still –

CHORUS.                    It stands as midnight stilled,
The finger falls.

MEPHISTOPHELES. It falls, all is fulfilled.

CHORUS. It is bygone.

MEPHISTOPHELES. A foolish word, bygone.

How so then, gone?
Gone, to sheer Nothing, past with null made one!
What matters our creative endless toil,
When, at a snatch, oblivion ends the coil?
'It is by-gone' – How shall this riddle run?
As good as if things never had begun,
Yet circle back, existence to possess:
I'd rather have Eternal Emptiness.

# BURIAL SCENE

LEMUR (*solo*). Who was it built the house so ill,
   With shovel and with spade?
LEMURES (*in chorus*). For you, dull guest, in hempen shift,
   'Tis much too handsome made.
LEMUR (*solo*). Who was it made the room so vile,
   No table and no chair?
LEMURES (*in chorus*). 'Tis but on loan a little while,
   So many claim a share.

MEPHISTOPHELES.

There lies the body: should the soul seek flight
I'll show him straight the bond, the blood-writ scroll;
But nowadays too oft the devil's right
Is thwarted by new means to save the soul.
The old way is offensive grown,
The new we find in favour lacking;
I, who once did the job alone,
Must look to minions for a backing.
   Our business is in evil plight:
Time-honoured usage, ancient right,
There's no more trusting in their laws.
Time was, the soul with last breath left the house,
I lay in watch and, as with nimblest mouse,
Snap! and I had her firmly in my claws.
And now will she, in darkness hesitating,
Still to the corpse's loathsome house cling fast,
Until the elements, each other hating,
Will drive her out ignobly at the last.
Long days and hours I've toiled with plaguey care,
Still nagging question asks How? When? and Where?
Old Master Death is feeble grown and slow,

And even loses grip on Whether or No;
On rigid limbs I'd often feast my eyes,
And all was sham, for they would stir and rise.
          (*With fantastic gestures of conjuration.*)
Come up, be quick, and double now your speed,
You lords of crooked or of straight-horned breed,
Chips off the ancient block, and bring as well,
You devil's-spit, the very jaws of hell.
Hell's jaws are many, differing in dimension,
They swallow folk according to their rank;
But after this last gala, to be frank,
We shan't give things like this so much attention.
          (*To the left, the ghastly jaws of hell gape open.*)
The side-fangs yawn; out from the arching jaw
A raging swill of fiery flood is spewed;
See, in the seething fume of that dread maw,
The town of flames eternally renewed.
Up to the teeth, the molten red comes rushing,
The damned swim wildly, hoping to be saved,
Then, where the huge hyena's jaws are crushing,
Renew their path with burning brimstone paved.
In nooks things unawaited still are lying,
In smallest space will greatest horrors teem.
You serve me well these sinners terrifying,
Too apt to think it lies and trance and dream . . .
          (*To the fat devils, with the short, straight horns.*)
Now, big-paunched rascals, you whose cheeks are
          burning,
And rank with hell's own sulphur all aglow,
You clumsy clods with bull-necks never turning,
Look out for streak of phosphor here below:
Psyche, that is, the soul on pinions stealing,
My stamp upon her first I will be sealing,

Her wings pluck off, leaving a squalid worm;
Then bear her off in fiery whirling storm.
Your duty, wine-skins, is to give
On lower planes a sharp look-out;
Whether she chooses there to live,
Remains in academic doubt.
The navel suits her well to make a stay –
Look to it well, from there she'll slip away.

*(To the skinny devils, with long, crooked horns.)*

You zanies, black-art loons of reach gigantic,
Stretch out your arms, your claws in action bring;
Grab through the air, with unremitting antic,
So that you catch the fluttering, fleeting thing.
Surely her old home seems a wretched sty,
Aspiring genius seeks to soar on high.

### GLORIA

*from above, on the right.*

THE HOST OF HEAVEN.

Follow, blest envoys,
Heavenly convoys
In halcyon flight,
Sinners forgiving,
Make the dust living,
And in your soaring
Be you outpouring
On all the living
Breath of delight.

MEPHISTOPHELES.

Jangling I hear, a foul discordant noise,
It comes with dawn unwelcome from above,

A mooncalf medley, fit for girls and boys,
In taste that sanctimonious persons love.
You know we planned, in pitchy hour accurst,
Destruction to the total human race:
Of those invented evils much the worst
Finds in their worshipping its proper place.

   They come, the lubbers, with their canting prattle,
Thus have they snatched from us full many a prize;
With our own weapons will they give us battle;
They too are devils – only in disguise.
Eternal shame is yours if here you flinch:
On, to the grave-side, not to yield an inch.

CHORUS OF ANGELS (*strewing roses*).
Roses that daze the eye,
Sweet fragrance bringing,
Fluttering, floating by,
From the spray winging.
Life new-breathed in a sigh,
Buds gently springing,
Swiftly your blossom show.

   Burst, Spring, into green,
In amethyst glow,
Let Paradise be seen
By him who sleeps below.

MEPHISTOPHELES (*to the Satans*).
Why jib and flinch? Works thus the hellish host?
Stand firm, their petals let them strow.
Go, every blockhead to his post!
They think, with such display of flowery wonder,
To snow the red-hot devils under;
Breathe and it wilts, it shrivels when you blow.
Now, devil-blowers, blow! – Enough, enough!
You scorch their flight and bleach their flowery stuff. –

Not so much force! Stop gullets, nostrils close!
Bless me, not one but far too wildly blows!
To keep a measure, never have you learnt:
Seared more than shrivelled, all is black and burnt.
They float, they come, with venomous clear light,
Pack close your ranks, and stand in their despite.
Our powers fail! Old courage all is spent,
And devils snuff strange glow, a flattering scent.

CHORUS OF ANGELS.
　　Blest blossoms acclaiming,
　　And joy's purest flaming,
　　With love they have sought us,
　　Bliss have they brought us,
　　Heart's sacred right.
　　Words of deep verity,
　　Ether's true clarity,
　　Evermore charity
　　To throngs of light.

MEPHISTOPHELES. Curse on the loons, the dismal band,
　　Upon their heads the Satans stand.
　　The fat-guts fall in somersault
　　Arse-over-tip down hell's old vault.
　　Good luck! You've earned your scalding bath!
　　But here I stay, and hold the path.
　　　　　(*He struggles to beat off the hovering roses.*)
　　False Jack o'Lanterns hence! You, ne'er so bright,
　　When caught are in a foul and sticky plight.
　　You'll flutter, will you? Off, you odious thing!
　　Like brimstone in my neck, like pitch you cling.

CHORUS OF ANGELS.
　　Things ill-fitting cease,
　　Yours to forswear them;
　　Things that rob inward peace,

Think not to bear them.
Comes the assault too nigh,
Must we our duty ply.
Love leads but loving-ones
To homes on high.

MEPHISTOPHELES.

I burn, head, heart, and spleen, a flaming evil,
This is an element of super-devil,
More sharp and keen than hell's own fire. –
Thus must you writhe, you creatures of desire.
You luckless lovers who, by true-love spurned,
Still for your sweethearts aching eyes have turned.

  Me, too! What is it drags my head aside,
When, sworn to combat, hate has been my pride?
This sight was always hostile, raw, perverse.
Comes something strange to pierce me, and engender
This joy in looking on their youthful splendour?
What weighs upon me, that I cannot curse?
And should I now in foolish leanings weaken,
Who would be dubbed then biggest fool henceforth?
They seem the bearers of a lovely beacon,
These miscreants who have had my hate and wrath.

  You sons of beauty, tell me, as I meet you,
Are not you too of Lucifer's great race?
A kiss, so fair you are, I'd give to greet you,
I feel you crown the day with special grace.
I feel at ease, all natural and trustful,
As if I'd seen you many times before,
In kitten-like desiring, sly and lustful,
With every glance your beauty moves me more.
Draw nearer, pray you, granting me one glance.

ANGELS. We come, and yet you shrink as we advance?
Lo, we approach, and, if you can, then stay.

*(The Angels hovering assemble, until the whole space*
*is filled with their company.)*

MEPHISTOPHELES *(who is crowded into the proscenium).*

Us spirits you call damned, and look askance.
Witch-masters, you, par excellence;
For man and maid you lead astray. –
What an adventure curst and dire!
Is this love's elemental game?
All of my body is on fire,
My neck can hardly feel a spurt of flame. –
You hover to and fro; but, pray you, settle:
A shade more earthly tame your limbs' high mettle;
Indeed it suits you well, this serious style,
But just for once I'd like to see you smile,
Something my hope of lasting joy to raise,
I mean the sort that lives in lovers' gaze:
A dimpling of the mouth and it is done.
With you, tall youth, I'd choose in love to fall,
This parson-visage suits you not at all,
Then give a wanton loving look, just one.
You could with decency appear more nude,
The surplice vaunts too much the acolyte –
And now they turn, and from behind are viewed –
Ah, how the rascals stir the appetite!

CHORUS OF ANGELS.

Turn, flames of love, once more
Pure light reveal.
Those who their lives deplore
Truth yet shall heal;
Rescued, no more the thrall
Of evil cares,
Soon with the All-in-All
Bliss shall be theirs.

MEPHISTOPHELES (*pulling himself together*).
  How is't with me? – Like Job, the man seen whole,
  With boil on boil, and sick of his own soul,
  His triumph, clear view of himself to win,
  When trusting in himself and in his kin;
  Saved are the devil's limbs by his control,
  The love-spell cannot pierce beneath his skin;
  The cursèd flames already are burnt out,
  And I, as is your due, curse you and all your rout.

CHORUS OF ANGELS.
  Over whom, most holy fire,
  You have swayed and stood,
  Henceforth will his life aspire
  In bliss with the good.
  Joined in maturity,
  Rise and extol.
  Ether wins purity,
  Breathes now the soul.

      (*They rise up, bearing away with them the
         immortal part of Faust.*)

MEPHISTOPHELES (*looking around him*).
  What may this be? And whither are they gone?
  You innocents now fool me and outbrave,
  And with your booty heavenwards are flown;
  For this you picked and nibbled at the grave!
  Filched from me is this lofty prize unmatched,
  A soul pledged mine, by written scroll it gave,
  This have they robbed from me, adroitly snatched.

    To whom then shall I carry my complaint?
  Who will restore to me my well-earned right?
  Fooled in old age are you, by fraud and feint,
  And have deserved it: yours a wretched plight.
  This thing have I most woefully mishandled,

And wrecked a deep-laid scheme in shameful sort,
Absurd amours, in gloating fancy dandled,
Have had the weathered devil for their sport.
And if to such a mad and puerile playing
The shrewd old master devil can descend,
No trifling folly this, beyond gainsaying,
That mastered him and beat him in the end.


## MOUNTAIN-GORGES, FOREST, CLIFF, WILDERNESS

*Holy Anchorites, scattered up the mountain-sides, dwelling
in clefts of the rocks.*

CHORUS and ECHO.
   Forest branches swaying,
   Mass of rock down-weighing,
   Wreathing roots immense,
   Boles in forest dense.
   Lashes wave on wave,
   Shelter gives deep cave.
   Lions around us stray,
   Silent and tame they rove,
   And sacred honours pay
   To the holy shrine of love.
PATER ECSTATICUS (*floating on high and below*).
   Evermore blissful fire,
   Glow of love's pure empire,
   Through the breast's seething pain
   God-loving ecstasies reign.
   Come, darts, and pierce me through,
   Lances my flesh subdue.

Maces, come batter me,
Lightnings, now shatter me:
Worthlessness drive afar,
Banned evermore.
Shine forth, enduring star,
Immortal love's core.

PATER PROFUNDUS (*in deep Region*).
As at my feet the chasm descending
Rests on the deep abyss below,
Or as the thousand streamlets blending
Plunge in dread fall, and foaming flow,
Or as the trunk, the forest gracing,
Lifts its own strength so nobly tall,
So is almighty love embracing
All it has made, to cherish all.

Around me whirls a sound of rushing
Like rock and wood in heaving gale,
And yet the gracious flood comes gushing
With wealth of waters down the vale,
The fields to bless; or with forked flaring
Lightning strikes from heaven sheer,
Once in its bosom venom bearing,
Yet purges now the atmosphere.

Heralds of love are these proclaiming
What powers eternal us enfold.
Come, holy fire, with inward flaming,
Where the poor soul, bewildered, cold,
Writhes, in the toils of sense repining,
Feeling the harsh chains' deadly smart.
O God, send peace and heavenly shining
On the dark desert of my heart.

PATER SERAPHICUS (*in middle Region*).
Morning cloud the pines are bearing,

Swayed in tresses of the trees.
What the inner life thus faring?
Spirit-throngs of youth are these.

BOYS, IN CHORUS OF THE BLEST.

Father, tell us as we wander,
Tell us who we are and where.
Happy we, no joy is fonder,
Being is so sweet and fair.

PATER SERAPHICUS.

Boys, with mind and sense scarce waking,
Born upon the midnight hour,
Parents' spell of grief forsaking,
Joy of the angelic power.
Feeling love at hand, and sharing,
Nearer come, in love and grace,
For indeed of earth's rough faring
Blessed ones, you bear no trace.
Come, alight, for I will lend you
Vision as of earth-born eyes.
Use the senses that befriend you,
See, what realm before you lies.
        (*He assumes them into his own spirit.*)
Trees behold, cliffs, rocks, and yonder
Spate of stream in mighty flow
Leaps the shortest way, with thunder
Plunging to the vale below.

VOICES OF BOYS (*within*).

Grand are these, but fear they waken,
All too dark the shadows grow,
Thus with awe our hearts are shaken:
Gracious father, let us go.

PATER SERAPHICUS.

Rise then higher: as you rise, shall

Growth unnoticed bless your throng.
As in pure eternal wise shall
God's own presence make you strong.
Thus sustained in spheres supernal,
Spirits find their heavenly food:
Love revealed, the love eternal,
Flowering in beatitude.

CHORUS OF BLEST BOYS (*circling the summits on high*).

Joyously wing ye,
Your hands entwine
Soar ye and sing ye
Heart's lore divine,
Taught by God's spirit,
Trust ye in grace:
Whom ye adore, ye
Shall see face to face.

ANGELS (*hovering in the higher atmosphere, bearing all that is
    immortal of Faust*).

Saved is our spirit-peer, in peace,
Preserved from evil scheming:
'For he whose strivings never cease
Is ours for his redeeming.'
If, touched by the celestial love,
His soul has sacred leaven,
There comes to greet him, from above,
The company of heaven.

THE YOUNGER ANGELS.

From fair sinners' hands these flowers,
Roses we have scattered wide;
Thus they made the victory ours,
Penitent and purified;
Flowers this soul, this prize have won us:
Fiends, as we strewed, would flinch, and shun us;

Devils fled, dismayed, sore-smitten,
Not as of old with hell-pangs bitten:
Love-pangs brought them to disaster;
Even that old Satan-Master
Shrank, pierced through with pain, defeated.
Sing, for victory completed!

ANGELS MORE PERFECT.

Bear we in cumbered flight
Earthly remains.
Were they of byssolite,
Still they have stains.
Has the high Spirit-force
Elements tended,
Not angels can divorce
Two closely blended;
Two natures single grown,
We must abide them,
Eternal love alone
Has power to divide them.

THE YOUNGER ANGELS.

As in the mist we veer,
Rocky height wreathing,
Feel we a presence near,
Spirit-life breathing.
Cloudlets float clear and free,
Eager the throngs we see
Of the blest boys.
Freed from duress of earth,
Ranging in poise,
Hail they the spring's new birth,
Bathed in the joys
Of this, the higher sphere.
Here let him then begin

  Fullness of life to win,
  Joined as their peer.
CHORUS OF BLEST BOYS.
  Him as soul's chrysalis
  Joyful receive we;
  For thus achieve we
  Angels' true pledge of bliss.
  Shake off the earthly flakes
  That yet enfold him;
  Strong in heaven's life he wakes,
  Beauteous behold him.
DOCTOR MARIANUS (*in the highest, purest cell*).
  Here is free prospect wide,
  The soul up-bearing.
  There women-figures glide,
  Heavenwards faring.
  With them the heavenly Queen,
  Majesty tender,
  In wreath of stars is seen,
  Clear in her splendour.
       (*Enraptured.*)
  Pavilioned in the heaven's blue,
  Queen on high of all the world,
  For the holy sight I sue,
  Of the mystery unfurled.
  Sanction what in man may move
  Feelings tender and austere,
  And with glow of sacred love
  Lifts him to thy presence near.
   Souls unconquerable rise
  If, sublime, thou will it;
  Sinks that storm in peaceful wise
  If thy pity still it.

Virgin, pure in heavenly sheen,
Mother, throned supernal,
Highest birth, our chosen Queen,
Godhead's peer eternal.
    Now near her splendour
Floats a light cloud,
Penitents tender
In gentle crowd,
Tasting heaven's ether,
At her feet kneeling,
For grace appealing.
    To thee, enthroned in holy awe,
Power is not denied,
That the lightly erring draw,
Trusting, to thy side.
    Hard to save whom lust bespake,
Weak, before his fire;
Who in single strength can break
Chains of dark desire?
    So the foot will swiftly slip,
On the slant way gliding,
Heart the fool of eye and lip,
In soft words confiding.

              (*Mater Gloriosa soars on high.*)

CHORUS OF PENITENT WOMEN.

    Heavenward faring,
To eternal realms soaring,
Hear our imploring,
Thou, mercy bearing,
Past all comparing.

MAGNA PECCATRIX (*St Luke*, 7).

    By the love that gave its tears,
Freely shed, as balsam sweet,

Braving pharisaic sneers,
To wash Thy Son's, the Saviour's feet;
By the precious box, bestowing
Fragrant nard the Saviour nigh,
By the tresses, drooping, flowing
Soft the sacred limbs to dry –

MULIER SAMARITANA (*St John, 4*).

By the well, the ancient pool,
Where Abraham his cattle brought,
By the pail whose rim so cool
Once the holy lips have sought;
By the living waters vernal
Springing from that sacred place,
Sending through the world eternal
Clear abounding flow of grace –

MARIA AEGYPTIACA (*Acta Sanctorum*).

By the hallowed tomb, the portal
Where they came our Lord to lay,
By the mystic arm immortal
Warning me to go my way;
By my forty years' repentance
In the waste and desert land,
By the words of bliss, the sentence,
Traced in parting, on the sand –

THE THREE.

Thou that from the greatly sinning
Turnest not thy face away,
And contrition's humble winning
Liftest to eternal day,
To this soul, that for a space
Fell, scarce knowing its transgression,
Grant, in merciful concession,
Thy divine forgiving grace.

UNA POENITENTIUM, once called GRETCHEN (*drawing closer*).

Ah, look down,
Thou rich in heaven's renown,
Turn thou the grace of thy dear face
On the fullness of my bliss;
For now my lover,
Earth's sadness over,
Comes from that world to me in this.

CHORUS OF THE BLEST BOYS

(*circling nearer*).

Transcending us he towers,
Great-limbed and vital,
Will for this care of ours
Make rich requital.
Too soon from life removed,
Its song could not reach us;
Much he has learnt and proved,
Now he will teach us.

THE ONE PENITENT, once called GRETCHEN.

Engirt by heaven's noble choirs,
With self new-born he scarcely knows
The life to which his soul aspires,
As like the angels' host he grows.
See, how he breaks from bonds of earth,
With every shackle shed at length,
And ether's raiment of new birth
Reveals his prime of youthful strength.
Grant me to teach and guide him here,
Him dazzled by new shining day.

MATER GLORIOSA.

Come, rise to seek the higher sphere,
And he, of thee aware, will take that way.

DOCTOR MARIANUS (*in prostrate adoration*).
   O contrite hearts, seek with your eyes
   The visage of salvation;
   Blissful in that gaze, arise,
   Through glad regeneration.
   Now may every pulse of good
   Seek to serve before thy face,
   Virgin, Queen of Motherhood,
   Keep us, Goddess, in thy grace.
CHORUS MYSTICUS.
   All things corruptible
   Are but a parable;
   Earth's insufficiency
   Here finds fulfilment;
   Here the ineffable
   Wins life through love;
   Eternal Womanhood
   Leads us above.